RAVES FOR M.D. LAKE'S
PEGGY O'NEILL MYSTERIES

AMENDS FOR MURDER
"A DAZZLER . . .
Lake has a way with language
that's rarely matched
and the protagonist is wonderful."
Drood Review of Books

COLD COMFORT
"OH, HOW I LOVE PEGGY O'NEILL!
M.D. Lake writes a good story
full of memorable characters . . .
Great fun—keep 'em coming!"
Barbara Paul, author of *In-Laws and Outlaws*

POISONED IVY
"ENJOYABLE, TOTALLY ABSORBING . . .
A pure, straightforward mystery
sure to appeal to those who prefer
a puzzle to mindless violence."
Toby Bromberg, *Rave Reviews* (Four Star Review)

A Gift for Murder

M.D. LAKE

AVON BOOKS ◆ NEW YORK

A GIFT FOR MURDER is an original publication of Avon Books. This work has never before appeared in book form. This work is a novel. Any similarity to actual persons or events is purely coincidental.

AVON BOOKS
A division of
The Hearst Corporation
1350 Avenue of the Americas
New York, New York 10019

First Avon Books Printing: December 1992

AVON TRADEMARK REG. U.S. PAT. OFF. AND IN OTHER COUNTRIES, MARCA REGISTRADA, HECHO EN U.S.A.

Printed in the U.S.A.

WCD 10 9 8

For Trudy and Doug Nichols,
and Betsy and Jane,
and Jo, again.

One

It was my night off. I'd had dinner with Paula Henderson and Lawrence Fitzpatrick and thought we were going to a movie afterward, but they talked me into going to a reading at the Tower instead.

A couple of months earlier, Paula had decided she wanted to learn to write poetry. Being Paula, she figured the most efficient way to go about it would be to take a course, so she enrolled in one of the evening courses offered by the Tower, a local writers' cooperative. Lawrence, being Lawrence, thought he'd like to try his hand at writing too, so he signed up for a course in nonfiction writing that met the same night as Paula's. If it had been a class in writing greeting cards, he would have taken it. Paula and Lawrence are called Night 'n' Day because Paula's black and Lawrence isn't, and also because you can't have the one without the other. Like me, they're campus cops.

Paula drove, and I sat in the backseat, contemplating the backs of their heads and wondering why there'd been the change in plan. They exchanged furtive glances and smirks, but that didn't make me suspicious, since lovers often look furtive.

We parked in the Tower's parking lot. As I got out of the car and looked around, I said, "I don't think little

1

kids would ever come trick-or-treating here. I know I wouldn't."

Although the Tower is close to the University campus, I'd never been there. What set it apart from the houses around it, and gave it its name, was the tower on the northwest corner that rose an additional story above the mansion's gabled roof. If you knew where to look, you could see the tower's peaked, copper green roof from many parts of the city.

Concealed floodlights threw the shadows of a large oak onto the building. The shadows moved in the warm late summer breeze, making the tower look like a snake writhing its way out of a basket.

Just inside the front door, a woman sat at a card table, selling tickets.

"Niobe Tigue," Paula whispered to me as we waited our turn.

I knew the name. It belonged to one of the few local writers who'd acquired a national reputation. She was a tall woman of about forty-five, with a strong face roughened by the sun and wind, and her thick, mahogany brown hair was pinned up loosely on her head. She sold tickets in a brisk, businesslike manner, not wasting time chatting with the customers. She nodded in vague recognition to Paula and Lawrence, but that was all. I accepted Paula's offer to pay for me since I was there under protest.

As soon as we'd stepped out of earshot, I asked her why a well-known writer like Niobe Tigue was selling tickets at the door.

"The Tower's a collective," Paula replied. "The members all have to help run it."

Double doors off the entryway to the left led into an auditorium that must have been the mansion's living and dining rooms before the place was remodeled. It looked as though it could hold about 150 people, but there weren't going to be that many people tonight. Black folding chairs faced a platform on which an elaborate podium stood. It looked like a pulpit. The folding chairs had been borrowed from a mortuary; stenciled on their backs, in white, were the words "Askew Funeral Home."

"Why are mortuaries called 'homes'?" I asked, trying to make myself comfortable on one of the chairs. "And, for that matter, why am I here?" I realized I was whispering, probably because of the pulpitlike podium and the funereal chairs.

"Let's see who I know," Paula said, ignoring the hard questions. She pointed to someone up front. "There's my teacher, Melody Carr, that woman with the curly blond hair."

Perhaps feeling that I was underwhelmed by it all, Lawrence said, "You know who Melody Carr's sister is, don't you?"

"No, Lawrence, I don't," I replied.

"Sandra Carr."

I gave him an expectant look.

"You mean you've never heard of Sandra Carr?" He was appalled.

I nodded. It's fun to appall Lawrence.

"She writes thrillers. She's world-famous."

"I thought only guys wrote those."

"Wrong as usual, Peggy. They're making a movie out of her last novel. It's about a serial killer."

"Is she here?"

"I don't see her," he said.

"She doesn't come to many of the Tower events," Paula explained. "She doesn't like the highbrow stuff—and most of the Tower writers don't like her kind of writing, either."

Too bad. Although I don't read thrillers, it would

have been interesting to meet a woman who wrote them.

"Her sister looks like the Woman in Jeopardy in a thriller," I said, my eyes going back to Melody Carr.

Paula started to say something, but a man stopped in the aisle next to us and put his hand on Lawrence's shoulder. "Larry," he said. "Glad you could make it." He turned to Paula. "Hi, Paula." And then he looked at me.

Larry? I'd known Lawrence a long time, but that was the first time I'd ever heard anybody who knew him call him Larry.

Lawrence didn't seem to mind. "Peggy O'Neill, this is Gary Mallory. Gary's my teacher."

We shook hands, exchanging smiles for maybe a tad longer than necessary. He was about my age and height, with dark, rough skin that was part sun and part the way he was. His brown eyes were deep-set. The effect was somber, even forbidding, except when he smiled. His smile was always sudden, and lovely, as I discovered later.

The three of them made stilted small talk for a few minutes. Then I saw Paula's and Lawrence's eyes meet, and suddenly I knew why they'd dragged me here.

The lights started to go down, and Mallory said he'd see us again after the reading. He walked up the aisle to the front rows, where, I guessed, the Tower writers sat. I tried to give Paula a frosty look, but she was staring at the empty stage.

After a few moments, a woman came out from a door behind the stage and stepped behind the podium. She looked about forty, attractive in a tall, willowy way. She introduced herself as Tamara Wallace Meade, the Tower's coordinator. Her hair was dark, with silver highlights like tinsel, and it fell nearly to her shoulders. She had a long neck and large, luminous gray eyes.

She favored us with the brisk, humorless smile of a woman with three names, and then expressed her pleasure at the number of people who had turned out. For the benefit of the newcomers among us, she gave a brief history of the writers' cooperative, from its small beginnings more than a decade ago as the Second Story to its present eminence as the Tower.

She also spoke of the appropriateness of the name. "Towers are useless," she said, "and yet it is from them that you can read the stars."

There was a smattering of applause and at least one audible groan—and another that wasn't.

"However, before we get on with the night's program, I'd like to take this opportunity to welcome back one of the Second Story's most distinguished members, a founding member, in fact, Cameron Harris. Cam, would you stand up, please?"

This time there was a lot of applause.

In the front row, a man stood up slowly, turned, and peered out at us, shoving his hands into his pockets. Even though he slouched, he was tall, with a shock of brown hair that fell down over his forehead. He had light-colored eyes under bushy brows, and he squinted, as if he needed glasses. His head seemed small, perhaps because of the length of his body.

He grinned at us, slow and easy, pulling one hand out of his pocket to give us a casual wave.

I knew who he was, of course—the local boy who'd made good. He'd had two best-sellers in the last four years, and his newest book, rushed into print to capitalize on his sudden fame, was climbing up the best-seller list.

"He's on television a lot, right?" I whispered to Paula. "Talk shows?" She nodded. "I could tell by the wave. I think he also tossed an air kiss to somebody in the third row."

He sat back down, and Tamara Wallace Meade said, "Even though Cam lives in New York City now, he's agreed to serve on the Tower's board of directors—provided the membership votes him in, of course." Everyone laughed at the absurd thought that it wouldn't. "If they do, Cam guarantees that we'll be seeing a lot more of him around here, and they'll be seeing less of him in the Big Apple."

We all applauded some more, and then the night's program began.

Until just before the end, the reading went the way they're supposed to—not that I'm an expert, but I suspect that if you've attended one, you've attended them all. It seems to be a convention that the authors act as if they've come unprepared. They carry notebooks and thumb through them casually, as if looking for something that might do. The audience, meanwhile, sits waiting, holding its collective breath and hoping they'll find something.

After six or seven authors had done that, I began to wish that one of them would look up with an apologetic smile, shrug, and say, "Nope, sorry. I thought I had something here, but I guess I was wrong," and go sit down. Nobody did.

I was interested in Gary Mallory's reading since, after all, he was the reason I was there that night. Tamara Wallace Meade introduced him, as she did all the authors. He'd been a reporter for a local newspaper, then a correspondent in Latin America for a news service. After five years, he returned here to write a book about his experiences. The book did well, and now he was working on a sequel. He was teaching a course in non-fiction writing at the Tower until he decided what he wanted to do next with his life.

He read an excerpt from the new book, a chapter dealing with the lives of coffee farmers in Colombia. It was a moving story, which he read quietly, letting the words do all the work. I liked his writing, and the sound of his voice too.

Niobe Tigue followed him. She was a good choice, I guess, since she wrote realistic stories that dealt with sturdy rural people beset on all sides by city slickers trying to seduce them into using credit cards and abandoning their old ways. She was tall and angular and paced back and forth on the stage as she read, like a backwoods preacher. I never have liked sermons disguised as stories, no matter how well done. Fiction like that holds no surprises.

The last reader on the program was Melody Carr, Paula's poetry teacher. According to Tamara Wallace Meade's introduction, Melody had one book of poetry published by a local press, and was teaching a course on how to turn journal writing into literature. She was also writing a book on the subject.

I turned to stare at Paula, who continued to look straight ahead, her nose tilted up, perhaps to hear better. She hadn't told me that part about the course she was taking. I wondered if she kept a journal too, and what she put in it if she did.

Melody Carr stood at the podium and paged through a thick notebook. Her fluffy blond hair resembled a sunlit dandelion, and she'd decorated the cover of her notebook with bright childish flowers, drawn in the newest shades of crayon.

"Here's one I like a lot," she announced finally, looking up at us. Her eyes were big and brown, like the eyes of a deer caught in a poacher's flashlight.

It was a pretty poem—something to do with longing—and she read several more just like it. She seemed surprised and happy each time she produced a poetic image. When she smiled, her teeth protruded slightly, as if trying to come out and play.

When she'd almost used up what I hoped was her al-
lotted time, she turned a page and stared at it for a long
moment and then said, "I wonder what you'll think of
this one."

She cleared her throat nervously and read a poem
about a penis. Her voice got stronger as she went along.

I'd never heard a poem on that particular organ before, so I gave it my full attention, interested in hearing
what somebody as ethereal as Melody Carr would make
of the subject.

Suddenly, a few rows in front of us, a chair scraped
harshly and a man got up. At first I thought he was going to start for the stage, and he did too, but then he
turned and strode down the aisle. He had a long face
with a scraggly brown beard that was starting to go
gray, and he was wearing starched and pressed army fatigues, and highly polished black combat boots. Fum-
bling loudly with the handle, he threw open one of the
double doors.

As he did, somebody in one of the front rows
laughed. In the silence, it sounded unusually loud and
obnoxious. The man at the door spun around and
scanned the room, searching for the source, his sunken,
close-set eyes blazing. Then he turned and disappeared
through the door, leaving it open.

"Would somebody please shut the door?" Melody
Carr asked quietly. She finished the poem and closed
her colorful notebook. Her eyes roamed around the
room as we applauded, and she looked pleased with
herself as she stepped off the stage and returned to her
chair.

I'd thought she was a poor choice to read last, but I'd
been wrong. She ended the reading with a bang, and I
admired her for it.

Tamara Wallace Meade stood up, her face expressionless. After thanking the authors, she urged us to

stay for refreshments and to pick up a schedule of courses offered by the Tower before we left.

I couldn't help teasing Paula. "I did get that right, didn't I? That poem did claim that the penis is just a vagina before it flowers?"

"Yes, it did."

"It's probably bad physiology."

"You don't have to go all sarcastic on me, Peggy. I didn't realize you were such a prude. Or is it because the subject makes you uneasy?"

Outraged, I started to protest, but decided against it, when I saw her stern accusing eyes on me. Paula hadn't been herself since she started writing poetry. I asked her who the man was who'd walked out.

"Her husband. He's a University professor."

We circulated for a while, and Paula introduced me to a few of her fellow students. Finally she said, "C'mon, let's go see what Lawrence and Gary have planned for the rest of the evening."

What a surprise, I thought, as I followed her across the room. Being single and unattached, I'd had to endure this sort of thing more than once.

In the middle of the room, Cameron Harris was talking to Niobe Tigue. Since they were both tall, they could stare right into each other's eyes. They seemed oblivious to the people crowding them and hanging on to their every word.

"I'd have thought," Niobe was saying, "that New York would've taken the oaf out of you by now, Cameron. But I guess I was wrong."

Harris laughed. It was the laugh that had followed Melody Carr's husband out the door. "I'd have thought you'd be happy to discover that the big city hasn't taken the country out of the boy, Niobe."

Paula dragged me away before I could hear any more

and led me over to where Lawrence was talking to Gary Mallory.

"You've got beautiful hair," Mallory said to me, after a brief, awkward silence, "and a light sprinkling of freckles."

"Yes," I replied.

I can usually come up with better lines than that. It wasn't long before I discovered that he could too.

Two

Four months later, in January, I was sitting opposite Cameron Harris at a farewell dinner in his honor at the home of Tamara Wallace Meade. I hadn't wanted to go, but Gary promised Tamara he'd come, and he asked me to accompany him. We'd been seeing each other since the reading at the Tower. Gary had a good sense of humor, although it wasn't as wicked as I would have liked, and he had an interesting mind. Sometimes he was too intense, but maybe that was because he was writing his book against a tight deadline. He wasn't comfortable living in a big city, and he talked a lot about returning to South America. I suspected he was working up the courage to ask me to go with him, although so far he'd only put out vague feelers.

According to Gary, the Meades' dinner parties were famous. They were perfectly composed, like a Mondrian abstraction. They required an equal number of men and women, or the composition would fall apart and the spices would fail to blend properly or the sauces would curdle.

"Why don't you ask Sandra Carr to go with you?" I asked him. In the time we'd been going together, I'd learned that Gary had dated Sandra, the famous writer of thrillers, before we met. I didn't know why they'd broken up, and it wasn't any of my business, either.

"Tamara and Sandra don't get along, for one thing," he replied. "Tamara doesn't think that what Sandra writes is literature, and Sandra thinks Tamara's a phony."

"And for another thing?"

"I'd rather go with you."

The Meades' low, sprawling home was on Lake Eleanor. I live on Lake Eleanor too, or almost: on the other side of it and up the hill a couple of blocks and down a couple of income brackets. We walked up the flagstone path to the front door, guided by little flames flickering in ceramic candle holders designed to look like paper bags. When I was a student at the University, I tried the same thing using real paper bags, but half of them burned up before any of my guests arrived.

John Meade, Tamara's husband, greeted us at the door. He was tall and silver-haired, only just beginning to lose the firmness around his chin and jaw. He was a lawyer and at least fifteen years older than his wife.

It was a pretty formal dinner: three wineglasses in front of each guest and a lot of silverware, some of which I never did use. In addition to Cameron Harris, Gary, and me, the guests included Melody Carr, Niobe Tigue, and Chris Ames, a family friend of the Meades'. Melody's husband, the man who'd stalked out at her reading in September, wasn't there. They'd separated right after that.

"Could I have some more of the noodles, please?" I asked Tamara. I'm not sure what made me say that. The formality, maybe, or the tension in the air, like heat lightning in summer that flickers without bringing the release of thunder.

Cameron Harris, sitting opposite me, laughed.

Tamara's eyes moved quickly from me to Harris. She

gave me an indulgent smile and said, "The *fettuccini al burro?* I'm so glad you liked it, Peggy." She turned to one of the caterers and asked him if there was more. He put a look of exaggerated pain on his face and said no.

"That's okay," I said, smiling all around. I hadn't actually liked the dish all that much, because it was cooked *al dente,* which is Italian for "underdone," and I hate that in a noodle. I was still hungry, though, having passed on the main course, which was veal.

"Noodles," Cameron Harris said, still laughing. "That's wonderful! Peggy what?"

"O'Neill," I answered.

"Well, I'm going to call you 'Red.' " He was quite capable of speaking normally, but whenever he thought he had an audience, he drawled. "I hope that's okay with you."

I didn't say anything, just gave him my best smile and turned to say something to Chris Ames, who was sitting next to me.

"Is it?" Harris persisted.

Four months before, Niobe Tigue had called him an oaf. She'd been right. "No," I said, and showed him most of my teeth, hoping he'd mistake them for a smile.

"Okay." Some of the good humor left his eyes. "Peggy it is."

He'd drunk a lot of the three different wines during the meal. Noticing things like that is one of my drearier habits. I also noticed that he'd flirted a lot with Melody Carr, who didn't seem comfortable with it, and then—perhaps to keep things even—occasionally dazzled Tamara with his attention too. Apparently now it was my turn to take the brunt of his charm.

"You're most certainly going to end up in his next novel as 'Red,' however," John Meade broke in, looking up suddenly at Harris. Meade had mostly kept his attention on his food, as if it held the secret of why he was there. I could have told him he was wasting his time.

"How would you know that, John?" Harris asked. "I didn't think you read my novels—or anybody else's, for that matter."

There was a moment's silence. "Even we philistines hear things, you know," Meade replied finally.

"I think a campus policewoman would be an interesting subject for a novel, or at least a story," Melody said brightly, looking around the table.

"Just don't forget the libel laws," Niobe muttered.

Harris laughed. Either he enjoyed the sound of his own laughter, or else didn't realize or care how loud it was. "I wouldn't write anything libelous about Red— Peggy, I mean."

"Then she's going to fare better than the rest of us," Niobe retorted.

"Nice dress, Niobe. Haven't I seen it before?" She was wearing a plain knit dress in an earthen color and a necklace of stones that looked handmade and heavy.

"Of course you have, Cameron. The last time we sat down to dinner together. You've got a good memory."

"Let's see. That would have been . . ." He used one of his forks to scratch his jaw thoughtfully. For all I knew, that could have been its purpose.

"Six years ago, right before you left for what Tamara likes to call The Big Apple."

Harris smiled down the table at Tamara. "Tamara's always had a way with words. Probably comes from all the classics she's read—the playwright Gibson, for example. Henry Gibson. Am I right, Tamara?"

Tamara's face seemed very pale. "Oh, Cam."

The man sitting next to me, Chris Ames, spoke up for the first time. "Ibsen," he said, softly but clearly. "Henrik Ibsen."

"That's what I said," Harris replied, looking at Ames as if he couldn't quite place him, "Gibson. Henry Gibson." He turned his attention to me again. "You could do worse than appear in one of my novels, Peggy."

"How, Cameron?" Niobe asked.

"She could appear in one of yours."

John Meade chuckled, a quiet, meaningless noise.

"Who would she be, I wonder," Harris went on, pretending to think. "I suppose the University has an agricultural research station somewhere out there in the sticks, where Niobe sets her stories. Maybe Peggy would be assigned to investigate a suspicious outbreak of cattail disease in the wetlands. She'd eventually discover that it was the dastardly deed of the local banker, Harvey Slyde, trying to force the swamp's owner, Blind Emma Grindhaugen, to sell out to him so he could put a strip mall on it, complete with a Sears outlet store, a movie theater, and a fitness center."

As he told the story in his mannered drawl, he kept his eyes on Niobe, as if measuring its effect on her. From where I was sitting, she seemed to shrivel up. Her face became bone, her lips a single thin line.

"Red O'Brien, girl cop, exposes the villain, thereby saving a choice piece of prairie somewhere—and Blind Emma too, of course—for future generations to enjoy." He stopped, took a big swallow of wine, and looked about the table, pleased with himself. We probably weren't the warmest audience he'd played to, but he didn't seem to notice.

Niobe said, "That's pretty much the story of the place where you grew up, Cameron. Have you forgotten, just because it's gone now?" Her eyes sparkled with tears as she forced herself to look at him.

"I'm sorry, Niobe." He tried to put one of his arms around her shoulder. "I meant it as a joke. I know how much I owe you."

"You don't owe me anything," she snapped, twisting away.

"You were my mentor."

She stared at him a long time, as if trying to decide if he was being sincere. I didn't blame her. I couldn't tell, either.

"About time for dessert, I think," John Meade said, glancing at his wife. Tamara got up quickly and went to the kitchen. A few moments later, one of the caterers followed her back and began clearing away our dinner plates.

Chris Ames leaned over and whispered to me, "I'm sorry you didn't like the 'noodles.'" He gave me a sly smile. He was short, about five five, with a shock of white hair, and small, dark eyes stuck like buttons in his face. "Or the *scaloppine al marsala* either, apparently."

"That's okay," I said, keeping my voice low too. "I'm a rather finicky eater. I don't eat anything that might taste like baby. What's your connection with the Tower?"

"I've been a friend of John and Tamara's for a long time, and John is my personal attorney."

"Mr. Ames is much more than just the Meades' friend," Melody butted in. "He's the reason we're no longer the Second Story."

"Although we still should be," Niobe Tigue said. "The Tower's a money pit."

"Don't pay any attention to Niobe," Melody said to me. "We'd grown out of the Second Story, Niobe. You know that."

"The Tower was yours?" I asked Ames.

"My father's, actually." The attention was making him uneasy, and he squirmed in his chair, like a child. "And it wasn't really so very generous of me, Miss Carr. I'm sure you know that. The house was much too large for a single man, so when my father died, I decided to sell it." He looked at me. "That was just at the time Tamara was complaining about how the writers' collective, the Second Story, had outgrown its space above the bookstore. So I offered my old place to them." He shrugged. "I think I actually made money on the deal, as a tax write-off. Did I, John?"

John Meade said something noncommittal, in lawyer fashion.

"Mr. Ames was a writer too," Melody said to me, "in his youth."

"Oh, well," Ames stammered, even more flustered than before. "I wouldn't call what I did writing."

"He wrote a novel," Cameron Harris said. "And after one rejection—destroyed it!" He snapped his fingers in the air, shook his head in disbelief. *"Destroyed* it."

Ames's face was pink and unhappy. Again he looked at me. "There wasn't a writers' organization like the Tower back then, you know, Ms. O'Neill, so I was on my own. And I didn't know anybody else who was doing anything as foolish and irresponsible as writing fiction. I took that rejection pretty hard, I'm afraid. But it was no big loss and it was a long time ago."

"Just up and destroyed it!" Harris repeated. "How—?"

"How would you know what it was like back then, Cam?" Melody turned on him with sudden fierceness. "You never had to write all alone. You got a lot of support from the other Second Story writers, back when you were starting out—from Niobe and from Tamara too. And from Sandra—" She stopped abruptly. Her lips trembled slightly.

"Hey, take it easy, Munk," Harris drawled. "Take it easy. You're right, of course." He turned to Ames. "I'm sorry if I offended you, Mr. Ames. But I'll bet you have a drawer full of unpublished fiction somewhere, don't you? You didn't just chuck it all when you went to work for your daddy? C'mon, 'fess up."

"I'm afraid I did, Mr. Harris," Ames answered, closing the subject.

Dessert arrived then. Unfortunately, it was something featuring egg yolks, sugar, and too much wine. I took one taste of it, then poked Chris Ames gently in the ribs and offered him my dish. When he finished with his, we switched dishes surreptitiously.

"I believe we do have more of the zabaglione," Tamara said, noticing the empty dish in front of me. "I'm sure you can have what's left, Peggy, if you're still hungry."

"No, thank you," I said.

Coffee and after-dinner drinks were served in the living room. I passed most of the rest of the evening talking to Chris Ames. He seemed impressed that I'd spent four years in the navy and was a campus cop. I found out that he was the son of the founder of a regional chain of hardware stores, and that he'd grown up in the mansion that was now the Tower.

Cameron Harris saw to it that he stayed the center of attention, with his loud laugh and voice. As Ames and I talked, I watched a little pantomime take place between Harris and Melody. She'd sat down at one end of a couch, slipped off her heels, and tucked her feet up under her. Harris came in after her and sat down beside her on the couch. She tried to put her feet back down on the floor, but he caught one, took it onto his lap, and began petting it, as if it were a cat. Melody blushed deeply and managed to twist the foot out of his grasp and tuck it back under her dress.

"Who's the old guy who limps around the Tower pushing a broom?" Harris asked Tamara, when she came over to refill his brandy snifter. "I tried to talk to him a couple of weeks ago when I was there, but I couldn't make out a word he said."

"That's Frank," she replied, "our custodian. Frank Ott." She looked at Chris Ames. "Frank was with Chris a long time, and before Chris took over the family business, he was with Chris's father. Isn't that right, Chris?"

"What's his problem?" Harris asked Ames. "A stroke?"

Ames shook his head. "No, he's always been like that. He runs his words together. But if you're around him a lot, and you take the time, you can make out most of what he says." He smiled at Melody. "Melody understands him."

"So do you, Mr. Ames," Melody replied.

"He slipped me something as I was making my getaway," Harris said. "At first I thought it was dirty pictures, but no such luck, it was a religious tract. Does he hand them out to everybody, Munk, or just to those of us obviously on the high road to hell?" For the second time tonight, he'd called Melody "Munk."

"He's harmless, Cam; it's nothing personal." She got up and sat down next to Niobe, over by the fireplace.

I caught Gary's eye and rolled mine. To make my meaning even clearer, I tapped my watch. He took the hint and went to get our coats.

"Not leaving so early, are you, Red?" Harris asked.

"Have to get to work, I'm afraid." That was a lie, for I had the night off.

"You work nights? I'm impressed. A woman walking those mean, tree-shaded paths alone in the night, sworn to keep the University crime-free. Make a great story." Looking from me to Gary, just coming back with our coats, he added, "I'll be spending a lot more time here now, you know, so we'll surely meet again. This semester at the U has reminded me of how much I miss the Midwest, and how little I really belong in New York. I have to get back to my roots." For a moment he sounded sincere. But then he ruined it. He called over to Niobe Tigue, "Is that the word I want, Niobe, 'roots'?"

She turned and glared at him, the shadows cast by the fire emphasizing the gauntness of her face, but she didn't say anything.

I pulled Gary toward the front door. Tamara and John Meade followed at our heels, making hostlike noises, and Harris came after them. "I hope you're bringing Peggy to my reading tomorrow night, Gary." He slapped Gary on the shoulder. "I just might put a campus cop with red hair into my story—a cameo appearance. Whatever else Niobe might think of my writing, I'm sure she'll agree I have a gift for improvisation."

The candles in their little ceramic sacks had all burned out when Gary and I retraced our steps down the Meades' flagstone walk to the car. I turned to him and muttered sweetly, "You owe me."

Three

Gary didn't take me to Cameron Harris's reading the next night, Paula and Lawrence did. Gary was already at the Tower, since it was his turn to help get the place ready and take tickets.

Paula, who was driving, said she'd heard that the novel Harris was working on was supposed to be all about his years as a member of the Second Story, before he went to New York. "A roman à clef."

"A 'novel with a key,'" Lawrence explained for my benefit.

"Thank you," I said politely. "Larry," I couldn't help adding.

"Did Harris talk about it last night?" Paula asked, glancing at me in the rearview mirror.

"He just promised me a major role," I said.

All the mansion's downstairs windows were ablaze with light, and the tower itself was floodlit as eerily as it had been four months before. The roof was covered with snow, the trees were bare, and the parking lot was full. Cameron Harris's reading was a sellout.

Gary was at the door. He looked at my ticket twice, took a bite out of it to make sure it was genuine, then waved us in.

Almost all the chairs from the Askew Funeral Home

were filled, so we couldn't sit together. We split up to find single chairs in different parts of the room.

Tamara Meade fluttered about on the stage, peering out at the crowded room from the podium, glancing at her watch. She looked considerably more nervous than she had the last time I'd seen her up there.

The man sitting next to me gave me a nudge in the ribs. "She fears the worst," he whispered. "She figured pretty prominently in Cam's love life, you know, back in the old Second Story days." He was big and loose-jointed and had a black goatee, the first I'd ever seen up close. "That's why she's sweating. Perspiring, I should say. Tamara Wallace Meade doesn't sweat. She thinks maybe she's going to see herself all too clearly in one of his characters tonight. Payback time."

"You poked me in the ribs with your elbow," I said. "You're going to have to be more careful. We're packed in here pretty tight. What do you mean by 'payback time'?"

"You don't know?" he asked, as if I'd just arrived from deep space. "Haven't you read her novel, *Romance and Reality?*"

I confessed that this was the first I'd heard of it.

"Ah, well." He settled more comfortably into his chair. "Then you won't get half the fun we're in for tonight. I was a member of the Second Story myself, y'know, back in the old days. I knew 'em all—knew Cam Harris when he was just an innocent country boy, cow dung still stuck to his boots."

"Speaking of which, there's egg clotted in your goatee."

He dug out a handkerchief and began rubbing it into his face. "Did I get it all?"

"Most of it." I glanced at my watch. It was past time for the reading to start.

A few minutes later, Tamara stepped off the stage

and began conferring with Gary and Niobe. The audience was growing restless, sensing that something was wrong. Then Tamara disappeared through the door at the back of the stage.

Gary stepped to the podium and tapped the microphone to get our attention. "We can't find Harris," he said, bluntly. "Please bear with us for a few more minutes."

The man with the goatee nudged me in the ribs again. "Maybe he had an accident, to shut him up. The way it happens in books."

We waited another five minutes. The first to get up was Melody Carr's husband. Instead of leaving, as he'd done at the last reading, he went up to the front of the room and began talking to Melody, quietly at first and then more animatedly. She listened, her face expressionless, her eyes fixed on his face, and then shook her head, giving him a gentle smile. She even touched his arm lightly.

He stared at her, looking incredulous, and shook her off. He stomped down the aisle, his tightly drawn mouth visible through his thin beard. The people standing in the back of the room moved aside for him. He was still wearing crisply pressed army fatigues and polished combat boots.

Other people began leaving too, those back by the double doors first, and by the time Gary stepped up onto the stage to announce that the reading had been canceled, only about a third of the audience remained.

"Did you try the bars on Central?" the man next to me shouted up at Gary.

The audience laughed uneasily. Gary waited for silence. Then he said, "No," and Niobe came up beside him and explained how we could get our money back.

When I found Paula and Lawrence, I asked them if

Cameron Harris was much of a drinker, since I'd seen him drink quite a lot the night before.

They didn't know. "Anyway," Lawrence said, "he's a big man, so he ought to be able to hold his liquor. No one's ever said he drank himself blotto before an important event. He isn't like Dylan Thomas," he added, as if he'd known both men well.

"We're taking off," Paula said. "I suppose you're going to wait for Gary?"

Gary finished closing up the Tower. We were putting on our coats when he said, "Nobody who knows Harris thinks this is typical behavior. He may not be the nicest guy in the world, but he's not known for standing up his fans."

I asked him if they'd tried the local hospitals.

"No, but Tamara called the police. They didn't take Harris's no-show very seriously. She was so upset, she finally made Melody drive her home, which was why I had to go out there and cancel the reading." Suddenly his eyes lit up and, leering, he asked, "You want to go up in the tower?"

"Sure, why not?" I replied. I'd never been up there, so maybe the evening wouldn't be a total loss.

"Follow me. I know where the key is."

It was hanging from a nail in the kitchen, a heavy, ornate key, dark with age. Gary took it and led the way back down the hall to the stairs to the second floor. "There's another way into the tower from a storage room across from the kitchen, but only the custodian, Frank, has a key to that."

"Maybe we should knock first," I said, "just in case Harris is up there, in the arms of a lover, time forgotten."

Gary looked at me as if he thought that might be a possibility. "It'll serve him right to get caught in the act, if he is." At the end of the hall, Gary opened the door and reached in. He flicked on a wall switch, and a light went on somewhere above us on the steep flight of stairs. A draft of cold, musty air came out at us. Another steep flight of stairs went down into the darkness below us.

"The tower was added after the house was built. It's pure decoration." He gestured for me to go ahead of him up the stairs.

I hesitated, feeling an inexplicable moment of panic. Then I remembered. The last time I'd climbed stairs like these was in an old house where I'd been trapped and nearly burned to death.

"It's okay," Gary said, giving me a little push.

Right. I climbed the stairs, resolved not to spend a lot of time up there. I don't mind heights, as long as there's a fire escape. There wasn't one on the tower.

Although the tower was round, the unpainted paneling made the room at its top square, with small windows in all four walls. The ceiling was high in the center and steeply sloped. There was a small door in one corner, to what I assumed was a storage closet. You'd have to duck your head to get inside. The worn planks of the floor made a hollow noise, and gave slightly as we walked across them.

"Look at that," Gary said, pointing to a wood-burning stove next to the door, squatting on the cast-iron paws of some animal. "It must be an antique by now."

I went over and touched it. It was as cold as the room.

"Probably hasn't been used since the thirties," Gary said. "I'll bet this was the servants' quarters."

We stood together at the west window, stooping slightly so that we could see out of it.

The view was wonderful. Because the mansion was

on top of a hill, the tower looked out over a sea of tree-
tops, mostly bare this time of year, the snow-covered
roofs of tall houses occasionally breaking the surface
like the keels of capsized ships. We couldn't see much
of the University, just the chimneys of Frye Hall, the
sloped tile roofs of some of the taller buildings on the
Old Campus, and the campanile, of course, on the mall.
Its clock showed almost nine. Farther away, across the
river to the south, the lights of the New Campus glit-
tered, and beyond that we could see the skyline of the
city, all lit up and beautiful in the dark.

Directly below, we saw the Tower parking lot, with
only Gary's car left in it. A residential street led down
and away from it to Central Avenue, with its cafés,
bars, and little theaters that catered mostly to the University crowd. Maybe the man with the goatee was
right, and Cameron Harris was down there somewhere,
in one of the bars. If so, somebody who'd been in the
audience would probably have found him by now, and
reminded him of what he'd forgotten.

But I didn't believe he was down there. I'd seen
enough of Cameron Harris to know he wouldn't miss
an event like this, no matter how superior he felt to the
local authors he'd left behind.

"What did Melody's husband have to say to her up
by the stage?" I asked Gary. "And remove that hand,
please."

The tower was a romantic enough place, but the
room was unfurnished and cold. And while the floor
gave a little, it didn't give enough for what Gary had in
mind. Why do men—even reasonably sensible men like
Gary—get so turned on when they're alone with a
woman in an unlikely, and usually uncomfortable,
place?

Gary snorted in disgust, either at me or at Melody's
husband. "I didn't hear all of it, just that he wanted her

to go for a drink. She said no. She's tougher than she looks."

"She'd have to be, just to get up in the morning."

"Maybe there's a blanket or something in that closet over there," Gary said hopefully.

"Sorry," I said, "there's no fire escape."

"I wasn't planning to start a fire."

"Then what's the point? C'mon, let's go now." Straightening up, I turned and pushed him back, playfully but firmly. He tripped over his own feet, lost his balance, and almost fell over backward, but I caught his outstretched hands before he did. We did some more or less amiable roughhousing—half wrestling, half dancing—across the room, before I got him pointed toward the stairs.

I'd taken only two steps after him when I heard a shriek of rusty metal behind me. I spun around, but it stopped as abruptly as it had started. The room was still empty, but now the closet door hung open, and dust floated in the yellow light around it.

"What was that?" Gary called up the stairs.

I went back to find out.

"Peggy? What's going on?"

Cameron Harris was in the closet, in a chair that faced the door. One hand was resting on a sheaf of paper in his lap; the other was holding a poker that trailed along the floor beside him, as if he was about to get up and stir the fire, except that there was no fire in that room. He seemed to be staring straight at me in his famous nearsighted way, but I knew that the glitter in his eyes was nothing more than a reflection of the naked bulb above us.

I heard Gary's sudden intake of breath and felt his arm around my shoulder, as he pulled me close to him. He didn't say anything. I appreciated it, the arm and the closeness, too. We stood still for a minute, as still as the dead man slumped in the chair, staring at us.

I didn't need Gary, of course. I've stumbled on bodies before, alone, and I could have dealt with this one alone, too. But it's a lot better to have a friend around, at times like those.

Four

Down in the Tower's kitchen, Gary and I sat at a table with Buck Hansen, a homicide lieutenant I've known a long time. Sergeant Burke, Buck's assistant, sat next to him, taking notes in his strange shorthand.

"Whoever put the body in the closet didn't close the door all the way afterwards," Buck said, "or else the latch didn't work properly. It's old. Your walking around up there must've been enough to jar the door open."

Buck's a little taller than me—about five ten—and he has silvery blond hair and a wide mouth that doesn't smile as often as his eyes do. His eyes are very blue.

I suddenly noticed how tired he looked. Buck has deep wrinkles at the corners of his eyes, like a lizard, a beautiful lizard. However, tonight his eyes were hooded and looked bruised. I realized I hadn't seen him in several months. We get together for dinner or lunch regularly, to catch up on what's going on in our lives, but he'd been busier than usual lately. It's become a bull market for homicide.

"Don't you ever get a vacation?" I asked him.

"It's been a while," he said. "There's blood on the poker Harris had in his hand, but I don't have to tell

29

you he didn't use it to kill himself. He was hit with it, more than once, from behind. The back of his head's a mess. From the marks on the floor, and the bloodstains, it looks like he was killed by the west windows and then dragged over to the chair and shoved into the closet."

He turned to Gary and asked him how he'd known where the key to the tower was kept.

"One of the first things I did after I joined the Tower was ask somebody if I could go up there," Gary told him.

"Who?"

"Who'd I ask? Whoever was around at the time, I guess—I don't remember. All the Towerites know where the key's kept, and a lot of visitors probably do too. I've taken a few people up there myself, besides Peggy."

I wondered who he'd taken up into the tower besides me, decided it was an unworthy thought.

Gary had been the first to arrive at the Tower that night, about six, since he was scheduled to open the place up and let the caterers in. Niobe Tigue, who had a van, was responsible for getting the folding chairs from the funeral home. When Gary arrived, only the custodian, Frank Ott, was there scraping ice off the walks.

Buck asked who else he'd seen come in, and Gary told him that Tamara Meade had arrived shortly after he had, probably a little after six. "That's pretty early, isn't it?" Buck asked. "The reading didn't start until eight. What did she have to do here so early?"

"Nothing, but she's the worrying kind. The last time we had a big-name author, the food never arrived. So she came early tonight, to make sure there weren't any screw-ups. She took Harris's failure to show up tonight as a reflection on her, and that's how she'll take his murder too."

After discussing the details of the reading for a few minutes, Tamara had gone to her office on the second floor, and Gary had gone into the auditorium to set up the sound system and test it. Niobe arrived in her van at about six-thirty, Gary guessed, bringing the folding chairs, and he went out back to help her carry them in from the parking lot.

"That's a lot of chairs," Buck said. "Did just the two of you bring them in?"

Gary grinned sourly. "If you mean, did Tamara or Frank offer to help, the answer's no, they didn't. I assume Tamara was busy, practicing her introductory speech and worrying."

Prodded by Buck, Gary figured it took ten minutes for Niobe and him to bring the chairs in and set them up. The caterers arrived while they were doing that. Tamara came downstairs and got in everybody's way. The next time Gary paid any attention, other Tower members and early birds were starting to arrive to get good seats.

Buck asked Gary if Cameron Harris had had a key to the Tower. Gary didn't know, but he didn't think so, since he wasn't one of the teachers or administrators.

Bonnie Winkler, an assistant medical examiner, came in to tell Buck they could take Harris's body away. Buck asked her for an estimated time of death, but she grinned and shook her head. Rigor mortis had begun to set in, she said, which meant Harris had probably been dead more than two hours before I'd found him, but how much longer, she couldn't say yet. The blood on the body and on the murder instrument was still sticky, but in that cold room, it could take a long time to dry.

Half an hour later, Buck let Gary and me go. He followed us down the hall and out the back door to the parking lot. Cameramen from the local TV stations were waiting for us, and as we came out the back door, their cameras rose up like donkeys' heads and reporters crowded around us, braying.

Buck made a brief generic statement that could have been filmed years ago and used for any murder. The reporters didn't seem to notice. Gary and I stood in the glare of television lights and the flash of strobes. A TV reporter hollered at me from the crowd, "O'Neill, right? Peggy O'Neill. Aren't you the campus policewoman who found Professor Adam Warren's body at the University two years ago?"

"Yes." It seemed longer than that. I recognized the reporter from that time, and wondered if I had aged as much as she had.

"What were the two of you doing up there?" she demanded, her bulging eyes darting from me to Gary and back again.

"Admiring the view," I said.

"Did you go up there expecting to find Cameron Harris's corpse?"

"No. That was just a bonus."

As Gary drove us out of the parking lot, I glanced back. The floodlights were still on, as they'd been the first time I'd seen the tower, giving the illusion that it was alive and moving against the dark winter sky. Up in the tower room, the brightly lit windows looked like the eyes of some prehistoric monster staring out over the city.

"You make a habit of finding the bodies of famous people?" Gary asked me, after we'd showered and climbed into my bed. It's a king-sized bed, because I like a lot of space, even when I'm with someone. I gave him a brief account of what the television reporter had been referring to, the body I'd once discovered on campus.

"There's still quite a lot about you I don't know, isn't there?" he said.

I hope so, I thought, as I switched off the light.

Five

I followed the case in the newspaper—I don't watch television news; there's too much noise—and left Buck alone with it. It was obvious he wasn't making any progress, at least none he was willing to talk about to reporters. After ten days, fresher corpses shoved Cameron Harris into the obscurity he'd dreaded in life, although he did make news when Chris Ames, who'd donated his father's mansion to the Towerites, announced a ten-thousand-dollar reward for information leading to the arrest of Harris's murderer. Ames had been my companion at the dinner party the night before Harris's murder and had made the evening almost bearable. A picture of him accompanied the article, a formal portrait that missed the twinkle in his small, round eyes and the mischievous smile. I'd enjoyed his company.

Two weeks after the murder, I invited Buck over for dinner. I fixed lasagna—like everybody else, I have a foolproof recipe—and salad, and Buck brought his own wine. I drank sparkling water with lemon. When we'd finished eating, we decided to skip dessert and walk around Lake Eleanor instead. It was a starry night without wind, and lots of other people were also out, walking around the lake on its lighted path, or skating on the rink.

Buck's one of my closest friends. His personal life's a mystery to the people on his job, and I don't know much about it either. A little over a year ago, I launched a trial balloon and watched as he let it sail right over his head. I'm glad he did, I guess. It's been my experience that the pleasures of friends last longer than those of lovers, and it's never the same, returning from the one to the other, if you can do it at all.

I asked Buck how the Harris case was going.

He looked at me, a glint of something in his tired eyes. Amusement, maybe. "Not enough suspects, too many suspects. A lot of people had good reasons for not liking him much, but none of them seems willing to confess to killing him. It's also hard to check alibis, when we can't even pin down the exact time of death."

"I suppose Gary's a suspect too."

"Every member of the Tower's a suspect. But I doubt Gary would have taken you up into the tower if he'd known his victim's body was there. Finding the body as quickly as we did is the only break we've had in the case. Unless, of course, Gary's among the weird ones. Is he?"

I assured Buck he wasn't.

"He also doesn't seem to have a motive," Buck went on. "He only joined the Tower a year ago, and claims he never met Harris until Harris arrived here last September."

"Gary dated Sandra Carr for a while," I said, playing devil's advocate, "and Cameron Harris dated her too, back in the Second Story days."

"Mr. Mallory confessed all that to you, did he? You think he did it, huh?"

"No, I just want to be sure you don't. Gary's not the jealous type. But maybe Sandra is."

"Maybe. A murder in a tower, the corpse set up the way Harris was—that's her style, all right. But she has an alibi, of sorts. She was in California, watching the filming of one of her novels. She only returned last week."

I knew that. A couple of days earlier, at Gary's place, I'd noticed an invitation Sandra had sent him to a party she was throwing to celebrate her return to town.

"Could she have made a quick trip back here, killed Harris, then returned to California?"

"We haven't been able to find anybody who'll say for sure she was in California the night Harris was killed. Have you ever read one of her novels? They're real page turners."

I told him I preferred cozier mysteries.

"Anyway, according to rumor, Harris was involved with a number of women here before he left for New York. They weren't all in the writing community, either. He got around."

Buck said he'd located a woman who'd gone out with him for a while. She'd thought the relationship was going somewhere, but about a month before he was murdered, he stopped calling her. When she called to ask what had gone wrong, he'd said something rude and hung up.

"Is she a suspect?"

"No. She has a solid alibi for the day Harris was killed, which is probably why she talked to us so freely."

"Does she know why he dumped her?"

"She thinks he found somebody younger. She said he always liked them young. She'd known Harris back in the Second Story days too."

I told Buck what I'd seen at the Meades' dinner party the night before Harris was killed, how he'd fondled Melody Carr's foot until she pulled it away and how he'd also flirted with Tamara Meade. I mentioned Melody's reading at the Tower four months earlier, when she'd read her poem about a penis and her husband stormed out in a rage.

Buck nodded, as he stepped over an icy patch on the path. "I've heard that story more than once," he said, smiling, "but not from any of the Tower writers themselves, who share a collective short memory. I've heard it from people who were in the audience. We haven't been able to find any connection between Melody Carr and Harris, if that's what you're thinking."

"Did anybody have any suggestions as to who might have owned the appendage in question?" I asked.

"None that I've heard. I gather the poem didn't offer much in the way of physiological detail."

This was a strange conversation. "Have you talked to her husband about it?"

"Oh yes. His name's Tony Verdugo, a professor of literature at the U. He just laughed in my face, said the poem wasn't about any real man, it was supposed to be about how love overcomes sexual differences, or something like that. I didn't take notes."

"Why'd Verdugo walk out, if that's all it was?"

"He said he had another engagement."

I laughed. So did Buck.

"He and Harris got in a fight at a party last fall," Buck went on, "and Harris knocked him down."

"Over Melody?"

"Not according to Verdugo. He claims he'd written a review of Harris's first novel that Harris didn't like. He made it sound as though Harris had more of a motive for murdering him than the other way around."

We walked on for a while without talking, watched a pack of little boys chase a pack of little girls across the ice on skates, laughing and screaming.

We were on the other side of the lake now, across the street from the sprawling home of Tamara and John

Meade. The downstairs was dark, but I could see lights behind the drapes in one of the upstairs windows.

I asked Buck why Harris had spent the last two weeks of his life at the Meades'. He explained that Harris had rented a house for the semester from a University professor who was away on leave. The only catch was that the professor and his family were returning in early January, two weeks before the semester ended. The Meades invited Harris to stay with them those two weeks, and he'd accepted.

According to John Meade, on the day Harris was murdered, he left the house a little before noon. He told Meade he was going to the University to turn in his grades and visit with some of his colleagues. From there, he would make his way to the Tower in time for his reading at eight. He didn't drive, and didn't even have a driver's license.

"Did he really go to the U?" I asked.

"If he did, nobody saw him—or will admit to it, if they did. He didn't have any friends among the English Department faculty. He mostly hung out with some of the students from his writing class."

"So either he lied to Meade," I said, "or somebody at the University is lying to you—or at least not coming forward."

"That's right. And he *did* lie to Meade about one thing: He didn't have any grades to turn in. He didn't give a final exam, so he'd turned in his grades on the last day of class."

I reminded Buck that he only had John Meade's word for what Harris had told him, and when he'd left the house.

"Isn't that usually the way," Buck said. It wasn't a question.

When I asked if the autopsy had yielded any clues, he said Harris had had something to drink about an hour before he was killed. "It was wine, by the way, but not enough to make him drunk."

"How do you know it was wine?"

"Bonnie said she could smell it during the autopsy."

Ugh. "If he'd been in a bar or restaurant," I said, "somebody ought to remember. Cameron Harris stood out in a crowd, and he'd been on quite a few talk shows recently. And he was loud."

We fell silent again.

After a while Buck said, "Tamara Meade and Harris used to be lovers. They lived together for over a year, until just before he left for New York. Mrs. Meade insists they parted amicably, but that's not what I've heard. I guess they must have made up, though, since he stayed at her place for two weeks. I wonder how much John Meade enjoyed that."

"What about the novel he was working on?" I asked. "Was it as full of nasty caricatures of Towerites as they expected?"

"We found the manuscript in his luggage at the Meades' home. It was going to deal with his early life, ending with his years as a member of the Second Story, before he left for New York. Some of it's surprisingly good—especially the chapters dealing with his childhood. The tone gets more recognizably Harris—'slyly mean-spirited,' as a reviewer called his last book—when he gets to the Second Story years."

"Could you identify any of the characters?"

"I couldn't, but with a little help from a few Towerites who aren't mentioned in the book and some Second Story hangers-on, we got some pretty good ideas of whom he was going to include. It promised to be quite a nasty dish."

"What about the manuscript on his lap? I assume that's what he planned to read from that night."

"It was going to be one of the last chapters, I think.

It's about an affair he had when he was younger, with a woman who jilted him and then wrote a novel about it. He implies that the experience embittered him, although it's quite a funny story too. The woman is a barely disguised Tamara Wallace Meade."

"Did you show it to her?"

"No, we spared her that, but we told her about it. She appeared shocked. He'd told her the novel was going to be a gift to the writers who had nurtured him, back when he was just starting out, a gift for the Tower. He'd abused her hospitality, she said. She was also quick to point out that if *she'd* killed him, she'd have taken the manuscript away with her, not made it part of a sick little tableau." Buck grinned. "John Meade said he might have sued Harris, if Harris had lived to read that chapter, or publish the novel."

I suggested that maybe one of them had put the manuscript in Harris's lap just to throw suspicion off themselves.

Buck said, "People only think like that in books."

We'd reached our starting point and turned up the street to my place.

"I'd like to read it," I said.

He looked at me, amusement, or the streetlamp, flickering in his eyes. "There's blood on it."

"I know. I was there, remember? It's probably dry by now."

"It's evidence."

"So make me a Xerox."

"Why?"

"Because I have access to the Tower, Buck, and I've met a lot of the people associated with the place. I'm going to start snooping around, whether you like it or not, and you know it. It would help if I could read that manuscript."

We were standing on the street where Buck's car was parked.

"I suppose the killer could have been somebody from the University too," Buck said slowly. "Somebody Harris met since he returned here."

"Exactly. A good point." If Buck hadn't brought it up, I'd been planning to. "And I'm not exactly a stranger to the University, am I?"

"No, you're not. I'd almost forgotten that." He avoided looking at me. We'd played these games before.

"So do I get to look at it?"

He waited a few moments before answering. "Okay."

"Thanks." I glanced at my watch.

"Am I keeping you from something?"

"No, but I have to call Gary before he goes to bed. Sandra Carr's throwing a party Friday night, and he's invited. I think I'd like to go, if you haven't solved the case by then. You never know whom you'll meet. Parties like that attract lots of creative people. And arranging Cameron Harris's corpse in the closet, with the poker and the manuscript, was creative, wasn't it?"

"Whoever killed Cameron Harris has to be a little crazy," Buck said, "crazier than most murderers. The way the corpse was arranged was a form of communication. We don't know what it means yet, but sane people don't send messages that way. So be discreet, Peggy, and don't take any chances."

"I always look both ways when crossing the street."

"Cameron Harris wasn't run down by a car."

Six

A few days earlier, I'd noticed a postcard on Gary's kitchen table. It featured a lurid drawing of a woman on a flight of stairs, flinching from a shadow holding a knife. I happened to have a butter knife in my hand at the time, which I used to flip the card over. It was an invitation from Sandra Carr.

"I'm not planning to go," Gary had said, catching me in the act of reading his mail. "With Sandra's parties, you don't need to RSVP."

After getting rid of Buck, I called Gary and told him I wanted to go to Sandra's party.

Long pause. "What's your sudden interest in Sandra Carr?"

"It just occurred to me that I live too sheltered a life. I need to meet a wilder and crazier type of person, and a woman who writes thriller novels sounds like just the ticket. You parted friends, didn't you?"

"She has cats. You're allergic to cats."

"Just enough so I don't want one in my house. But I can put up with them at somebody else's house, if I'm sufficiently entertained, and they don't crawl on me. C'mon, Gary. You owe me, remember. She must still like you, if she sent you an invitation to her party."

"She just didn't bother to remove my name from her

42

party list. She's got it computerized, and when she decides to have a party, she cranks out invitations to the entire list. Cameron Harris's estate probably got an invi—" He broke off. "Does this have anything to do with Harris's murder, Peggy?"

"Gary. I didn't put up this kind of a fuss when you asked me to go to the Meades' ghastly dinner party, did I?" That wasn't an answer, of course, but what would an answer have gotten me but more questions?

When I got up the next morning, I went to the nearest public library and looked up Tamara Meade's novel *Romance and Reality*. The dust jacket featured a woman standing in an art gallery, staring at two portraits hanging on the wall, one of a man who looked like the young Byron writing a poem in a high wind, the other of an older, more serious man in his study, perhaps balancing his checkbook.

When I took it to the librarian, she looked at me curiously and asked if I knew the writer. I asked if only the author's friends checked out the book.

"Oh, no, that's not what I meant. It has a rather steady circulation—but to a somewhat older reader." She looked a little uncomfortable, as if she'd expressed herself badly.

"Women who don't wear jeans and down jackets, you mean."

"Exactly."

Romance and Reality wasn't a long book, and I'm a fast reader, but it still seemed to take forever, like driving across South Dakota. The heroine's name is Alyssa—always something to be deplored in fiction, if not in life. She's a woman of stunningly ordinary sensibilities who finds herself torn between two men: one creative and obsessed with his art, penniless and apt to stay that way; the other a solid member of the upper middle class, a pediatrician. As the novel grinds on, Alyssa gradually begins to sense the destructive self-absorption of the creative man, and her disillusionment with him is completed when she finds him making love to her younger sister in a clump of lilacs in late spring. Running roughly parallel to this strand of the plot is her growing discovery of the pediatrician's goodness. Alyssa finally decides she wants an ordered, secure life, a life that will give her the stability to develop her own potential, rather than live to develop the potential of another. It never occurs to her to develop her potential without either man.

I might have thrown *Romance and Reality* across the room, if it hadn't been a library book and if I hadn't been reading it for clues. While neither the artist in the novel nor the pediatrician resembled Cameron Harris and John Meade in appearance, there were obvious similarities. John Meade couldn't have enjoyed reading the novel much, unless he had a great sense of humor or tolerance, neither of which I'd noticed in him.

While the pediatrician does win Alyssa in the end, the artist gets all the best lines—and all the love scenes too, some of which were pretty well done, in a breathless way. Alyssa seemed especially fond of the dramatist Henrik Ibsen, and of his demand that people be true to themselves, whatever the cost. I remembered that Ibsen had been mentioned at the Meades' dinner party. Cameron Harris called him Gibson. I'd read *A Doll's House* and *Hedda Gabler* in college and found him boring, but maybe I read bad translations.

I wondered if Tamara Meade had a younger sister, or hated the smell of lilacs, or both.

That evening a cop came to my door with a fat manila envelope, compliments of Lieutenant Hansen. It contained a Xeroxed copy of the chapter Cameron Harris planned to read the night he was murdered, and a copy of the rest of the manuscript too.

I read the chapter before leaving for work that night. It was a strange experience, and not only because of the Xeroxed bloodstains. It basically told the same story as *Romance and Reality* but from quite a different point of view. Whereas Tamara's novel was sentimental and humorless, Harris's story was the rough sketch for what might have become a small comic masterpiece. The focus was on the naïveté of the earnest young narrator, who is led astray by a cynical and grasping woman who enjoys playing, for a time, at the bohemian life of the artist. When he finally sees through her, he still can't break off their affair. In the end she tires of being poor and throws him over for an older man, a smug and boring member of the upper middle class. She does it, she announces, because she wants to be true to herself.

To someone who hadn't read Tamara's novel, or who didn't realize there was another version of the story, Harris's story might be nothing more than funny and, in places, touching. To someone who knew the real people involved, it was a devastating portrait of Tamara and her husband, John. If it was going to be a chapter in a book that Harris was calling a gift to the Tower, then his sense of humor was even nastier than I'd thought. What was he going to do—wrap it up and give it to them?

The chapter wasn't finished. It stopped just as the unnamed woman finishes explaining to the narrator why she's dumping him, using words and concepts much too big for her. Either Harris had planned to read just the fragment, or else he'd intended to improvise an ending.

I put the first chapters of the novel, the ones Buck said dealt with Harris's childhood, aside and skimmed through the notes he'd written for chapters on the Tower, which he'd planned to call the "Garret." They were mostly just fragments of sentences and phrases, and occasionally the names of characters with a sentence or two describing them. Only two names rang any bells for me. One was a character called "Mentor." Beside this name, Harris had written: "Who was Mentor? The goddess Athena disguised as an old man. My Mentor is an old man disguised as the goddess Athena!"

At the Meades' dinner party, Harris had called Niobe Tigue his mentor. This was apparently his way of paying off that debt.

Another character was called "Trisha Payne." Next to her name Harris had written: "If cucumber sandwiches could write poetry, they'd sound like Trisha."

"Trisha Payne" was Melody Carr. I knew that because that was how I felt about Melody's poems—with one notable exception.

I was patrolling the Old Campus that night, my favorite beat. Almost from the start, I've taken the dog watch, from 11:00 P.M. to 7:00 A.M. I love the night, perhaps because it's a dangerous love for a woman. And I enjoy being alone. Of course, a cop on duty is never truly alone, since she wears a uniform and carries a pistol she knows how to use. The walkie-talkie on her belt keeps up a soft metallic chatter that's company of a sort. All women should be allowed to dress the way I do; it would be a way of taking back the night.

The moon cast the shadows of trees across the snow and reflected off the windows of the old, ivy-covered buildings. I'd spent most of my time as a student in and around these buildings, and I'd only crossed the river to the New Campus when forced to take a lecture class in science to satisfy a requirement.

We enter buildings at random, just to let people know we're there. If we're lucky, the loneliness is broken only by an occasional student or professor who's stayed on campus late. If we're not so lucky, we might have to deal with a burglar or vandal looking for something to steal or trash, or one of the homeless who manage to get into buildings and live in them for weeks—months sometimes—before they're caught.

Spring semester had only just started and the early February night was cold and quiet. I spent my time thinking about Tamara Meade and Cameron Harris and their two contrasting love stories.

Tamara had seemed to be looking forward to Harris's future involvement in the Tower and his more frequent returns to town. She gave a dinner party in his honor the night before he was murdered and let him stay in her home for two weeks, in spite of the fact that he'd cheated on her when they were lovers.

I shook my head angrily. I was confusing reality and fiction. What I meant was, if there was any truth to her story, Harris had cheated on her. But it was commonly believed, by the writers and ex-writers who knew them, that Tamara's novel was based on at least a grain of truth.

Maybe they'd agreed to let bygones be bygones. After all, their affair ended a long time ago, before Harris left town and became famous. And besides, in her novel Tamara comes off the victor—morally, at least. So why shouldn't she throw a party for him and invite him to stay with her and her wealthy husband? And why shouldn't Harris accept—knowing what he was going to read at the Tower?

Whatever the truth of either version of their love story, Tamara had gone from Cameron Harris to John Meade. I wondered if she ever regretted her choice, once Harris had become famous, and started making lots of money.

And how did John Meade feel?

However, the Meades were only two suspects among

many. The chapter Harris planned to read may not have had anything to do with his murder. He was carrying the story because he intended to read it that night; his killer might simply have taken the opportunity to confuse the police by placing it on his lap, rather than leaving it scattered around, as the bloodstains indicated.

It was a little after two in the morning. Paula's voice crackled suddenly from my walkie-talkie, jarring me out of my brooding. She and Lawrence were working the dog watch that month too, not because they liked it, as I do, but because it was Paula's turn. I told her where to find me, and a few minutes later, she pulled up in the squad car, Lawrence beside her. We drove off to an all-night diner near campus, the Donut Whole, for coffee and to warm up for the rest of the night.

I asked them how their writing was coming along.

"Paula's written a great poem about little kids skiing along the crest of a hill," Lawrence said. "Crows in scarves and stocking caps, streaking across the upside-down sky. They're black kids."

"Right, Larry," I said.

"The sky upside-down," Paula corrected him.

"I like it better my way. Her teacher thinks she's got a great talent for imagery."

"How about you?" I asked. "How's the nonfiction class going?"

"Pretty good," he said. "I'm revising a piece on Creeping Charlie, maybe for publication. Gary thinks it's good."

Creeping Charlie was a campus flasher. He got away with it for almost six months, until Lawrence figured out a pattern in his behavior and, just before Christmas, caught him pursuing his avocation in a campus parking ramp. It's hard being a flasher here in the winter, but Charlie figured a way: Under his long overcoat he wore only boots and trouser legs held up with suspenders.

One of his victims said she wasn't sure what in all that she was expected to admire.

"What about you, Peggy?" Paula asked me. "What're you doing in your spare time?"

She was fishing to find out how things were going between Gary and me. I couldn't tell her what I didn't know. "A little racquetball. A lot of skiing. And I thought I'd snoop around a bit, see if I could find out anything that might help solve the Cameron Harris murder."

"Oh, Peggy!" Paula exclaimed, her voice full of resignation. "Not again!"

I just smiled at her over my coffee cup.

"Hey, Paula," Lawrence said, "lighten up. Peggy found the guy's body, so it's her responsibility to find the killer. Makes perfect sense, when you think about it, especially when you remember that she's Buck Hansen's friend, and he's not doing so well on this one. Right, Peggy?"

I couldn't tell if he was being sarcastic. "Thank you, Lawrence," I said, giving him the benefit of the doubt.

Seven

When I woke up the next afternoon, I showered, dressed, and ate a couple of bananas with my coffee. Bananas go with coffee almost as well as chocolate, but they're better for you.

I drove up to the Tower and parked in its nearly empty lot.

At night, brightly lit and framed in darkness, the old mansion looked a little like a fairy-tale castle. During the day, washed in weak sunlight, it looked almost like all the other old mansions in the neighborhood. Its gingerbread trim was badly in need of work, and the tower itself was a comic appendage out of proportion to the size of the rest of the place.

I stood at the base of the tower and looked up. Thin clouds were sailing fast across the sky, creating the dizzying sense that the tower was falling on me. I shook my head to clear it and went over and rattled the mansion's side door. It was locked, with a faded sign tacked on it that said to use the front entrance. I continued on around to the front, climbed to the porch, pushed open the door, and went in.

The hallway was empty and silent. The double doors on the left, leading into the auditorium, were open, and light fell through the windows onto the figure of a man with a mop and a bucket of water, his back to me. Without the folding chairs, I could see that the floor needed sanding and a coat of varnish.

The rooms used for classes and offices were in both the basement and on the second floor. A directory, consisting of typewritten scraps of paper under glass, told me where the various writers had their offices. Melody's office was in the basement. Tamara's was upstairs.

Something touched my shoulder and I spun around. It was the man with the mop, Frank Ott, the Tower's custodian. He was about sixty, heavy, but not fat, and about six feet tall with a full head of gray hair and long sideburns. I suspected he'd had to work at coming up behind me so silently.

"You're into mime, aren't you, Frank?" I said, annoyed. "Poems of silence. Scaring people."

He waited until I'd finished, and then he said something in which all the words overlapped, as if he were trying to say them all at once. The only word I thought I understood was "scare," and I took it to mean he hadn't meant to scare me. His eyes looked apologetic too, which helped.

He didn't say anything else, just stood and waited, a smile on his face, hopeful or idiotic, I couldn't decide which. Everything about him was gray, from his messy hair and the stubble on his face to his mournful eyes.

"Okay," I said, and smiled back at him. I asked him who he was, pretending I didn't know.

He gave me a reproachful look and said something softly, making a "for shame" gesture with long, thick fingers.

"What?"

He repeated the words exactly as before, but more slowly, asking me why I'd asked him who he was, when I'd already called him "Frank."

I felt my face turn red. "I don't know," I told him. "Just making conversation. I'm sorry."

He liked the fact that I'd blushed. He beamed at me and then started on a long speech. I caught the name "Harris." Then he pointed to me again and said more words, one of which was "television."

I nodded, assuming he was telling me that he knew I'd found Cameron Harris's body. "Were you here that night?"

More excited explanation. At the end of it he grinned at me. However, since I'd understood only one word, "police," his grin meant nothing.

"Aren't you ever scared," I asked, "having to work in a place where somebody was killed?"

He shook his head. A sudden look of anger appeared on his face. "I've been good!"

I thought about that for a moment. "You mean, Cameron Harris wasn't?"

He started in on another long, jumbled speech, his voice rising. The words "God" and "Bible" were clear, as was "hell." Then he stopped abruptly, looking over my shoulder, at the stairs. I turned around. It was Tamara Meade. She stopped on the landing when she saw me. "Oh, hello, Peggy." Her large eyes jumped from me to Frank, who turned and stalked back into the auditorium.

"Well, at least now you can say you've met Frank," she said, as I followed her back up the stairs. "I heard him talking, and going on rather too long and loudly, so I thought I'd better come down and see what was going on. He isn't my idea of an appropriate receptionist for the Tower. Could you understand anything he said? He takes a lot of getting used to."

I followed her down the hall and into her office.

"I think he was trying to explain why he didn't think Cameron Harris was a good person. There seemed to be some talk of hellfire and damnation too. But he didn't slip me a tract or anything, the way he did Harris. I could probably get used to the way he talks, with a little time."

"I'm sure you could." Tamara sat down at her desk. Without waiting to be asked, I sat down in the chair next to it. "Frank doesn't think any of us are good, I'm afraid," she continued. "In the gospel according to Frank, only God should have the power to create, so that makes us blasphemers in his eyes."

"He's told you that?"

"Oh yes, and not just me. He waxes eloquent on the subject—if you have the patience, and curiosity, to listen. Some people do. For some reason Frank adores Melody, although he wants her to repent too. He plays no favorites in that respect."

"Repent and give up writing," I said.

"Well, he has other sins in mind too, of course. Frank's got rather a lurid imagination. He holds the all too common belief that creative people are immoral." She shot me a quick glance, perhaps to see if I agreed with Frank.

"What's his problem?"

She shrugged. "He's been like that since childhood. He thinks faster than he can speak, gets all his words confused. He's got rather the opposite problem from most of us." She laughed again. Her laugh sounded nervous every time I heard it. She had once been extremely beautiful, but up close I could see that the effort to stay young was starting to age her. Her eyes were so striking that you might overlook their lack of warmth.

I asked her why she kept Frank around, if she disliked him so much.

"Oh, I don't dislike him. Besides, we can't get rid of him. Chris's only condition—Chris Ames, you remember—when he gave us the Tower was that we keep Frank. The Tower's curse," she added, with another little nervous laugh. "Anyway, he's harmless, and we don't have to pay him very much. Part of his salary is covered by a special program to mainstream people with handicaps. Incidentally, I want to thank you for finding Cam—Cam's body. I know that sounds absurd, and it must have been terrible for you, but the thought of him up there, all alone, is horrid. But that's what his killer intended, wasn't it, that we never find his body. That he be up there, almost over our heads, forever!" She rolled her eyes toward the ceiling. "And it would have made it so much harder for the police to catch the killer too, if you hadn't found him so quickly. Not that they're doing such a good job of it anyway. I'm babbling, aren't I? I always start to babble when I get on the subject of Cam." She rummaged around on her desk, found a Kleenex, dabbed at her dry eyes with it. "I imagine you're looking for Gary. He's not here today. He doesn't spend much time here, except when he's teaching his classes. But of course, you must know that." She looked at me expectantly, having finally talked herself into wondering about my visit.

"I was just driving by, and thought I'd stop in, on the off chance Gary was here. I've read your novel, by the way," I added. "I enjoyed it."

"Really?" She raised an eyebrow, not unlike the librarian who'd checked it out to me.

"Very much." I attended Catholic schools as a child, so lying comes easy. "Are you writing a sequel?"

"A sequel? No, I—" She paused. "I don't have much time for writing nowadays. A few years ago, I discovered that I have a talent for administration and fundraising. For the moment that gives me the same satisfaction that writing does. And, of course, the Tower needs me, if it's going to survive—and I want it to survive."

"It needs work," I said. "It's starting to look a little run-down, inside and out." Except for her office, of course.

Tamara's office was furnished as a kind of study, with a beautifully maintained antique desk, oak bookcases and file cabinets, an Oriental rug on the floor, and heavy drapes that covered not just the window but the entire wall. An antique lamp fixture hung from the ceiling in the middle of the room. Her office contrasted dramatically with the spartan appearance of the rest of the Tower.

As if reading my mind, she said, "I furnished this with my own money. I spend a lot of time here, on Tower business, and I like to be surrounded by beautiful things. But I agree, the Tower is beginning to look run-down. Until recently, there was a lot more grant money available for the arts. Both federal and state money have dried up. But that's my job, you know, to find new sources of funding. And it's very time-consuming."

"I suppose Harris's reading was to bring in extra revenue," I said.

She nodded. "That was part of it. But quite frankly we'd hoped to get more from Cameron than one night. You saw how many people came to hear him read. We hoped to use his name to attract more students and also to use his contacts to bring in writers with national reputations to teach and read. So whoever killed him also struck a blow at the Tower. I know that sounds selfish, to think of Cam's death in terms of our loss, but I can't help it."

"He'd never been here until he came to town last fall, had he?"

"That's right. He left for New York before Chris

gave us the mansion and didn't set foot in here until about four months ago."

That meant that the mansion—and the tower—had been a curiosity to Cameron Harris too, as it had been to me. Had he met somebody who offered to take him up into the tower and show him the view?

Tamara glanced at her watch. "I thought you were a campus policewoman. Is this your day off?"

"Oh no, I work nights. The dog watch."

"I see. I suppose, after you've been there awhile, you'll get a better watch." She stood up, making her wish to see me gone even clearer.

Taking the hint, I stood up too. "Can't Mr. Ames help the Tower financially?"

The question offended her. "Chris has done his share. We can't go on asking him for money forever, it wouldn't be fair. The Tower has to make it on its own now. Chris gave us this wonderful place; now it's up to us to make a go of it."

"And we're doing a piss-poor job of it, if you ask me." That came from Niobe Tigue, standing in the doorway, tall and rawboned, looking like a settler's wife in a film about pioneers. "This dump's a white elephant. We should never have left the Second Story. We could afford that."

Tamara tried to smile. "Niobe was the only one who wanted us to turn down Chris's gift."

"But you wouldn't listen," Niobe said, "and here we are. I'm here for my paycheck." She looked me up and down. "You on duty?"

"No," I said. "I just came over to see if Gary was here."

"Don't you have a phone? The phones still work in the Tower, don't they, Tamara? We can still pay the phone bill?"

Niobe Tigue was one of those people who have a

sixth sense about lying. They make life hard for people like me.

"I was in the neighborhood—"

"A couple of summers ago," she interrupted me, "you found the dead body of a man I knew slightly, I'm sorry to say. Adam Warren. A rat. And now you've found Cam's body. You make a practice of turning up corpses?"

"No, I—"

"And you're a friend of the homicide detective who's in charge of the case—he's talked to all of us, with that little man who follows him around taking notes." She meant Burke. "I could see it from the way the two of you looked at each other on television. Gary mentioned it too, so it wasn't only good detective work on my part." She paused. "Gary's a fine writer. I wonder if he knows that you're using him to get to us, to help your inept policeman friend figure out which one of us killed Cam. What'd she get out of *you,* Tamara?"

"Niobe, I don't think—" Tamara said.

"Right." Niobe snatched the paycheck out of Tamara's fingers and turned on her heels. She stopped. A man stood in the doorway. "You!"

"Hello, Niobe," he said. "How're you doing?"

"As if you gave a damn!" Her voice sounded thin and cold. "What're you doing here, Arthur? Isn't Melody in her office?"

"No, she's not." He turned to Tamara. "Tell me, Tamara, what's that janitor of yours got against me? If looks could kill, I'd have dropped dead on the stairs coming up here. Is he afraid I want to examine his psyche? If so, assure him that I wouldn't go near the thing."

Tamara started to say something, but Niobe beat her to it. "Unless he had the money to pay for it," she said. "Frank doesn't seem to think you're good for Melody,

Arthur. I guess he's a lot more perceptive than he appears. Maybe he thinks you're trying to take her over, body and soul. I'd look out for Frank, if I were you. Now, out of my way!"

She pushed by him. Pink-faced, he called after her, "Thanks for the warning, Niobe."

Tamara returned to her desk and began scribbling on a yellow legal pad, as if we weren't there anymore. The man looked me up and down as if trying to judge the freshness of a fish.

He was about my height, lean and graceful in his movements. His pencil-thin mustache outlined his long upper lip and then came down the sides of his mouth to do the same for his jawline, as if to hide, or flaunt, what seemed to me to be his weakest features. His teeth were too large, too square, and, when he smiled, too numerous. "Did I hear Niobe say you're a police officer investigating Harris's murder?"

"No," I said, "not really. She got it wrong."

"It wouldn't be the first thing she got wrong. 'Not really'? Does that mean you're 'sort of' or 'just a little bit of' a police officer investigating Harris's murder?"

He had Niobe's talent for not letting his victims off the hook. "I'm a campus cop, and I haven't been assigned to investigate Harris's murder." Who says I can't tell the truth when I have to? "Who are you?"

"Dr. Arthur Tigue. As you might imagine, I was once married to Niobe." He gave me a smile that asked for sympathy, then turned to Tamara. "Have you seen Melody anywhere? She's got an appointment with me at four. I thought, since I was in the neighborhood, I'd offer her a ride."

Without looking up from her desk, Tamara told him that Melody had left the Tower half an hour ago.

"Ah, well," he said cheerfully, "I'll see her at my office then." He nodded at the top of Tamara's head, stared hard at me, and left. I waited until I heard his footsteps on the stairs and then, ignoring Tamara's look of exasperation, asked her who he was.

"He told you. Arthur Tigue. Niobe's ex-husband."

"I got that, but what does he do? Is he a dentist?" I hate being stonewalled.

"No." In spite of herself, she asked, "Why?"

"Well, he said he's a doctor and Melody's got an appointment with him at four. Besides, he looks a lot like a dentist."

"That's close enough. Now please, I have work to do."

I wanted to ask her about Alyssa's younger sister, in *Romance and Reality*, and about lilacs too, but something told me now wasn't a good time. Wishing her a pleasant afternoon, I went back downstairs. Frank Ott was there, waiting for me. He said something I couldn't understand and shoved a piece of paper into my hand, before retreating to the basement.

"Thanks," I called after him.

It was a pamphlet with a devil on the cover in cheap, lurid colors. It urged me to forswear lying and graven images, and to live in truth. About the last thing you'd want to read, if you were a writer—or a snoop.

Eight

It was late afternoon when I left the Tower, and starting to get dark. According to Buck, Harris and his students had regularly gone to a bar on Central Avenue after class. The bar's name was the Whale, perhaps because it had swallowed up so many shipwrecked people. It was a two-minute drive down the hill from the Tower. Maybe I'd find one of Harris's students, there for old times' sake.

The Whale is located in the middle of a business community supported mostly by faculty and students: one expensive clothing store for the fraternity and sorority crowd and a used-clothing store for the rest of the students, a copy center, four or five cheap Asian restaurants, a good bakery, bars for every taste and pocketbook, a coffeehouse that serves great espresso, and a great used bookstore owned by the meanest man alive. Across the street from the Whale is a comedy theater, a Laundromat, and an Italian restaurant I like a lot, the Via Appia.

For a nondrinker, I knew the Whale pretty well. I'd been called there often enough, to break up fights and haul drunks off to detox. I hadn't been called there much recently, however, since the new owner had transformed the place from just another student bar into

something resembling an English pub. Now it specialized in beers and ales from the British Isles. The prices
kept the consumption of alcohol down and most of the
candidates for detox out.

It was dark inside, and hushed, but in another hour or
so it would be crowded with customers drinking British
brew and eating greasy baskets of fish and chips, which
actually taste pretty good. Right now only a few people
sat at tables scattered around the room.

"Hey, Peggy," the bartender, a lean, freckled woman
named Kyle called out. "It's been a while. You're out
and about early. I didn't think you got up before the sun
went down. Coffee?" She knew me well enough to
know I didn't want a beer.

I said no, thanks, I recognized the coffee in the pot
at the end of the bar; it had been there the last time I
came in. I told her I'd heard that Cameron Harris used
to hang out there.

"Sure. I knew him. He was a regular, right up till his
death. Came here with some of his students." Her face
darkened. "That was a terrible thing. He was a nice
guy. We joked around, and the money he left in tips
didn't clink, it rustled. You know, the homicide boys've
already been here, and I told them everything I know,
which is nothing. Harris wasn't here at all that day."

"What about his students? Were any of them here?"

She stopped wiping the bar counter with a rag and
pointed to somebody behind me. "He was. Rich Something. But some detectives talked to him already, so
he's old news."

The man she'd pointed to was standing in front of a
dart board, his back to me, carefully aiming a dart. I
thanked Kyle and went over to him.

"Damn!" He aimed another dart, launched it, and
said "Damn!" again, for the same excellent reason.

He turned to me. "You any good at this?" He spoke with a slight drawl, like Cameron Harris.

I'd played a lot of darts during my years in the navy. It was something I could do while my friends were drinking. "I used to be."

He pulled the darts out of the board and handed them to me. I wasn't as sharp as I once was, but I was still pretty good. I made the game close, for he had the soft, porky look of a boy who doesn't like to lose even in the little things.

I couldn't tell how old he was. Thirty, I guessed. About five eight, but because he was wearing cowboy boots with high heels, he looked taller. He was also wearing a cowboy shirt with mother-of-pearl snaps instead of buttons, and jeans that had cost a lot because they'd been designed to look worn. The effect he was trying to achieve was either ruined or enhanced, I wasn't sure which, by granny glasses and baby fat.

I told him I was a campus cop and that I was helping with the Harris murder investigation.

"Oliver, comma, Rich," he said, offering me a soft hand to shake. "My guess is, you're a journalist looking for sensation and column inches. 'Cameron Harris ruts with his students and winds up dead.' A cop would have a badge."

I brought out my shield and let him see it. He raised one eyebrow. I've always wanted to be able to do that, but no matter how hard I try, I end up looking startled. "University?" he said. "I didn't realize you people stuck your noses in murder."

"If it involves the University, we do."

"Cam wasn't murdered on campus."

"No, but there's an obvious campus connection."

"Ah. You mean someone like 'The Mother of the Prairie Renaissance,' Niobe Tigue, might've done him in for trampling on all her cherished causes, getting lucrative book contracts, and appearing on all the talk shows too. I suppose you have a point. But the city cops have already talked to us—Cam's students."

"I know, but I got your information secondhand. I'd like to hear it directly from the horse's mouth. It's always possible that, in the retelling, you might recall something you didn't tell them."

"My God," he exclaimed, "that's exactly what cops say on television! Are you required to memorize lines like that as a part of your training, along with the Miranda?"

I smiled, Sphinx-like. Oliver was an interesting study for something, though I wasn't sure what.

He lifted the empty mug in front of him, pretended to be surprised it was empty, and set it down. "Same again?" I asked.

"Why don't you make it an Old Nick this time," he said casually.

I went back to the bar and ordered one. It came in a pretty bottle, with a lurid devil on the label, and cost four dollars and some change. The devil looked a lot like the one on the pamphlet Frank Ott had slipped me at the Tower, urging me to repent and live in truth.

"Be gentle with him," Kyle said.

"Cam was an okay teacher," Oliver told me, after he'd carefully poured ale into his glass and taken a hefty swallow. "Too easy on the wannabees—the ones without talent—but he knew a lot about the politics of publishing, and that's what I wanted from the class. Once you reach a certain level of competence, the only difference between success and failure is who you know and how well you can manipulate your agent, your editor, and your publisher."

I wondered if that had been on the final exam, then remembered that Harris hadn't given one. I asked him how well he'd known Harris.

"Not very well, actually. None of us did. To tell you the truth, I don't think there was a private Cam Harris. I think that what you saw was what you got. My guess is that those of us who drank with him knew him as well as anybody. Of course," he added modestly, "I may be wrong."

"When was the last time you saw him?"

"Two days before he died, Wednesday. Right here. This was our regular table."

"But classes were over. They ended the previous Friday."

"Yeah, right, but we kept meeting here at the usual time. Cam was still in town, because of his reading at the Tower on Friday, and we knew that sooner or later he'd come strolling in too. He enjoyed talking to us. Frankly, he liked being adored. He didn't come Thursday because he had to go to a dinner that night."

That was the dinner at the Meades'. "Did he tell you on Wednesday that he wouldn't be coming on Friday either?"

Oliver shook his head and knocked back a slug of ale. "No, but don't jump to any hasty conclusions. You have to remember, there wasn't any agreement to meet here that last week, it was just a spontaneous thing. And not all of his students showed up either. Some went home for semester break as soon as they were done with finals. So it was just me and four or five others."

"But if he didn't plan to see you on Friday, wouldn't he have made a bigger deal when he left on Wednesday? I mean, you'd been his students and drinking buddies for nearly four months."

Oliver shrugged. "Maybe he wasn't big on saying good-bye. Or maybe something unexpected came up. Who knows?"

"You said that the week after classes ended, Harris

would show up here 'sooner or later.' What does that mean?"

"Just what it sounds like. He'd come in anywhere between six-thirty and seven."

"But during the semester he came earlier?"

"Well, sure. During the semester we always walked over from the classroom together. It doesn't take more than ten minutes, so we'd get here around four-twenty, four-thirty. We once tried to talk Cam into holding class here, but he nixed that. Too many distractions. But we always came here straight from class. Once classes were over, Cam didn't have any reason to come here at all, much less at the old time."

Right, but he did go to the Whale, where he knew his students would be waiting for him. There was no reason why he wouldn't go at the usual time. What was he doing to kill time during that last week?

Oliver grinned at me. "You're like a vacuum cleaner, aren't you? Sucking up the slightest particle of dust. You're looking for clues in the fact that he didn't say he wouldn't be here Friday night, and the fact that he got here late during finals week. You must be desperate to earn that reward." He drained his glass, checking the bottom against the light to make sure he'd got it all.

Two other people, a woman and a man, came into the Whale. They got a pitcher of draft beer from Kyle and came over to our table.

"Be careful what you say," Oliver said to them. "She's a cop, looking for Cam Harris's killer."

"Is he lost?" the man asked in a bored voice. They looked like brother and sister, both about Oliver's age, with long, lusterless hair and pasty complexions. The similarity was probably generic, not genetic.

"My name's Peggy O'Neill."

Unimpressed, they lit cigarettes. The woman's name was Liz. Gesturing to her companion, she said "Eric."

Oliver asked them if they could remember Harris saying anything about coming to the Whale before his reading Friday night. They both studied gouts of smoke in front of their mouths for a moment, then sucked them back in and let them trickle out through their noses. Smokers are a form of life that gives me lots of watching pleasure.

"Why would he?" Eric asked, pouring beer.

"I don't remember if he said anything about it," Liz said, "but I expected to see him on Friday. I was planning to walk up to the Tower with him for his reading. I'd bought a ticket and everything."

"I still think you're trying to make something out of nothing," Oliver said to me.

He was probably right. But Harris's whereabouts were unknown the afternoon of the last day of his life. What kept him away from his favorite bar and his admiring students? He told John Meade he was going to campus to turn in his grades and say good-bye to some of his friends. But at least part of that was a lie, since he hadn't given a final exam and had turned in his grades on the last day of class. And there wasn't anybody on campus he was close to, at least nobody who had come forward and admitted to seeing him.

Rich Oliver stomped over to the bar on his high-heeled boots. He seemed to have trouble directing them. Liz and Eric resumed an argument they must have been having before joining us, concerning the possibility of a distinctive female voice in literature in a phallocentric world.

When Oliver came back with a pint of Bass, I asked him if Harris had ever talked about his friends in town.

"What friends?" Oliver asked. "To hear him talk, he didn't have any local friends, just people he was going to put into stories and that novel he was writing. I finally figured out he was probably going to use some of us too." He looked as though he found it hard to believe he could be material for fiction.

"Don't forget that guy Cam told us he beat up," Liz said, turning away from her partner for a moment, "the one who wears a combat uniform. What's his name?"

Oliver frowned. She'd upstaged him. He took a swallow of ale. "Cam had a thing about this guy, a professor. Tony something, whom I'd never heard of."

"Tony Verdugo," Liz said. "A big man in Comp. Lit. Only his closest friends can understand a word he writes, and they're only pretending. That's what Cam said about him, anyway."

"Cam always called him a 'tenured radical without balls,'" Oliver said, wresting the story from Liz. "Sorry if you find that offensive. As Liz said, he always wore some kind of combat uniform. Cam said he thought his teaching would bring about the revolution, and he had to be properly dressed for it."

"Tell me about the fight," I said. Buck had mentioned it.

"I told the homicide cops about it already," Oliver said, "but maybe I'll remember something I forgot, if I tell it again—like this Tony Verdugo chap always carried a fireplace poker around."

"The story seemed a little corny to most of us," Liz said, "Cam Harris trying to come off like Hemingway, or something, punching out an intellectual. *For Whom the Bell Tolls*. It was at a party, he said."

"*The Sun Also Rises*," her friend corrected her, yawning smoke.

"Did he tell you what the fight was about?"

"I got the impression there was a woman involved," Liz said with a shrug of infinite boredom.

"Isn't there always?" Oliver asked. "This guy comes in here sometimes, by the way. Cam spotted him once at the bar and went over and talked to him. I couldn't hear what they said, but Cam came back grinning. And I didn't see Verdugo in here after that—at least, not when Cam was here. He's been here a couple of times since Cam was murdered, though, looking like he's in mourning or something, but I don't think it's over Cam Harris."

I looked around the bar, wondering how much of his student days Rich Oliver spent in the Whale.

Liz had once again lost interest in us and was telling her friend how the words "pen" and "penis" were related, making writing more difficult for women than men.

I asked Oliver if Harris had talked about anybody else. He thought a moment and then shook his head. Harris gossiped about some of the celebrity authors he'd known in New York and mentioned a few local people Oliver had never heard of. He couldn't remember their names.

"Did you tell her about Niobe Tigue?" Liz asked him. "Cam really had a thing about her. It sounded like there was more to it than simply disliking her writing. We wondered if they'd been lovers, back in the old days, when he lived here, although she would've been a little old for him, even then."

"Right," Oliver agreed. "Whenever Cam started in on Niobe Tigue, he wasn't very funny. He told us she tried to make him write the way she writes. He warned us against her. If we let her influence us, we'd end up writing stories for the *Reader's Digest*—'Life in these United States.' "

"I'm taking a class from her right now," Liz told me. "It's too early to tell, but I think she's got some good ideas."

"Cam told us once," Oliver said, "that Niobe Tigue thought she had him. And then he said, 'She was wrong about that, boys and girls. It was I who had her!' "

"I remember that," Liz said. "His eyes were glittering. Very dramatic. I sort of wondered what he meant by 'had.'"

"You would," Oliver said. "Come to think of it, Cam said pretty much the same thing about somebody else at the University." A crafty look appeared on his pasty face.

"Who?" I asked.

"Do you remember, Liz?"

She shook her head.

Oliver spun his empty mug on the scarred tabletop in front of him and said, "I'm trying to remember."

I took the hint and his empty mug back to Kyle at the bar and got a refill, another draft for a dollar, not an Old Nick for four.

Kyle shook her head at me. "Is this ethical?"

When Oliver had taken a swallow and wiped foam off his lips with the back of a soft, white hand, he said, "Niobe Tigue's husband, rather, her ex-husband. Cam told us he'd tried to get him too, but Cam had got him instead, just like he'd got Niobe. When we all looked confused, he just laughed, his usual booming laugh, and said we'd have to wait for the book."

I waved good-bye to Kyle, who was busier now, and walked out into the fresh air and the night. What had I got for the time and money I'd spent in the Whale? Not much. Cameron Harris once had a fight with Melody Carr's husband, Tony Verdugo. I already knew that. Since Verdugo was still at large, and the case still open, it obviously hadn't led Buck anywhere, or anywhere he was going to tell me about.

Liz, at least, had expected Harris to come to the Whale before his reading, and I thought Rich Oliver had too. Oliver also mentioned that Harris hadn't been coming to the Whale at the usual time—four-thirty or so—during his last week in town. He'd come at least an hour and a half later. That didn't have to mean anything, either. But where had he spent that time? And why did he lie to John Meade about turning in his grades on Friday? If he'd been working on his story for the reading, wouldn't he have stayed at the Meades' to do it?

So far, none of what I'd learned added up to anything. Some of it might not have been real, but even imaginary crumbs can make your mouth water, if you're hungry enough.

I was curious to see the house Harris had lived in during most of his stay in town. I drove to a gas station with a pay phone and called Buck.

He wasn't in, but Sergeant Burke was, and he gave me the address. He told me they'd already talked to the people who'd rented it to Harris, and hadn't learned anything of interest from them. They'd also talked to the nearest neighbors, but most of them didn't know Harris had lived there for over three months.

The house was a couple of miles from the University, at the end of a cul-de-sac, and bore a vague resemblance to a rustic lodge. Light glowed through the drapes covering the front windows. Around it on three sides was a dense woods that came right up to it. It seemed an idyllic private spot, perfect for a writer. Harris could have thrown wild parties every night of the week, complete with rock bands and a fleet of white stretch limos lining the curb, and the nearest neighbors would not have known.

The house looked so innocent. Hard to imagine that one of its tenants had been murdered. Of course, he hadn't been murdered there; he'd been murdered in the Tower.

A shadow crossed in front of the draped windows

and a woman's face peered out from a corner of the drape. I made a U-turn and drove out of there, hoping I hadn't upset her. I didn't want her to think I was a ghoul visiting the home of a famous man who'd got himself murdered. Especially since that's pretty much what I was.

and a woman's face peered out from a corner of the
paper. I made a face and drove on to a more...

Nine

The next afternoon, I called a friend of mine in the Humanities Department, Edith Silberman, to find out when
I could come over and see her. "For what?" she demanded. "As if I didn't know. You found poor
Cameron Harris's battered corpse, so you think you're
obliged to find his killer too. I don't approve of this
way of thinking, Peggy. However, office hours will be
over by the time you get here, if you leave now."

Since the weather was good and the roads clear of
snow and ice, I biked over to the Humanities Building
on the Old Campus. It's the University's oldest building. In winter the leafless ivy that crisscrosses its age-
darkened brick looks like scaffolding. Inside, the cool,
dimly lit halls are lined with heavily veined marble that
gives the building a subterranean feeling.

Edith was the best teacher I'd had in college, and she
was my adviser too. Perhaps because I'd been older
than the average undergraduate student, or because I
preferred reading to television, Edith and I kept in
touch after I graduated and we became friends. And last
spring, I'd helped her out of a jam.

I knocked on her door and entered. She gave me a
big hug, then led me to the other end of her office,
where she has two old overstuffed chairs separated by

a battered coffee table on a threadbare piece of carpet. I'd spent a lot of time there, with one or another of my papers between us on the table. Edith's a sturdy woman with cropped black hair threaded with gray and a burst of white, like a ball of cotton, at her left temple. She doesn't know she's short.

"Help yourself to coffee," she said, "but it's just as instant as ever."

I shuddered and declined. "I was going to call you soon anyway. It's not just Cameron Harris."

"I'm deeply moved. Besides, it's my turn to have you over. We had that wonderful lasagna at your place last time. I never get tired of it." She's a kind person.

When we'd exhausted our store of pleasantries, she settled back in her chair and said, "Nobody ever introduced Cameron Harris to me, but I knew who he was. He got his picture in the paper a lot, and I even saw him on a late-night talk show a while back. I thought his head was a little small for that body, making him look rather snakelike. He was a visiting writer in the English Department, which means you'd better go over to Frye Hall and find somebody to help you round up suspects. Niobe Tigue, for example."

"She's on my list of suspects."

"Oh, of course she is; I should've realized that. Both she and Harris write about small-town life, but her stories are full of bran and fiber. She writes as if progress were simply an error in judgment on some liberal's part, whereas Harris wrote as if small-town life existed only for the amusement of him and the yuppies who created him. You think she knocked him over the head because he was trampling on her ideals?"

"Could be. But they knew each other before he went on to fame and fortune in New York, and he planned to include her in his next novel, which was about his years with the Second Story." I told her about the character in Harris's novel called "Mentor."

"At least he knew his classics," she said, grudgingly. "And you think Niobe Tigue might not have been able to take a joke? You're probably right. I don't think she can. You know, I *want* to like her, and I feel as though I should. But I hear dreadful things about how she teaches writing. She apparently tries to teach her students how to write nineteenth-century fiction, and what's the good of that?"

"You're sounding a little like Cameron Harris," I said. "I was at a dinner party where he parodied her writing."

"I wouldn't be surprised. He had a wicked way with words. Anyway, I don't know anything much about her. I don't think she's nutty enough to kill somebody frivolously, but she might resort to violence in order to achieve what she considers a high moral purpose."

"Like saving a piece of prairie from being transformed into a strip mall," I suggested, thinking of Harris's story.

"Exactly. If you could show me that Harris was investing his royalties in a project like that, I'd say Niobe's the one who did him in. I don't suppose her ex-husband's a suspect?"

"Arthur Tigue? You know him?"

She made a face. "I'm sorry to say, I do. A professor of psychology. He pulls down an enormous salary from the U, has an office five times the size of this one, and he's listed as teaching a course or two a year, although it's mostly his grad students who do that. He uses his University connection primarily to attract patients to his private practice. He's a therapist."

"I met him yesterday at the Tower. He came in looking for one of the writers. Niobe was there. She can't stand him."

Edith nodded. "A colleague of mine went to him for therapy once. A bright woman, but troubled. After two sessions, she decided she'd rather have the problem if Tigue was the solution. She called him a manipulator, a Rasputin for the nineties."

Recalling Tigue's pale face and eyes, his thin mustache and beard, I could see the resemblance. Did Buck know about him?

I asked Edith if she knew a Tony Verdugo in Comparative Literature.

She looked surprised. "Tony? Of course I know him! Why would he want to kill Harris?"

"Verdugo's married to Melody Carr, the writer Arthur Tigue came looking for yesterday. I saw Cameron Harris fondling Melody's foot the night before he was murdered. And I also heard Melody read a poem about a penis at the Tower last fall that Verdugo may have suspected wasn't his. He stalked out, and they've been living apart ever since. Finally, Harris punched Verdugo out at a party last fall—apparently because he didn't like something Verdugo wrote about him."

Edith was laughing before I'd finished running through my list. "The plot thickens, or, at least, becomes more turgid. I wish I'd been there to see Tony's face when his wife read that poem. He's chairman of Comp. Lit., you know, and he holds everything I love in literature in contempt, so we're not what you'd call bosom buddies. He insists that literary criticism is as creative as—possibly more important than—the fiction it feeds on. I once suggested that the difference between fiction and criticism is that fiction isn't usually an embarrassment to its author five years after it's published. He almost hit me. His office is just down the hall, but it's bigger and has a nicer view."

"I don't suppose you happened to see Harris over here, on the day he died, for example?"

"No, sorry. Why?"

I told her that Harris's whereabouts were unaccounted for the afternoon of his murder. "He said he was coming to the U to turn in grades and see friends. But he turned in his grades on the last day of class, and he didn't have any friends here that we know about."

Edith thought about what I'd told her. "You think Harris was having an affair with Tony's wife, and Tony killed him on account of that? Not likely, Peggy. He might plan a murder, down to the littlest detail, but he'd never carry it out. He's like Harris; he uses the power of the pen to destroy his enemies. And he has a lot of power, deciding what's literature these days and what isn't, and who gets to talk about it." She frowned. "I remember now. Tony wrote a devastating review of Harris's first novel, in the *New York Times*. He must have been chagrined when the novel succeeded anyway."

I told her about the novel Harris was working on when he was killed. I didn't know if Verdugo was going to be in it, but his wife Melody certainly was.

Edith nodded grimly. "You can be sure Cameron Harris was planning some revenge on Verdugo for that review. Have you ever seen Tony Verdugo, Peggy?"

I told her I'd only seen him stalk out of the Tower. "He was dressed for combat."

"He's been wearing paratrooper garb ever since his Marxist days, when all the literary scholars were going around claiming solidarity with the struggling masses. Now that the revolution's failed, he's a post-Marxist—or perhaps Marxist-*faux*—I can't keep up with the terminology anymore. He still wears the uniform, but with a difference. Now he has it cleaned and pressed. He's 'quoting himself.' He's a 'text,' which means he doesn't have to be responsible for what he does."

"Even murder?"

"I wouldn't be surprised." Edith looked at her watch. "You want to observe Tony in action? I saw him a few minutes before you arrived, heading into his seminar. There's a window in the classroom door. You might find it amusing, given all that noise he makes about subverting the dominant culture. He sits on top of his desk, legs crossed, which forces his students either to look down, in obedience, or up, in awe. If they elect to look straight ahead, as you'd do with an equal, they find themselves staring at his crotch."

I laughed and got up.

Edith followed me to the door. "It's your friend Buck Hansen who's in charge of the Harris murder, isn't it? He doesn't seem to be making any progress on his own. Has he asked you to help?" She'd had a bad experience with Buck and didn't talk about him with much warmth.

"Not in so many words," I said.

"Let him do his own work. Harris died violently, and it's obvious it was someone from his past, more than likely someone connected to the Tower or the University. Also, from what I read in the newspaper, Harris's body was posed after he was killed, with a manuscript in his lap and the weapon the killer used in his hand. That means you're trying to find a maniac."

I told her I knew that and that I wanted to do whatever I could to get that maniac off the streets.

"You're snooping," she said, "and Harris's killer might have already noticed. You're a person who walks around alone at night, Peggy. That makes you different from the policemen who are hunting him. You're vulnerable."

She was hard to argue with. I reminded her of my gun and told her that until Harris's killer was caught, I'd be extra careful.

I walked down the hall to Verdugo's classroom, conscious of Edith watching me from her doorway. I stopped when I got to the classroom door and glanced in the narrow window.

Edith was right. The angry man I'd seen leaving Melody's reading and Harris's nonreading was sitting on top of his desk with his legs crossed at the ankles. He was dressed for battle. His students, earnest-looking young men and women, sat in rows in front of him, some looking up and some looking down, a few staring straight ahead.

His head turned suddenly and his eyes met mine. I was standing in a pool of light from the fixture overhead. I moved away quickly, half expecting to hear the classroom door burst open behind me.

Edith had said Tony Verdugo didn't have the guts to commit murder. But she didn't say he wasn't a maniac, and madness sometimes gives cowards courage.

Ten

I left Edith a little after three. Since Niobe Tigue already took it for granted that I was investigating the murder of Cameron Harris, I decided to try her office and see if she'd talk to me. Frye Hall isn't far from the Humanities Building, so I walked my bike over, threading my way through students hurrying to classes in the icy afternoon air.

As an English major, I'd spent a lot of time in Frye Hall, which is where I found my first murder victim, the distinguished professor the TV reporter had referred to. I'd almost joined him there myself. But Frye's a massive old building, built to shrug off the vagaries of history.

Niobe Tigue's office was located on the third floor, home of the creative writing program. I climbed the two flights of stairs, scarcely noticing the place where I'd once tripped and fallen over a stretched wire meant to kill or maim me. I passed the office where Cameron Harris had spent fall semester. His name was still on the wall next to the door, scrawled on a piece of cardboard in what I recognized as his own handwriting. It was odd that nobody had removed the little sign, and sad, too, that nobody had taken it for the autograph.

I knocked at Niobe's door and entered when she hollered "Come in."

Afternoon winter light fell through the sloped skylight, softening Niobe Tigue's angular features. She watched me approach her desk with a smile of satisfaction, as if she'd won a bet with herself.

"You get around, don't you?" she said. "You're at Cameron Harris's last supper, and the next night you stumble on his corpse. Yesterday you're at the Tower badgering Tamara, and now you're here. I didn't hear the bloodhounds baying, but they must have been right at my heels. You have any official standing?"

"No." I pulled a chair up next to her desk and sat down, just as if I'd been asked. "As you guessed, I'm a friend of the homicide cop in charge of the Harris case. I know the University pretty well, so I offered to help him."

"And did he agree to let you?"

I thought about my answer before replying. Niobe Tigue seemed to require that. "Not in so many words."

She surprised me with a lovely grin. "How like a man. And what of any value do you hope to get out of talking to me?"

"I won't know until we've finished."

"When we've finished, you'll know what I've told you and nothing more."

"I'll also know what I think of what you've told me. That'll be something more."

She blinked, then nodded. "I daresay it will. Whoever killed Cameron is somebody I know. That's a scarifying thought. I've spent a lot of time thinking about who it might be."

I asked her if she'd come up with any answers, and she shook her head. "Far too many, unfortunately. I loved Cameron, you see, even though that was a difficult thing to do. It would have been easier to hate him,

and most people, in my experience, take the easy path."
Niobe's eyes were blue and clear, with lines around
them, as if she'd spent a lot of her life squinting into
bright sunlight as she walked the harder path. They
were resting on me now, measuring me.

I told her about the story Harris had planned to read
the night he was killed, and described how it had been
found on his lap. I was curious to see how she'd react.
If anything, the expression on her face became stonier
as I talked. "It was a devastating portrait of Tamara
Meade."

"Serves Tamara right. She was one of those who encouraged Cameron to think he was a natural genius
who didn't need discipline. And then, in that foolish
novel of hers, *Romance and Reality*, she blamed him
for the breakup of their relationship."

"You don't think it was his fault?"

"No. She dumped him for John Meade, who'd been
hanging around for months, ever since his wife died,
hoping she'd notice him and his money."

"That's not how her novel reads."

"I know that," she snapped. "I forced myself to read
the damned thing, and I almost croaked for laughing.
Instead of having the guts to admit the truth, that she
was afraid to stay with a man whose genius could take
him either to the heights or the depths, she had to stick
in a 'younger sister' that her heroine found in the lilac
bushes with the 'artist.' She should have confronted her
own cowardice in that book. That would have been a
novel."

"You don't think there was another woman?"

"Hell, no!" A strand of her rich dark hair had es-
caped from the pile on her head, and she brushed it
away from her eyes impatiently. "Obviously, you've
read *Romance and Reality*, so you remember all the ag-
onizing Tamara's heroine does over her choice between

the struggling and irresponsible genius and the stolid older man. It's sentimental and unconvincing, but whether that's because Tamara doesn't know how to write or because she doesn't know how to feel, I'm not prepared to say. Both, probably. Tamara had read some Ibsen. You remember Ibsen, don't you?"

I told her I'd read a few of his plays and that I remembered how Harris had made fun of him at the Meades' dinner party.

She got up suddenly. I thought she was going to get one of Ibsen's plays from her bookcase and offer it to me. Instead she went to a window and looked out. "Right," she said, her back to me. "Cameron was teasing Tamara for having stolen ideas from Ibsen to try to make her heroine 'deeper.' Ibsen wrote plays about men who betray love for power and glory. It's meant symbolically, of course." She spoke more slowly, making sure I understood this difficult idea. "Love, which is feminine, is a part of a man's psyche, and when he sacrifices it for power and glory, he destroys his psychic balance and all hell breaks loose. And Ibsen was right." Niobe sounded fierce as she turned to glare at me. "Just look at what the men who have betrayed love for power have done to our planet."

I've never cared for literature that uses women to symbolize the softer aspects of the male psyche—I can't imagine using men to symbolize the harder aspects of mine—but I didn't tell her so. In Tamara's novel, I reminded her, the woman, Alyssa, betrays love for power, or at least for money, which is the same thing.

"Exactly. In this day and age, women have the same opportunities to betray their essential natures as men have. That's fine, but it's too damn bad that's what we have to do to get ahead! It was a heavy blow to

Cameron when Tamara dumped him for John Meade. It embittered him, killed something of value in him."

I realized that, not far under her crusty surface, Niobe Tigue was as much a romantic as Melody Carr. "What about Tamara's feelings for him? She may have dumped Cameron Harris for a wealthy man, but do you think she still loved him?"

"Tamara loves only one person in all the world, and that's the woman she sees every morning when she brushes her teeth." Niobe came back to her desk and slumped into her swivel chair.

"Do you think she regretted the choice she made, once Harris became successful?"

"I hope so," she said.

"I can't believe *Romance and Reality* was a joy for John Meade to read."

"Nobody'll ever know what John Meade thinks about the book. As far as I know, he's never read it. He just paid to have it published."

"What?"

My surprise pleased her. "You think Tamara could have had it published on its own merits? I never asked, of course, but I assume John had to shell out plenty. It was published by a local press that's not above doing the occasional vanity novel, if the price is right. John's either a saint or a fool. I can never decide which."

"According to a librarian I talked to, *Romance and Reality* is still checked out occasionally."

"So are the novels of Mrs. Humphrey Ward." Then she laughed, reached over, and patted my hand, resting on her desk. Her hands had once performed hard work, and years of writing hadn't softened them much. "It's not going to be easy, trying to find a murderer among a bunch of prima donnas who are largely out of control, is it?" Her tone was mocking. "You think Tamara killed Cameron because he'd become successful and was going to make fun of her in his next novel? Well, she might have wanted to—who knows what Tamara wants—but in my opinion, murder's too common for her, and too risky. Of course, John Meade might have done it, to keep Cameron from writing that novel, except that I assume murder is still, even in these corrupt times, too exciting for men with heart conditions. Who else, Peggy?"

"At the Tower last fall," I began, "Melody Carr read a poem—"

"In which a penis flowers into a vagina!" Niobe snorted. "Just what you'd expect from a twenty-five-year-old child."

"Do you think it could have been about Cameron Harris?"

She looked surprised, as if she hadn't thought of that before. "No." Her eyes moved away from me, into the shadows of her office. "No, she was just following the example of some of the better-known women poets on the East Coast, who, for a time, were much given to writing poems about the male member. Literary fads take a while to get here. Also, she wanted to shock Tony. She achieved that, if nothing else." Niobe smiled grimly.

"But Cameron Harris was flirting with Melody at the Meades' dinner party. You saw it."

"Of course I did. I'm no more blind than you are. But that was more of Cameron tormenting Tamara for dumping him. He wasn't interested in Melody—or vice versa."

"Wasn't it a little late for Harris to be paying Tamara back for a relationship that ended a long time ago? Besides, they were supposed to be friends. Otherwise, what was Harris doing staying with the Meades those last two weeks he was in town?"

"Tamara thought the Tower needed Cameron, if it

was going to survive." Niobe snorted again. She snorted well. "The Tower's not going to survive, not unless Chris Ames chips in some more of the family fortune to help it. And word is, he can't afford to. Apparently, Daddy didn't cut him enough slack in his will."

"You don't like Chris Ames, do you?"

"Not much escapes those cold green eyes and those big ears of yours, does it, Peggy O'Neill?"

"I hope not." I've got green eyes, true, although I wouldn't call them cold. And only one of my ears is what might be called big. "Ames seemed pleasant enough to me."

She shrugged. "Mind you, I don't have anything against people who sell hardware—it's as worthwhile as writing stories—but I don't trust people who give up their dreams. Chris gave up his dream, in order to do what his daddy wanted him to do. It was Chris, by the way, who encouraged Tamara to read Ibsen's plays, thus making *Romance and Reality* even more pretentious than it might otherwise have been."

I laughed. She looked as if she couldn't see anything to laugh about.

"I couldn't help noticing," I said, "with my cold green eyes and big ears, that there's no love lost between you and your ex-husband."

Her face went hard again. "No, I don't suppose you could. I imagine Tamara told you all about us." She stopped just short of making it a question.

I tried to look noncommittal. Tamara had said as little as possible about them.

"Arthur and I were married for fifteen years," Niobe said. "We spent the first eight on a farm he'd inherited from his father. He tried to be a writer, a poet, while I did the chores."

She looked down at her hands, clenched into fists on

her desk and then picked up a pen, a real fountain pen, and unscrewed the cap. "What he tried to write poems about was the joy one feels when living close to the soil. When he failed at that—the farm animals made so much noise, he couldn't concentrate—he decided he needed a college degree. Without consulting me, he sold the farm and we moved here. He studied psychology at the University, thinking it would give him greater insights into the human condition." She laughed.

"He discovered the power in psychology, the power it could give you over people. He couldn't move anybody with his poetry, so he decided to become a therapist instead."

She glanced at me to see if I was paying attention. "He got a Ph.D., hung out his shingle, and went to work. Arthur has a good couch-side manner, if you're into long teeth and smarm. He wrote one of those psychobabble books on getting to know your inner child—and it was very successful. He also published articles in professional journals and gave countless talks at conferences, and after a couple of years, the University hired him. Oh yes," she added, as if as an afterthought, "somewhere in there he dumped me for a fellow graduate student who later dumped him for one of their professors."

Niobe Tigue recounted all that dispassionately, as if it were somebody else's story. She doodled on a piece of white paper as she talked, sharp angles and squares. Her fountain pen had red ink.

"Did Arthur ever have Harris as a patient?" I asked, remembering something Rich Oliver had mentioned at the Whale.

"Well, Arthur thought he did. Just after he started his practice, he suggested to Cameron that he could free more of his creative energy by putting himself into Arthur's capable hands. After all, didn't Arthur know what the creative life was all about, with its tensions, et cetera? Much to everyone's surprise, Cameron went along with the idea—or seemed to. But it was only a pretense. Cameron stayed in therapy with Arthur a month, and then quit. You see, he'd got what he wanted—material for fiction, for a comedy." She paused. "Where'd you hear that Cameron was in therapy with Arthur?"

I guessed it from something one of Harris's former students had said, I told her.

Niobe nodded. "Arthur made a brief appearance in Cameron's second book, *Lost Letters Home*. One of the fictional letters is addressed to the hero's former shrink, whose office is decorated like a nursery, with an oversize playpen and toys for his clients."

"Is it really?" I asked. "I mean, is Arthur's office like that?" I was blurring fiction and reality again.

Niobe grinned at my confusion. "How should I know? But it wouldn't surprise me. After all, 'the child within' has become a growth industry among the shrinks—as if we don't have better things to do with our lives—and Arthur got in on the ground floor."

"He must have hated Cameron Harris."

"I'm sure he did." Niobe's eyes glinted, as if she were challenging me to make something of it.

"And now he's Melody Carr's therapist," I said.

She nodded.

"I got the feeling yesterday that you thought Arthur was more than just her therapist."

"Did you?" She seemed amused. "I have no doubt Arthur would like to be more than Melody's therapist, but I don't know that he is—yet. She's certainly his type, though. He's always been fatally attracted to the sweet young things. A lot of Tower men have been in love with Melody over the years."

"You make it sound like Melody's been a Towerite forever. She can't be more than twenty-four, twenty-five."

"She lived with her sister when she was in high school, and sometimes Sandra would bring her to Second Story events. Melody was already writing poetry, dreary stuff about unrequited love for guys on motorcycles, and moons laden with promise. She was quite precocious," Niobe added, dryly.

"Has Arthur ever got any of the other Towerites into therapy?" I asked.

"A few, I think. He can be very persuasive. I know a little about that."

"Tamara?"

"No. He tried, but she'd have none of it. He was infatuated with her years ago, but she never liked him. And besides, she was going with Cameron." Niobe gave me her sudden, beautiful smile. "You're getting to know us all quite well, aren't you? As if you've been a part of the Tower forever yourself. It's kind of spooky."

I smiled back. "I think so, too. Cameron Harris gloated to his students that your husband once thought he had him, but in reality, he had Arthur. You've told me what that meant. But Harris said the same thing about you. Can you tell me what he meant by that?"

The smile left her face. "That wasn't very generous, but why should that surprise me? Yes, I guess I thought I 'had' Cameron too. My taste in men is really quite remarkable, isn't it? First Arthur, then Cameron." She crumpled up the piece of paper she'd been doodling on and threw it into a wastebasket.

"Were you in love with Harris?"

"No. At least, not in the way you mean. For a time Cameron pretended to share my values, and perhaps he really did—I don't know anymore!" She was fighting tears, as she had at the Meades' dinner. "I even allowed myself to imagine that we were going to be a team, a writing team. I taught him a lot about writing, and he was a good student, at first. But he had no discipline. He could toss out stories faster than anybody I've ever known, almost finished, publishable. He was an improvisor—that's what he always called himself too. Had he stayed here, he might have learned to use his gift, instead of letting it use him. But when Tamara dumped him for John, he fled to New York, and I lost him. He took the easy path then. He betrayed his gift, his genius."

She got up suddenly. With a half grin on her face and fire in her eyes, she glared down at me. I didn't like that, so I got up too. Although I'm five nine, she still glared down at me.

"Betraying your genius has a way of revenging itself," she said sternly, but she wasn't speaking to me. She was looking through me. "It always revenges itself."

She pressed the fountain pen hard into the blotter covering her desk. The ink spread around it slowly, like blood.

Eleven

I biked home in the dark and called Buck. Although it was after six, I caught him at his office. He sounded tired. I thanked him for sending me the copy of Harris's story and novel notes. He said something noncommittal and asked if I'd figured out who'd done it yet. "No, but Niobe Tigue seems to think Harris was done in because he betrayed his genius—if that's any help."

"From what I've learned about Ms. Tigue, that would make her the prime suspect, wouldn't it?"

"I think she thinks Henrik Ibsen's the prime suspect."

"Who's Henry Gibson?"

"The playwright."

"You mean Ibsen."

"That's what I said." I'd been through that routine once before, though not as a participant. I explained to Buck Ibsen's connection with Harris. Buck wasn't impressed. Since he hadn't even heard of Arthur Tigue, I repeated what Niobe had told me. I heard Buck sigh and scratch something on a piece of paper. I'd impressed him with that, at least.

"Although he's got a private practice, he also teaches at the U. According to Niobe, he makes piles of money introducing people to their inner child. A kind of adoption service."

" 'Inner child,' " Buck echoed dully. "A layman's term for a much more difficult concept, don't you think?" Buck tries not to keep up on these kinds of things.

"No, I don't." I told him what I'd learned from Rich Oliver, that Harris had been arriving late at the Whale the week before his murder. Even though the semester was over, Harris was still at loose ends, hanging around town until his reading at the Tower. Why would he come to the bar later, especially when he knew his students would be waiting there for him, and he seemed to enjoy talking to them?

"But he knew some of them would be there whenever he showed up, so he didn't have to hurry," Buck reminded me.

"But hurry from where, damn it? How'd he spend that last week? Do you know?"

Buck said that, according to the Meades, he stayed in his room at their place and worked. Tamara usually left for the Tower before Harris got up in the morning, but John Meade often heard Harris pecking away on his typewriter, probably working on the story he was going to read the night he was killed. Then, around lunchtime, he would leave the house. John Meade didn't know where he went. Eventually he'd make his way to the Whale and return home at ten or eleven at night, except on Thursday, when he didn't go to the Whale because of the Meades' dinner party for him.

"But on Friday he didn't show up at the Whale at all. And he lied to John Meade about what he was going to do that afternoon. Why? Where was he until I found his body? You said he'd been drinking wine—who'd he been drinking it with?"

"We don't know."

I asked Buck if he knew how serious Harris was about moving back here from New York.

"Very serious, I guess. We talked to people who knew him in New York, and they all agreed he was unhappy there, and often talked about returning here to live. With jet planes, electronic mail, and fax machines, nobody needs to live in New York City anymore."

"I wonder how many people weren't thrilled at the thought of having him back."

"Quite a few."

"Do you think that story on his lap will ever be published?"

"I wondered about that too. I showed it to an agent here in town, and he didn't think so. It was a first draft, with no ending. Harris must have intended to do a lot of improvising that night. I guess he was good at that. In this agent's opinion, Cameron Harris's books were only as good as his last television appearance, so the literary world probably isn't going to scramble to publish every scrap of paper he scrawled something on."

"Killing Harris was the same as killing the story, then."

"Right. Whoever killed him could safely leave the story in Harris's lap, even if it was someone like Tamara or John Meade, who didn't want it published."

"Which reminds me," I said. "Those dark blotches on some of the manuscript's pages. That was blood, right?"

"I told you it was."

"That means the manuscript must have been scattered over the floor, doesn't it? And the killer had to gather it up in order to place it in Harris's lap?"

"Yes. He apparently didn't want Harris's body found right away, so he couldn't leave the manuscript on the floor, in case somebody came up to the tower—as you and Gary did."

"Yeah, but he didn't have to place it so neatly in Harris's lap."

"No. We'll be sure to ask him about that, when we catch him. Or her."

In my mind's eye, I saw again Cameron Harris sitting in that chair, the poker that had killed him in one hand, the manuscript in his lap. It was a work of art of sorts, a private act of creative destruction, not unlike the manuscript itself. I wanted to hear the killer's explanation for it, but only after he was safely behind bars.

I asked Buck if he found anything odd about the house where Harris had lived for most of the semester.

"Curious, you mean," he said, after a pause.

"Odd, curious—what's the difference?"

"Sherlock Holmes would have said 'curious.' He would have said, 'Watson, I would like to draw your attention to the curious fact that the house was a perfect setting for a murder.' "

I grinned, finally getting it. "But the murder wasn't committed in that house, Holmes," I said, in my tweediest British voice.

"That's the curious fact, Watson."

Why hadn't Cameron Harris been murdered while he was still living in that house? The killer could have driven up, parked, gone right up to the door, and knocked. If it had been night, nobody would have seen the car drive down the cul-de-sac, and even in daytime, who would have noticed?

However, people plotting murder have to assume that everybody is watching. In that case, the killer could have come through the woods behind the house.

Yet Harris had lived peaceably in that isolated place for over three months—and then been brutally murdered after he left it, and in a very public place, too. Which probably meant that whoever had killed him hadn't decided to do it until Harris had moved to the Meades' home.

Finding out who Harris had been with the afternoon of his murder was, therefore, even more important. The small inconsistencies in his movements, such as when he showed up at the Whale, took on a new significance.

I microwaved a frozen dinner without looking at the label. Chicken, possibly, or fish, I thought, savoring it, or maybe something entirely unknown, mutated especially for the microwave. I made a cup of French roast coffee in my little French plunger pot and was deeply involved in a good book when the doorbell rang.

It was Gary. He noticed the remains of my dinner and rolled his eyes. His big brown eyes rolled well. The microwave, with its attendant labor-saving food, was one of the things he didn't like about modern life, and one of the things I liked a lot about it. I mean, how far back did Gary want to go? A nice mammoth chop singed over an open fire in a cave? We argued about it all the way down to Lake Eleanor, where we skated on the rink until it was time for me to get ready for work.

Twelve

It was snowing when I left my apartment the next afternoon, so I drove to the University. I parked my old Rabbit illegally in front of the Psychology Building, hoping that, if a campus cop spotted it, it would be one who knew my car and had nothing against me.

Once, a few years before, I'd known the Psychology Department pretty well, because I'd gone out with a guy who got a Ph.D. in psychology. George Something. I've repressed his last name because he wanted to inflict it upon me. He wanted me to abandon the campus cop idea, marry him, and be a faculty wife. Thinking about it makes me shudder, even now.

During my time with George, the Incomprehensible Mistake, I'd figured out that the Psych Department is primarily a factory dedicated to generating grant money to keep its faculty living in a style beyond the average person's wildest dreams. It's a rare undergraduate psych major who ever sees a professor or is asked to write a complete sentence.

The department has its own building, a modern, nearly featureless four-story square. Ivy would help a lot; rumor has it that the chairman of the department holds his graduate students responsible for keeping it off the walls. He's a compulsive neat freak, who

95

smokes two packs a day and, understandably, has a twitch. Since none of the faculty teaches undergraduates, there are no classrooms, only spacious offices, laboratories, and seminar rooms. Undergraduates are taught in large auditoriums elsewhere on campus, usually by long-gone and occasionally dead professors whose lectures were filmed years ago. Other than the Administration Building, the Psych Building is the only air-conditioned building on the Old Campus, the expense justified by the enormous investment the department has in rats.

The receptionist wasn't anybody I knew, but the nameplate sitting on her desk said Pamela Reardon, who'd been the department's receptionist back when I was going with George.

"I'm trying to get hold of Professor Tigue."

"Who?" She was a blond woman with a sharp nose and stubborn chin.

"Arthur Tigue," I repeated, hoping that, by putting the man's two names together, they'd ring a bell.

"Tigue, Tigue." She turned to the two women and one man at desks behind her. "Anybody here know a Professor Arthur Tigue?"

"I've heard rumors," the black man muttered, not pausing in his typing.

"He's in clinical psychology," I said, puzzled. Then I noticed they were all trying not to laugh.

"Of course he is," the receptionist said, "but why look for him here? As you so astutely point out, he's a clinical psychologist. That means he has a private practice. And that means he only comes in on the fifteenth and the last day of the month."

"To pick up his paycheck."

"No, no, no!" she said, throwing up her hands. My cynicism seemed to shock her. "That's when he holds his seminars. It's only a coincidence that those also happen to be paydays."

"If you believe that," one of the secretaries behind her said, "I've got a nice bridge I'd like to sell you."

I shook my head. "Nothing ever changes around here, does it?"

"You were in this department?" The receptionist looked me up and down, as if checking for the physical evidence.

"I once went with a guy who got his Ph.D. in psychology."

"That's worse, somehow."

"He's behind me now. Now, how do I get hold of Tigue?"

"We're strictly forbidden to give out faculty phone numbers," she said, "and it wouldn't do you any good anyway. He'd demand to know how you got it, and if you didn't give him a satisfactory answer, he'd bite your head off and hang up on you. Unless you want to offer him a lucrative contract for another of his feel-good books. Do you?"

I didn't.

She tapped her pencil on the desk. "You could always try his office. That's where he is today, seeing patients at a hundred dollars per fifty-minute hour, to supplement his University salary of eighty-five thousand dollars." She scribbled down the address, handed it to me. "What're you going to sell him? 'Cause I don't think you're going to him for help."

"Nothing. Where's Pamela, by the way?"

"Who? Oh, Pam. She left nearly a year ago."

"Her nameplate's still on your desk."

"True, but most of the professors called Pam 'Mary,' the name of one of her predecessors. They didn't notice that Mary'd left years ago. I won't settle for Mary, so

I'm trying to train them to call me Pam instead. I took it on as a challenge."

"Why not try to train them to call you by your name?"

"That would mean writing a requisition for a new nameplate for my desk. Which would be a waste of my time, since I don't plan to be here very long anyway. So far, I've taught six professors to call me Pam. I'm thinking of writing it up and submitting it to one of the behavioral journals."

The fifteenth of the month would be the middle of next week. She told me he taught from six to ten at night. "You can't expect his clients to come to his office at night. So that's when he schedules his seminars. His students don't complain, believe me—not if they ever expect to get jobs like his."

As I walked back to my car, I wondered how I'd get to meet Arthur Tigue. Through Niobe, he'd known most of the Towerites, back when they called themselves the Second Story. He'd even tried to get his claws into some of them, including Cameron Harris, and now he was Melody Carr's therapist—and maybe more than that. He'd made a cameo appearance in one of Harris's novels, *Lost Letters Home,* and might have been lined up for a bigger role in Harris's new novel.

I decided it would be worth my time to drive to his office and try to get in to see him.

His office was on the second floor of a two-story building in a recently constructed strip mall north of town. According to the directory, the building housed a dentist, a chiropractor, a tax accountant, a lawyer who specialized in divorce and bankruptcy, and two therapists. All this and the fast-food restaurants down the block probably took care of most of the needs of the people who lived around here.

As I walked into Tigue's waiting room, a crisp gray couple glanced up at me nervously, as if afraid I might be somebody they knew, and then ducked back down into the old magazines on their laps. Copies of Tigue's latest book, *Making Friends With Your Self,* were scattered around the room. The receptionist, a small woman with sleek dark hair and a sleek bright smile, asked me how she could help. I told her I wanted to talk to Dr. Tigue.

"Are you a patient?" she asked.

"No, I wanted to talk to him about a private matter."

I could see that she was about to say, "What else would anybody want to talk to Dr. Tigue about?" but good breeding clicked in. She opened her appointment book and ran a finger down the day's schedule.

"Dr. Tigue has no vacancies today." She flipped to the next page. "He isn't in tomorrow, but I see that he is booked up on Friday too. There's always the possibility that somebody will cancel, if you'd like to give me your name. You'll have to fill out a credit form too." She offered me one. "May I ask who recommended us to you?"

"That's okay," I said, "it's not important."

As I started to turn away, a door behind her opened and a man and a woman, both in their early forties, came out. The man looked angry and ready to kill; the woman was red-eyed, her shoulders slumped, but she managed to turn back and say to Tigue, who was sitting at his desk making notes, "Thank you, Doctor."

From where I was standing, his office looked like a day-care center. On the wall behind his desk, an egg yolk on a poster told me to have a nice day. Toys, crayons, and large beanbag seats were scattered around the carpeted floor. Cameron Harris had got it right.

Tigue glanced up from his desk. It took him a moment to place me, and then, frowning, he got up and came quickly out of his office. He stopped about a foot closer to me than I'm comfortable with, but maybe he didn't mean anything threatening by it. Maybe he'd freed the child within, and the child had turned out to be socially inept.

"At the Tower yesterday," he said, gazing down at me sternly, "you told me you were not investigating Cameron Harris's murder." His dark, caterpillarlike mustache seemed to inch its way along the top of his long upper lip. "I would be interested in hearing an explanation, brief and simple, of your appearance here today."

"I'm investigating Cameron Harris's murder," I explained, briefly and simply.

"I don't remember your name." When I told him, he went on, in a tired voice. "I teach a seminar at the University, Ms. O'Neill, the preparation time for which is long and exhaustive. I see patients here three days a week, which takes its toll as well—and I have kept these good people here waiting too, for which I apologize." He turned and bowed to them. "And I am committed to writing a book against a very short deadline. I have no time to help an amateur detective try to earn a reward for the apprehension of Harris's killer. So please, Ms. O'Neill, go away." He turned on his heels and walked back to his office.

That was succinct. "What's the name of the book?" I asked his retreating back.

He turned, then caught himself, suspecting perhaps that the question hadn't been meant entirely seriously.

"You may come in now," he said to the couple who'd been waiting there before me, and held the door for them.

"You're the woman who found Cameron Harris's

body in that awful tower, aren't you?" the man said as he passed me. "You were on TV."

"Spenser!" his wife called back to him.

"Yes," I said. And, hoping I wasn't practicing psychology without a license, I added, "Have a nice day!"

Thirteen

The snow had stopped when I got outside, leaving powder blowing on the streets in a gentle breeze. I headed back toward the University, and when I got to Central Avenue, turned up the hill to the Tower. It was a little after four. I knew from Paula that Melody Carr's poetry class began at six but that she liked to get to the Tower early to prepare.

The downstairs was empty and still, giving the impression that everybody had moved out. Melody's office was in the basement. I knocked on the door and went in.

It was a small office, made smaller by the cardboard boxes and grocery bags scattered around the room. The bags were overflowing with clothes and what looked like odds and ends from kitchen drawers. I maneuvered my way through the mess toward her desk. The same happy face poster I'd seen in Tigue's office hung on her wall, stuck on with tape, instead of framed like his.

"It looks like you're moving in," I said.

"I'm in transit—in more ways than one." She didn't seem surprised to see me. "I'm renting an efficiency, until I get my finances in order and I can find a larger place."

Melody was about five five, a blonde with curly hair

102

that bounced when she nodded her head, which she did a lot to indicate seriousness of purpose. Her small mouth and slightly bucktoothed smile gave her face an innocence and vulnerability I distrusted. "It's nice to see you again, Peggy," she went on, "even though I know you're here to talk about Cam's death."

"How do you know that?"

"Oh, it's common knowledge now. You were here the other day, pretending to look for Gary, but you were really asking Tamara all kinds of questions about the murder, weren't you?"

"Did Tamara tell you that?"

"It doesn't matter who told me. I just don't think it's very nice, the way you're doing this."

I had various options: I could continue to insist that I'd only come to the Tower on Tuesday looking for Gary—in which case, why was I here tonight?—or try to skate around the question.

"Murder's not very nice," I said.

She wasn't having any of that. "Are you helping the police?"

"I'm trying," I admitted. "Why not? I've met some of the Towerites. I know my way around the University. That gives me a little edge over the police, don't you think?"

She sucked on a pencil for a moment, then nodded. "Arthur, Dr. Tigue, advised me not to talk to you."

"Why? Doesn't he want Cameron Harris's murderer caught?"

"Of course he does. We all do—even those who didn't like him. His murder was a terrible thing." Her small, firm chin began to tremble, and her eyes filled with tears. "Dr. Tigue's my therapist, and he's also advising me on my book, *From Journal To Poem*."

I tried to suppress a shudder. "But why doesn't he want you to talk to me?"

She looked away. "He doesn't think amateurs ought to be trying to help the police, especially if they're only doing it for the reward. He also doesn't think it's good for me to talk to strangers about—Cameron."

"It's true, the reward would be nice. But I'd be trying to find out who killed Cameron Harris even without it. After all, I found his body. That was a horrible shock to me too, you know. I keep seeing his face . . ."

She nodded, for that was something she could understand—relate to, I mean. She looked at me with new interest. "I can imagine," she said. She sighed and shook her head. "Poor Cam. If not for you, he might still be up there, in the tower."

"That's right," I said. "So in a sense, you Towerites owe me a little, don't you?"

She seemed to mull that one over. As she did, I studied her desk, which was as messy as the room, covered with thin volumes of poetry, books on teaching creative writing, and typed and handwritten poems—student work. There was also a book by Arthur Tigue with his picture on the back cover. The smile on his face was electric, like that of a used-car salesman or a TV evangelist.

I spotted Paula's name on one sheet of paper and twisted my head around to see that Melody had written in the margin, in purple ink, "Do you really think the adverb is necessary here?"

Melody caught me trying to read the poem and delicately turned it over.

"Paula's a friend of mine," I explained, not at all embarrassed.

"I know. She's a very good writer, and she has a wonderful sense of imagery, but I wish she'd open up more. Sharing feelings doesn't come easily, you know. Irony is so much safer. It's like medieval armor or a turtle shell. I try to get my students to realize that irony is one of the inauthentic voices and to take the risk of giving it up."

People who use crayons to express themselves talk like Melody Carr. In my opinion, being able to use irony appropriately is what separates us from the sandbox. "For some reason, I don't think your husband would agree with you."

"Tony?" She looked startled. "You've already talked to him?"

"No, not yet, but I'm going to. How long were you two married?"

"Three years. We're still married, but only in name."

I was surprised; Melody seemed glad to be rid of Verdugo. "What possessed you to marry him in the first place?"

"Oh, I was very young." She emphasized the "I," implying that Verdugo had no such excuse. "In fact, we met at my graduation." She laughed at the memory, a noise like the highest keys on a piano, the ones nobody writes music for anymore. "Tony was the convocation speaker, very Marxist and dashing, and afterwards, while we were all milling around looking for our family members, he came up and asked me who I was. A week later, he called me up and asked me on a date. I said yes."

She shook her head, wiser now, and her fluffy hair bounced. "Arthur—Dr. Tigue—has shown me that I was blinded by Tony's status. That's easy to see now. I'd been one of those faceless, nameless students in black gowns lined up in rows behind him as he stood at the podium and spoke to that huge crowd, and then suddenly I was singled out by him. I was overwhelmed. Meanwhile, Tony saw me as the child-woman he could project his emotional needs onto, instead of developing an emotional life of his own."

Someday, I thought, we'll know everything there is

to know about ourselves, thanks to the Dr. Tigues of the world, and won't that be wonderful! I noticed that Melody couldn't make up her mind whether to call him "Dr. Tigue" or "Arthur."

She suddenly looked concerned, her eyes bright and inquisitive. "But you surely don't think Tony's a suspect, do you? Why would he want to murder Cam?"

I counted four beats. Then I said, "I was here last fall, the night you read the poem your husband walked out on."

"I don't see—oh, you think my love poem was about Cam. Well, it's not."

"Tony might have thought it was."

"Oh, I'm sure he didn't."

"How do you know?"

"Because we talked about it when I got home that night. Tony demanded to know who the poem was about. He said he had a right to know. I just laughed. The great professor of literature, treating a poem as if it were about something real. I told him I had no particular man in mind, that I was expressing my dream that someday we will transcend sexual differences. That's all."

Involuntarily my eyes went up to the happy face on the wall, then quickly back to Melody.

"I'm glad I'm not the only one around here who's having trouble keeping reality and fiction separate," I said. "Did he believe you?"

"Well, he said he did," she replied, her eyes avoiding mine.

"Cameron Harris was flirting with you at the Meades'. Was he just having an experience that he would later transform into art too?"

Her pale face turned bright red. "That's exactly what it was. That's exactly what he would do. He wasn't interested in me or anybody else. He was only interested in his writing. If you think there was anything between us, you're wrong!" Her hair was bouncing all over her head.

"I also wondered why he called you 'Munk,' " I said.

"It's a nickname, short for 'Chipmunk.' " She glanced at her watch.

"Who gave you the name?"

"I don't remember. I've had it a long time." Her hands began moving things around on her desk, making a soft rustling noise, like mice, or chipmunks.

It wasn't a nice nickname for her. "Did Harris give it to you?"

"I said it was a long time ago. I don't remember!"

I turned quickly at a sound behind me. Frank Ott, the custodian, was standing in the doorway, tall and gray. He paused there a moment, his eyes going from Melody to me, and then, without saying anything, he came in and went over to Melody's desk. He picked up her wastebasket and took it out into the hall.

When he came back, he said something to her that I didn't catch.

"I'm fine, Frank, thank you," Melody said. "She's asking me a few questions about Mr. Harris's death. I'll tell you all about it later, I promise."

He left, his expressionless eyes skittering over me as he passed my chair.

I asked her if he always barged in like that, without knocking.

"I don't mind. He cleans my office more regularly than the others. He knows how allergic I am to dust, and it's pretty bad down here, especially now, with all my stuff." She waved at the boxes and paper bags scattered around the room. "We're very fond of each other, Frank and I. Tony thinks it's because we're so much alike; he says neither of us knows how to use language intelligently."

"Frank didn't like Cameron Harris," I said, deciding not to comment on that one. "He said something to me that implied he thought Harris deserved to die."

"I hope you're not part of a police conspiracy to try to pin Cam's death on Frank. Just because he's different from the rest of us. The police questioned him a long time—longer than anybody else I've talked to. That wasn't fair."

I said that was probably because no one else here went around mumbling threats to blasphemers and other sinners.

She shrugged. "It's getting late, Peggy. I've talked to you long enough, and I still have several journals to read before class."

"Journals? Your students keep journals?"

"Yes, they do. That's what I teach, how to transform your experiences into poetry. I require my students to keep a journal and to develop poems from that. I read both their journals and their poems."

So it was true. Paula was keeping a journal. There were depths to my best friend I didn't even know existed.

As I got up to go, I said, "Your sister Sandra once had an affair with Harris. Was that before or after his affair with Tamara?"

The little social smile she'd put on her face to honor my departure vanished. She sat up in her chair. "Before or— What difference does it make?"

"Just curious."

"Why?"

"Well, in her novel, Tamara describes how she—I mean her heroine, Alyssa—finds the artist in the lilacs with another woman. I was just wondering—"

"Tamara's novel is fiction." She tried to keep her voice steady. "Surely you don't believe a word of it is true, do you?" She laughed, achieving the sound of a small window breaking. "Really, you are just as poor a reader as Tony."

"Everything's fiction around this place!" I blurted out, frustration I hadn't been aware of bubbling over. "Your penis—excuse me, *love*—poem doesn't refer to anything; Tamara's younger sister rolling in the lilacs with the artist doesn't either; Frank's hellfire and damnation is only his way of letting people know he's around. I suppose Cameron Harris's death was fiction too."

She watched me carefully. I could have sworn I saw a little glitter of amusement behind her wide-open, innocent eyes. "I'm sorry I can't be of more help. Really, I am." She sounded concerned for my sanity, and with good reason.

At the door, I said, coldly, "Cameron Harris didn't take Tamara's novel as 'just fiction.' He wrote a story of his own that was going to appear in his next novel—a novel that was going to make fun of the Tower and everybody connected with it. He was going to read that story the night he was murdered, and it dealt with his affair with Tamara."

"Really? How do you know that?"

"Because I read it. And the manuscript had blood on it." I didn't mention that on my copy, the blood was Xeroxed.

"That's awful." She looked as though she was trying not to laugh. "I mean, that you had to read a manuscript with blood on it. How did you know the story was about Cam and Tamara? Did he use their names?"

I could either lose my temper again or get out of there, so I left. Frank was outside, in the hall, dumping something into his trash barrel on wheels.

"How much of that did you hear?" I snarled.

His mild gaze stayed on me as he reached into his shirt pocket. He pulled out a tract and held it out. I snatched it from him and kept going. A crudely done black-and-white woodcut on the front page showed a man standing on a street corner. He was staring into a bright ray of light, about to learn something important. I envied him.

I continued down the dimly lit hall, past rooms with students in them, waiting for class to begin. I spotted Paula, her head bent over a notebook, writing furiously, the point of her tongue sticking out the side of her mouth.

On the first floor, Gary was starting up the stairs to his office.

"Sleuthing?" he asked.

"Yeah."

"Any luck?"

I showed him the tract Frank had given me. "Just this."

"Gives you something to think about," he said.

I told him I was working that night. I had to trade with Jesse Porter so I could have the next night, Friday, off, for Sandra Carr's party.

"The reason for your sudden interest in the literary life isn't a secret anymore, Peggy," he said. "People are making sure I know they know."

I apologized for putting him in an embarrassing position. He shrugged and said it didn't matter much. Tower gossip rolled off his back. He waved and strolled off down the hall. I watched him go. I really liked him. He wasn't going to be around much longer, though. What would I say if he asked me to go to South America with him? I wondered what I'd do there, if I were nuts enough to go.

I went out into the cold night. In the parking lot, I saw a large American car, maroon and at least ten years old—one of the real gas guzzlers—parked in front of the side door, its motor running. I started to go around it when the driver called to me. It was Chris Ames, my table companion at the Meades' dinner party.

He gave me his impish smile, which put dimples in his cheeks, and asked if I was taking a writing class. At least someone didn't seem to know I was playing detective.

I told him no, that I'd just come over to talk to Gary. The old lie was on its last legs now. "How about you?"

"I'm here to pick up Tamara. We go to my club sometimes and play tennis after she's finished with work. It helps her relax, and it keeps us both in shape. She's had to work late a lot recently. There's a deadline for some kind of grant proposal. By the way—" he lowered his voice conspiratorially "—I saw you on television the morning after you discovered Harris's body. What you said to that reporter gave me a laugh. Not an appropriate response, but I couldn't help it."

I told him I couldn't help it either.

"Noodles!" he said.

Tamara emerged from the Tower and came up on the passenger side of the car. "You do get around," she said to me. She might have been an epidemiologist, speaking to a test tube full of some loathsome virus, and her large gray eyes were as cold as the night. She slid into the car and closed the door. "Let's go," she said to Ames. She leaned her head back against the headrest without looking at him.

Ames didn't let her mood bother him. "Do you play tennis?" he asked me, a smile still on his round face.

I told him I played racquetball.

He said he'd never played the game, but maybe he wasn't too old to learn. I said good tennis players made awful racquetball players, but added that I hoped we'd meet again.

"I do too," he said. "Why don't you give me a call at my office, some day when you're free, since I know you work nights. I mean it. I'm not exactly overwhelmed with work these days."

"She wants to earn your reward, Chris," Tamara said, her eyes closed.

"I know." He was still smiling up at me. "And I'd like to help her do it."

After I promised I'd give him a call, he waved and drove off. Tamara looked as if she were asleep.

I watched the taillights of his car disappear down the hill. Where did Chris Ames, the old family friend, fit in? How much did he know about what went on in the Tower, his childhood home? And what was his relationship with Tamara Wallace Meade, his lawyer's wife, anyway?

Fourteen

The next night Gary and I went to Sandra Carr's party. It was a drop-in affair to celebrate her return from Hollywood, where she'd watched them make a movie of one of her novels. Gary had been to similar parties before, to celebrate her birthdays, returns from long trips abroad, the completion of a novel, and so forth. "She works like a fiend," he told me, "no pun intended. Locks herself away, and you don't see her for weeks, sometimes months. And then, when she's finished a book or a story, she can't stand to be alone. That's when she goes into what she calls her 'party frenzy.'"

She came as a surprise. She had red hair and freckles, which was the first thing Gary had noticed about me. But "red hair and freckles" doesn't really say much, at least not to those of us blessed with them. Sandra's hair was redder than mine—she would have looked much more dramatic steering the back end of a ladder truck at high speed than I, for example—and her freckles had been scattered carelessly all over her face, some of them leaving skid marks on contact. She was taller than I too, almost six feet, and long-limbed, appearing both gawky and graceful at the same time. She had an angular face with a strong chin, china blue eyes, and a quick smile.

Gary introduced us, trying desperately to be formal about it. She greeted him with a big hug and then pushed him away, grinning at his embarrassment. She stuck out her hand and shook mine. Her blue eyes were bright, and she used them to quickly assess me.

"Toss your coats on my bed," she said. "Gary knows where it is."

Somebody behind me laughed. Gary turned the same color as Sandra's hair, and we both looked to see who it was.

Tony Verdugo, in his usual fatigues and polished boots, was sprawled in an overstuffed chair, with a plate of canapes balanced on one knee and a drink in his hand. He said, "Hey there, Gary!" and then looked at me. "I've seen you someplace before, haven't I?"

"I don't know."

"She's a campus cop," Sandra told him. "Maybe she's been stalking you, the way she's been stalking everybody else who knew Cam Harris. Have you, Peggy?"

"Like a bloodhound," I answered.

"Yes," Verdugo said, recognition dawning, "that's right." He stared at me a little longer, a disbelieving smile on his face, and then he said to Gary, softly, "Show Peggy where to toss her coat, Gary."

Before Gary could inflict damage on Verdugo, I took him by the arm and led him to the circular stairs that I guessed went up to Sandra's bedroom. Behind us, I heard Sandra say, "I've missed you, Tony. There's nobody like you in Hollywood, where everyone is so polite to everyone else. It gets so damned oppressive."

They both laughed.

Gary muttered, "The son of a bitch. And did you notice how he stared at you?"

"Take it easy." We dumped our coats on Sandra's

bed. It jiggled slightly, like Jell-O. I looked at him inquiringly.

"You, too," he said.

Sandra lived on one of the top floors of what was once a grain elevator. It had recently been recycled into very fashionable and expensive condominiums. Sandra's had probably been designed for chrome and glass and perhaps leather furniture, but she'd overridden that with her own taste, which leaned strongly toward textured, striped wallpaper and early American clutter interspersed with lurid posters of thriller movies and equally lurid framed covers of her own books.

She liked indoor plants too; they were hanging everywhere and in pots on the floor. That was something else she had on me, besides the clutter. I've got something given to me by my Aunt Tess, dying slowly in a pot in my kitchen, but that's it. The noise of plants photosynthesizing drives me nuts.

As Gary and I were going back down the stairs, two cats darted past us. They got to the bottom, stopped abruptly, turned, and gave their black coats a quick, nervous lick as they waited for us. When I tried to step around them, one of them stepped into my path and leaned against my leg. Cats are like that; they have a sixth sense for people who are allergic to them.

"They have names?" I asked Gary.

"The one curled around your ankles is Jim Bob. The other's Pierre."

The cats followed us into the living room. I pretended to ignore them.

"Sandra's sister, Melody, is allergic to cats, too," Gary said. "A lot worse than you. That's one reason why you won't see her here tonight." He glowered across the room at Tony Verdugo, the other reason.

"I'll be fine," I said, "as long as the cats stay away from me, and you stay away from Verdugo. Cameron

Harris apparently clobbered him at a party last fall. Look what happened to him."

"Scat!" Gary bent down and clapped his hands in front of Jim Bob's face. The cat looked up at him curiously, as if expecting an explanation. Then, looking mildly disappointed, he sauntered off. The other one, Pierre, followed in his wake, turning rejection into an opportunity to delicately sniff his companion's butt.

We'd been among the first to arrive, but soon the place was packed with people. A trio played dance music in one corner of the room, and two caterers kept a long table full of things to eat and drink. Gary followed me around for a while, dutifully introducing me to people he knew, most of whom were writers or otherwise involved in the arts, and then he disappeared. I spotted him occasionally, hovering in the vicinity of Sandra Carr.

Not many of the writers were members of the Tower. Most of them wrote fantasy and science fiction or horror and mystery. One woman, her large body surrounded by a brightly-colored dashiki, wrote romantic suspense.

We'd been there about half an hour when I glanced up and saw a tall man with a thin mustache and equally thin beard come in. Arthur Tigue. I stepped behind a local literary agent who'd kept his ankle-length fur coat on and watched as Tigue glanced around the room until he spotted Sandra. He gave her a big hug that she seemed to endure rather than enjoy.

"Damn!" she said, in a loud voice. "First Tony and now you, Arthur! My mailing list needs some serious weeding, doesn't it? Nice to see you again, by the way." She turned back to the people she'd been talking to before Tigue came in.

A little later, as I was standing in front of Sandra's floor-to-ceiling picture windows, admiring the view of the city, I was cornered by a writer of hard-boiled mysteries, a small, mild-mannered man in his mid-fifties with thinning hair and a nose like a toucan's. I'd read a novel of his one summer, lying on the shore of Lake Eleanor. After talking to him for a few minutes, I realized that his hero, a tough private eye named Boxx, was probably modeled on the bully who used to beat him up in high school. I wondered if that's where all the hard-boiled private eyes came from.

"What'd ya write?" he asked me.

"Nothing, but I have a friend who's interested in writing."

"Tell him not to write mysteries," he said morosely. "There's no money in it. There's too damned many of us all doing the same thing, and the formula's growing old as we speak."

"It's a she," I said.

"I never read books by broads."

"Not even Sandra's?"

"Oh, well, Sandy." He perked up. "She's a whole other ball of wax. Sandy can do terror!"

"Can't you? What does it take?"

"I'm working on it," he said, launching a haunted look at me over his nose.

I felt somebody standing next to me, too close for comfort. It was Arthur Tigue. He took a sip of his drink, watching me over the rim as he did. His cold gray eyes in his white face didn't blink. I could do that too, with my cold green eyes, and I did.

After a half minute of this, he said, "You do get around, don't you, Ms. O'Neill? Still trying to earn that reward, I imagine. But in your efforts to do that, you don't seem to mind upsetting people. You upset a patient of mine, Melody Carr, yesterday."

The mystery writer looked at Tigue, looked at me,

raised his glass to whatever he saw between us, and faded away.

"I'm sorry if I upset Melody," I said, "although she didn't seem upset to me. In fact, I think I was more upset. She ended up laughing at me. And I don't care about the reward. I'm simply a concerned citizen." I flashed him my best concerned-citizen smile. I have sincere teeth. I wondered if Tigue's thin brown mustache was meant to obscure or emphasize the fact that his upper lip looked like a skinny worm.

"You did upset her, although she may have dealt with her feelings by—as the current slang will have it—'stuffing it.' But don't let that fool you. She is currently in a delicate emotional state. Understandably so, after all, for a man she knew and admired has died violently, and she is divorcing her husband."

Tigue's voice was like New Age music, urging me to relax, get in touch with my feelings. "The man she knew and admired didn't just die violently," I said. "He was murdered, and his killer's still on the loose. Melody's a suspect, and for that matter, so are you. Also, I didn't get the impression she was terribly upset over the breakup of her marriage."

"Melody—Ms. Carr—has not yet worked through the loss of her husband," he droned on, as if accustomed to this kind of childish hairsplitting. "She is in a state of denial still."

We should all be in such a state. "She looked to me as though she had other irons in the fire, bigger fish to fry." Give me a couple of good clichés over psychobabble any day.

"Again, Ms. O'Neill—" he bowed his head "—I must ask you to defer to a specialist in the field."

"Okay." I gave him the smile I use when deferring to specialists in the field. "Didn't you once have Cameron Harris as a patient too?"

He stiffened. "I don't know where you heard that. Most probably from my ex-wife, Niobe. As you may have noticed from her behavior at the Tower the other afternoon, she isn't very balanced in her dealings with me. She has not worked through—"

"I know. Losing you. I can understand that. But Harris was your patient, wasn't he?"

"Briefly, yes. But he was not ready for therapy. And I was too inexperienced a therapist to realize that. Too bad, really; therapy could have helped him. And helping him might have saved his life."

"How?"

"It might have helped him understand, among other things, the nature of the power he had over people, both in person and in his writing. As you may have heard, Ms. O'Neill, he was often—" Tigue searched for a word "—unkind to his friends, both in his writing and in reality. He had such a poor self-image that he could not believe in the reality of his power. I could have taught him to believe in that power, and to use it more creatively. I know you met Harris. Perhaps you'll agree that he had a curiously blank face. It acted like a screen onto which you could project your fantasies, your longings. He didn't understand that, the ability he had to be all things to all people. And so, inevitably, he disappointed them. One by one, he disappointed everybody he ever got close to."

On the two occasions I'd seen Harris—alive, that is—I'd been busy trying to make his features add up to something rather than projecting my fantasies onto them.

"You think his killer was someone who felt betrayed because he couldn't be what he or she wanted him to be."

"I do think so, yes."

"You have anybody in particular in mind?"

He smiled down at me. "Oh, quite a few people fit the description, I believe." He looked around the room, as if the people he had in mind were all within eavesdropping distance. "Niobe, for instance, comes easily to mind in this connection. She thought she was going to be Harris's guide, his mentor. He was supposed to join her cause, saving the prairie through literature, or whatever it is now. But, in all fairness, there were many women, and some men too, who came under—rather, put themselves under—Cameron Harris's spell."

"Tamara Meade?"

He pursed his lips knowingly.

"Perhaps you yourself come easily to mind in this connection," I said.

"Me?" He seemed startled. He looked closely at me, as if noticing me for the first time. "You think I had some reason for wanting to kill him?"

"He betrayed you, didn't he? Led you to believe you had him. You thought he'd put himself into your hands, and then he turned around and made fun of you in a novel."

As I spoke, his pale face turned pink, like the inside of a clamshell. "Oh dear." He tried to keep his voice mellow and condescending. "You have been picking up some irresponsible notions, haven't you? That comes from talking to Niobe. I wonder what other distorted information you've gathered."

"I realize Niobe's biased. Probably a lot of the people I've talked to are," I added. "That's why I'd like to hear your story, Dr. Tigue, and get your insights into the people around Cameron Harris. After all, you're a trained psychologist, and you've known all of them for at least ten years."

My words were like spilled milk to a sponge. "I know you're not at the University often," I continued, "so I thought I could talk to you at your office—perhaps for just a few minutes."

"You're a very hard woman to turn down, aren't you, Ms. O'Neill? I like tenacity in a woman." He rubbed his mustache with a long finger. "Not at my office." He looked at his watch, a Rolex that cost more than the new car I'd been considering. "It's Friday today, isn't it? I teach on Wednesday night. The seminar lasts until ten, so if you're really interested in getting my version of the story Niobe fed you and my insights, for what they're worth, why don't you come to my office at, say, a quarter past the hour?"

Roll call wasn't until eleven, so I'd have plenty of time. I told Tigue I'd see him there.

"I don't suppose you know where Harris was the afternoon he died?" I asked.

"No, why?"

"Nobody seems to know. I wondered if maybe he'd come to see you, at your office."

Tigue looked worried. "Did he tell anybody he was going to see me that day?"

"Not that I know of."

"He was staying with the Meades, wasn't he? Surely they must know where he was."

"They don't."

"Well, I didn't see him that day," he said firmly. "In fact, I didn't see him at all during the months he was here." His eyes moved away from me, back to the view from Sandra's window. "My guess is he spent the afternoon down there somewhere, on Central, in one of the little bars he used to love so much." He pointed out the cord of yellow light that was Central Avenue. "But the police must have asked around down there, and if he'd been there, they'd know by now." He shrugged, as if it wasn't any of his business. "Well, it's been nice talking to you, Ms. O'Neill. I'll see you Wednesday night. I'm looking forward to it."

An arm went around my waist. "I'll bet you are, Arthur." Tony Verdugo looked at me and added, with a smile, "But you'd better ask him to quote you a price, Peggy, before you ask him for help."

Fifteen

During the past few minutes, I'd been watching Verdugo make his way toward us through the crowd, drink in hand; still, he managed to sneak up on me. I slipped out of his grasp and stepped away, smiling sociably. After all, I was there to learn, not teach.

"I'm jealous," he said. "What's Arthur got that I haven't? Or are you going to consult Dr. Tigue professionally Wednesday night?"

"I was getting around to you," I assured him.

"But first you want to get Arthur's trained insights into our psyches, is that it? You know, I finally remembered where I'd seen you before. You were staring into my classroom the other afternoon. Naughty, naughty!"

I gave him my best baffled look. "I don't know what you're talking about."

"Now, now! Don't play the innocent with me, honey. You were right outside my classroom door, staring in. You want to be incognito, you better do something about that red hair. You're on a quest for knowledge, aren't you?" He lowered his voice. "But what you don't realize is nothing's knowable."

"How do you know?"

"Give it up, Peggy," Sandra said, joining our little group. "Nobody can stop Tony from trying to convince

123

the world of the absurdity of trying to convince the world of anything. It pays too well and it's how he gets all those big grants of his." She smiled at me. "Maybe you're really gathering material for a true crime story. You should, if you aren't. It'd pay a lot more than your campus cop job." She looked out the window. "Did you know you can see the Tower from here?"

With her help, I could see the apex of the pointed roof of the tower, poking out of the trees. I was surprised at how close it seemed.

"Creepy, isn't it?" Sandra said. "Cam Harris murdered in that little room. What the hell was he doing up there? Who'd he go up there with?"

Verdugo said, "Uh-oh. Sandy's starting to think about it 'aesthetically.' I smell another made-for-TV-thriller on the way. Maybe this one'll have some substance to it, being based on so much intimate knowledge of the deceased."

Sandra brought one long arm around in a fast arc. Her open hand landed on the side of Verdugo's face with the noise of a rifle shot, rocking his head back.

"Jesus, Sandra." He'd spilled his drink all down his clothes, but still held his glass. "You can dish it out, but you can't take it."

"There are limits, Tony," she said, only slightly breathless from the exertion. "Why don't you write your own novels, instead of living high off the work of people who do?" She turned to me, as if what just happened were nothing more than an aside. "I suppose you think you know Cameron Harris pretty well now, even though you never knew him when he was alive."

"I met him. I thought he was a jerk." I braced myself for a possible attack, but instead she laughed.

"Yeah, he was that! And wore the label proudly too. Or wanted us to think he did. But he was a pretty talented guy."

"He started out pretty talented, you mean," I said.

"No. I meant what I said. You don't get your books on the bestseller list by a fluke. Cam discovered what he was good at writing, and he wrote it. A lot of people liked it and bought it. In my eyes, that makes him a pretty talented guy. His first novel, at least, was wonderful; it had to be, to survive Tony's patronizing *Times* review."

Verdugo was off getting another drink. I told her I'd heard about the review.

"It was mean-spirited," she said. "Tony used Cam's novel as an excuse to show off how clever he is, and the novel didn't deserve that. I was surprised that Cam didn't do a number on Tony in *Lost Letters Home*, the way he did on Arthur." She grinned at Tigue, whose pale face turned pink again. He started to say something, but Sandra didn't wait for him. "I suppose you've managed to pick that up too, on your rounds?"

"I've managed to put names to some of the slurs," I said, trying to be tactful.

"Did you get Harris's satire on Arthur's peculiar forms of therapy?" Verdugo was back, with a fresh drink. "Why didn't you sue him, Art?"

"I wouldn't dignify his attack on me with a lawsuit," Tigue replied.

"You mean you *don't* encourage your adult patients to play with blocks on your office floor?" Verdugo pressed. "I've never been fortunate enough to see Melody in a diaper, but I'll bet she's quite fetching." He took a step toward Tigue. "Is she, Dr. Tigue?" His face was twisted, and starting to swell where Sandra had slapped him. Tigue quickly stepped behind me, out of reach. He started to say something, but changed his mind.

The writer of hard-boiled mysteries had crept into the circle, next to Sandra. "You think maybe somebody killed Cam Harris on account of what he wrote in one of his books?" he asked her, one professional to another. "The revenge motive?"

"No, Clyde," she replied, "nothing in real life is quite as simple as your plots. I think he was murdered on account of his next book, the one he never got the chance to finish. *Lost Letters Home* was just finger exercises. In the next one, everybody who'd ever come to the attention of Cam's jaundiced eye was in for it. Too bad he didn't have the time to finish it." She was staring levelly at Verdugo as she spoke.

"You'd have been in it too, Sandy," Verdugo said.

"I should hope so," she replied. "I would've sued the bastard if I wasn't!"

"Really?" Verdugo sounded skeptical. "You and Niobe Tigue are the only Towerites with national reputations to worry about."

"Maybe Niobe, who's totally devoid of a sense of humor, worries about her reputation, but I don't worry about mine, except when I'm not getting any publicity at all. It's people like you, Tony, who have to worry about that little boy showing up to shout that the emperor's naked. He's going to someday, you know."

"How about your sister, Sandy? How'd you feel about her making an appearance in his novel?"

Sandra opened her mouth but closed it and started over. "Melody was only a child when Cam lived here, Tony. He didn't know her well enough to put her in a book. You know that." She turned away from Verdugo and looked out the window again. "Against all odds," she went on softly, "the country boy found a way to become a success. Quite a story, for someone who started out writing like Niobe, part of what she called the 'New Prairie Renaissance.'" Sandra shuddered at the memory, as if she might have started out that way too.

Verdugo said, "Melody told me once that, as soon as

he got all he could from Niobe, he turned and mocked everything she stood for. I imagine that might rankle a bit, don't you?"

Sandra nodded, laughed. They were suddenly the best of friends again, working against somebody other than each other. "That's how Niobe tells the story, at least. Is it true, Arthur? You were still married to her, weren't you?"

"I know nothing about that," he said. "We'd parted ways before she took on the education of Cameron Harris."

"And yet," I put in, "Niobe thinks Harris became cynical and bitter because Tamara dumped him for John Meade's money and status."

Sandra burst out laughing. " 'Cam Harris, the clown with the broken heart.' What a joke! Under that crusty exterior, Niobe's a romantic. All reactionaries are, I suppose."

"Then you think there really was a woman in the lilacs?"

"No!" Sandra said, quickly. "That's Tamara's version of the truth. It was obvious to anybody who was there that she was going to dump Cam for old John Meade. Even Cam saw it coming, before he—" She broke off suddenly.

"He what, Sandy?" Verdugo asked her. "Took some femme fatale into the lilacs for a little slap and tickle?"

Before Sandra could speak, the woman who wrote romantic suspense came rushing up, her bright dashiki fluttering, her gold sandals flapping.

"Isn't it wonderful, Sandra," she gushed. "You were gone a month and didn't lose so much as a single plant! I went from room to room and looked at all of them. Not a brown leaf anywhere."

"I should hope not, Ursula," Sandra replied. She seemed happy to change the subject. "My sister came in and watered them for me. She's very good with plants. I believe she even talks to the damned things."

"You asked Melody to water your plants for you?" Verdugo exclaimed. "God, Sandra, that's going too far, even for you. Even if you'd taken your cats to California with you, or boarded them out somewhere, Melody would've died a little bit every time she came into this place. Some of us, you know, think you keep cats just to keep her out of your life."

"It's me she's allergic to, not my cats," Sandra snapped. She turned to Tigue. "What about it, Arthur? Aren't allergies psychosomatic?"

"They can be." He seemed to take the question seriously. "How long has she been allergic to cats? Surely not when she was living with you."

"I didn't have cats then. I waited until she'd graduated from high school and moved out. Then I got Jim Bob and Pierre. Where are they, anyway?"

I could have told her. I'd been keeping track of them. At that moment they were in the laps of some people across the room, licking shrimp dip off toast points.

"But you asked her to come in and water your plants while you were in California?" Arthur Tigue persisted.

"It didn't hurt her any. It doesn't take long to water a few plants and feed a couple of cats. Besides, it was only for a month."

"You made her feed the cats too!" Verdugo laughed. "My God, Sandra!"

"I *paid* her. She was glad to have the money, Tony," she added pointedly. "C'mon, let's go get something to drink and find a place to sit, and I'll tell you all about L.A." She took another glance out of her big picture window. "The tower's dark. No high culture taking place down there tonight. It's all happening up here." She put her arm around Tony's waist, as if they were lifelong buddies, and they walked away.

That left Arthur Tigue and me alone at the picture window again. He'd listened to the conversation between Sandra and Verdugo with interest, as if taking notes, but now he was staring out into the night, as if he found the view of the city fascinating. His hawk nose went well with his pencil-thin beard and mustache. A Rasputin for the nineties, Edith Silberman's friend had called him.

He became aware of me watching him and turned quickly away.

"What's your office number?" I asked him.

"My office number? Oh, 243."

"I'll see you Wednesday night, then," I said.

"What? Oh, yes, Wednesday night." He headed toward the bar.

After a while, I drifted over to where Sandra was entertaining an adoring crowd, Gary among them, hanging on to her every word.

We stayed until after midnight. I watched Tony Verdugo attempt to balance getting plastered with picking up a young woman who bore some resemblance to Melody Carr, and then I watched Arthur Tigue, who'd drunk very little, move in on her when Verdugo was safely asleep in a chair. I wondered what Tigue had that I couldn't see in him. I'd never understood Rasputin's power either. Both men had deep-set eyes with lots of white showing, like silent film stars.

I decided I'd seen enough of the popular fiction crowd when I noticed my eyes itching from the cats. I went upstairs and got Gary's and my coats and brought them down.

Sandra followed us to the door. She gave Gary a hug. Then, before I could avoid it, she gave me one too, and said we'd have to get together for lunch sometime.

I smiled and said I'd like that. I believed her when she said Cameron Harris couldn't hurt her, and I doubted that she'd resort to killing anybody except in self-defense. But I wondered if protecting her sister would constitute self-defense in Sandra's mind. I remembered what Harris planned to call Melody in his novel—"Trisha Payne"—and what he'd said about her poetry. Had Sandra known about that? What else did she know about his plans for her sister? It would be useful to talk to her alone sometime.

In the car, Gary was subdued, but after a few minutes of silence, he asked me if I'd learned anything useful. I told him I had an appointment to meet with Arthur Tigue the following Wednesday.

"I've heard he's a real manipulator," he said. "You'd better be careful, or you'll end up in therapy with him, getting to know Peggy O'Neill when she was a little girl."

"I know all I want to about little Peggy. I don't need to find out any more." Like Niobe Tigue, I had better things to do with my life.

Sixteen

I couldn't think of anything more I could do to help solve Cameron Harris's murder, at least, not before my meeting with Arthur Tigue on Wednesday night.

Monday night, our night off, Paula, Lawrence, and I went with Gary to see a flamenco dance troupe that was passing through town. Gary had acquired a taste for, and a large record collection of, flamenco music in South America. I enjoyed it too, although maybe not for the same reason he did. If machismo always meant that combination of grace, fire, and humor I wouldn't mind it at all. Afterward we had a late supper at Paula's place. She took up gourmet cooking once, with the same seriousness of purpose that she was now devoting to poetry, and always seemed to have the ingredients on hand to whip up something tasty. I've never understood it.

As she thrust something into the oven, she asked me what I got out of Melody on Thursday afternoon.

"Only that you should place the adverb 'darkly' after 'glass' instead of before 'through.' "

"That's from the Bible," Lawrence said, surprising both Paula and me with his cultural breadth. "I guess you didn't get anything helpful out of her."

"That's because Melody doesn't know anything helpful," Paula retorted.

"I sure hope I didn't upset her so much that she couldn't teach that night," I said. "At her sister's party, her therapist told me she was decimated after my grilling."

"You didn't upset her at all," Paula said smugly. "Tigue's a real creep, isn't he?"

I asked her how she knew, and she said she sometimes saw him at the Tower, either dropping Melody off or picking her up after class. "He's a psychologist, and yet he drives a bright red convertible. You'd think he'd know what that means!"

"A Porsche," Lawrence said enviously.

I smiled. "You really like Melody, don't you?"

Paula looked at me with her big, serious eyes. "Yes, I do. I know she's not a great poet—not yet, anyway—but she knows good poetry when she sees it. And she knows how to teach poetry. Not all great poets are good teachers, you know, and vice versa."

"It's the same way with batting and pitching coaches, Peggy," Lawrence put in, "in baseball."

"Thank you, Lar," I said.

"Melody has the ability to get into a student's poem," Paula went on, "no matter how bad it is. She takes a poem on its own terms, instead of imposing her own standards on it. And she's very sweet. In that respect, Peggy, you could take a page from her book."

"From her journal, you mean. Maybe I could learn to decorate my arrest reports with big sunflowers and rainbows. I hope you're not trying to tell me that an excellent poetry teacher can't be a murderer too."

"Melody feels terrible about Harris's death. I think it was a growing experience for her."

"Murder as a growing experience!" I snorted, like

Niobe Tigue. When, oh when, was Paula going to pass through this phase?

"She's just finished a poem about it," Paula said, unfazed by my snort. "It's very moving. She read it to us a couple of days ago, and also the entries in her journal that deal with Harris's death, so we could see how poems grow from experience. Harris's death affected Melody terribly."

I wondered why. They hadn't been all that good friends, had they? At least, I hadn't found anybody who'd said they'd been. Melody had been only a child, according to Niobe, when Harris was a member of the Second Story.

I asked Paula how come I never saw her carrying around a journal.

She sniffed. "A snoop like you might 'accidentally on purpose' open it to see what I've written. I wouldn't want to hurt your feelings."

Gary didn't say much the whole evening. Maybe he was bogged down in the book he was working so hard on, or maybe he was tired of discussing literature and murder. Most likely, though, he was thinking about South America. He'd liked living in primitive villages, and told me often enough that writing about it was a distant second to living it. Writing was "just a way to pay the bills." He looked hurt when I pointed out that if he were really living it, he wouldn't have any bills to pay.

Gary was an observer; in that respect, we were alike. He had a wonderful talent for putting what he observed into words. To be anything other than a writer would just be that—*other,* something he had no way of knowing if he would like being or not. So many people think they want to be either/or when, in fact, the glory and the despair of being human is that we're always both/and. With Melody's longing to recover childhood, and

Niobe's demand that we return to the ways of the past, they were just trying to become something that's less than human.

I don't know how much I really like being me. I know even less, though, about how I'd like to be somebody else.

When we left Paula's, we went to my place for the night, and I could tell that the flamenco rhythms were still echoing in Gary's head, so I tried to imagine I was Conchita O'Neill, with a rose clenched in my teeth. I almost giggled but managed to control it. Some men get touchy when you giggle in the wrong places, and I knew that Gary was that kind of man.

"Give me a call," Chris Ames had told me when I saw him last Thursday. Why not? I didn't have anything else to do with my time, and he'd obviously enjoyed my company at the Meades' dinner party as much as I'd enjoyed his.

I called the main office and got a secretary who sounded as if my request to talk to Ames was not in her job description. When I persisted, she transferred me to Ames's secretary, who sounded friendly. I was on hold for no more than fifteen seconds before Ames came on the line.

"I wondered if you'd call. Tamara gave me quite an earful about you in the car that evening. I was hoping you wouldn't overlook me in your pursuit of Mr. Harris's murderer."

"Oh? You think you have something of interest to say on the subject?"

"Not at all. I doubt that I have anything useful to tell you. But I must say that I do enjoy the company of waggish young people like yourself. One meets so few of them anymore. We could have lunch someday, since

I'm obviously not fit for racquetball. There's a lovely restaurant here in the building. It would be on me."

I told him I didn't get up in time for lunch on the days after I worked, but I'd very much enjoy seeing his office. "How about now?"

"You'd like to see the kind of digs they provide the chairman of the board of a nuts-'n'-bolts empire, would you? I assure you, they'll knock your socks off. And I think today would be an especially appropriate time to see my office." He laughed at some private joke.

"What's so special about today?"

"Perhaps I'll tell you when you get here. Is it a date?"

I'd never known anybody who said "digs" and "knock your socks off," or who thought I was waggish. I agreed to be at his office at three that afternoon. He sounded like he really wanted my company.

Seventeen

His office was in what had been the tallest building in town for a long time, and the first with an exterior solely of glass panels that reflected the world around it. Originally that included a great deal of sky; now there are so many other buildings like it that they only reflect one another.

The offices of Ames Hardware were on the twenty-second floor. The elevator took about that many seconds to get there, with no sense of motion at all. I rode up with a woman and a man for whom business fashion had obliterated all traces of personality, and with stares that didn't encourage small talk.

The receptionist's office of Ames Hardware was as large as my living room and even less cluttered. The walls had dark oak paneling, and over the door behind the receptionist was a freshly polished brass plate with "Ames Hardware" embossed on it. Hallways led off to the left and right.

"You're expected." The receptionist was an older woman with a pleasant smile. "Mr. Ames warned me to be on the lookout for the saucy young woman with the red hair. That's got to be you."

Saucy, too! She spoke my name into the intercom. Almost immediately the door behind her opened, and

Chris Ames came bustling out. He looked happy to see me. Putting one arm around my waist and taking my elbow with his other hand, he steered me into his office, speaking welcoming inanities the whole time, as if trying to keep me from panicking as he guided me through a minefield. He had to look up to see my face.

He deposited me on a burgundy leather sofa, soft with age, and sat down next to me. Like the outer office, his was paneled in dark oak. Concealed lights in the ceiling illuminated oil paintings on the walls. The painting of a man on the wall behind Ames's desk looked a lot like him. A brass plate on the frame identified him as Christopher Ames Sr.

Ames saw me looking at it. "He died just a little over ten years ago, there, at that desk. He was ninety, and I don't think he missed a day of work in his life."

"He looks nice." I wasn't just being polite; he really did. But portraits can lie.

"My father wasn't just a nice man. He was a wonderful man. I doubt he had an enemy in the world. He took over his father's hardware store in the depths of the depression of the thirties, and he almost went broke. He tried to sell out, but nobody had the money to buy, or wanted to. Nobody was building then, nobody was buying hardware. So he hung on by his fingernails, cursing the business, until the war ended—the Second World War—and suddenly construction boomed, as did the need for hardware. He borrowed capital and began to expand." Ames gazed up at his father's portrait, smiling. "He took as little credit as possible for his success, always pointing out that he'd tried to unload the business, but couldn't."

He broke off and asked me if I'd like coffee. "I could offer you a drink, of course, but I suspect that would be a waste of breath. Are you by any chance a teetotaler?"

"No. I just don't drink. But I don't mind other people drinking around me—if they know how."

Ames poked his head out the door and spoke to the receptionist.

"Ames Hardware is yours now," I said.

"No, unfortunately, it's not. A few years before he died, Father took the company public. It was against my wishes, but he thought we needed to continue to expand in order to stay competitive, and that takes capital. He was right, in the short run. But our stock became very attractive. Too attractive. A corporate raider got hold of a significant block of it and made a successful takeover bid. Fortunately, Father didn't live to see it."

The receptionist came in and set down a tray with a thermos of coffee and cups and saucers.

"But you're still chairman of the board," I said.

"Oh yes. I'm the chairman of the board, all right." He sounded slightly bitter. Then he laughed and looked at me, merriment in his button eyes. "That's the little surprise I promised you. I've decided to resign."

"Why?"

"Because I no longer have duties or responsibilities, I sit at the head of the table at meetings, allowing myself to be patronized by toadies who know where the real power lies. I have a nice little nest egg of my own, and a diversified stock portfolio, so I don't imagine I'll starve, even after I pay someone the reward for bringing Mr. Harris's murderer to justice. You, for example." He pointed a finger at me. "As we were talking on the phone, I thought you would be a delightful person to test my decision on, before I announce it this afternoon and tell them what I think of them. I haven't told anybody else yet, not even Tamara."

"What's Tamara got to do with it?"

"Oh, I assumed you knew. You must know a great deal about the Towerites and their friends by now."

"I know only what I've been told," I said, finding it hard not to sound grumpy. "And from a bunch of writers, that's worse than nothing. But I've heard that you and Tamara are good friends."

His button eyes twinkled. "Yes, we are. I feel—in these coarse and cynical times—that I must add that we are good friends in an old-fashioned, chaste way. Can you accept that, Miss O'Neill?"

"Sure. I have a similar relationship with a homicide cop. Some people find it hard to believe that two adults of the opposite sex can have a close relationship that's not sexual in nature."

He nodded. "I've known Tamara's husband, John, since we were children. We went to the same school, and we were chums. When he graduated from law school, my father employed him, and he continues to handle my personal affairs to this very day. I pretty much have the run of their home. I'm a bachelor, you know, but frankly I enjoy the company of beautiful and intelligent women. And I don't wish for any real 'entanglements.' I suppose one could say that I am a very selfish man. It's a harmless selfishness, I think."

"What does Tamara get out of it?"

"Oh, I suppose she thinks of me as 'the good father,' one who observes life from a height and can put troubling things in an appropriate context for her. She's much too emotional to do that herself, and John is too absorbed in his books and his hobbies. Tamara and I also play tennis at my club regularly, now that John is unable to engage in strenuous activities."

"Your relationship has a long tradition," I said. "The courtly love tradition of the Renaissance. Do you write poems to your lady too?"

"No, no. Nothing quite so exalted. I got writing out of my system a long time ago."

I got up and walked around the room. I sat down in

the big dark leather chair behind his desk and swiveled it this way and that. His father had died in it; I felt myself disappearing into it.

"How does it feel?" Ames asked me, smiling.

"It makes me feel puny." How did Ames, who was smaller than I, feel behind it? I decided not to ask. There wasn't much on the desk, just a phone and a pair of photographs in a leather frame. One showed a child playing with toys on a bare wooden floor; the other was of Ames's father, a somewhat younger version than the portrait behind me.

"There're no pictures of your mother," I said.

Ames came over and stood behind me. He shook his head sadly. "I never knew her. She died when I was born."

"You were a cute kid." I nodded to the photograph.

It was a clear afternoon. From the windows, I could see a long way. I found the river and followed it up through the University, with the Old Campus on the east bank, the campanile in the middle, and the New Campus a harsh sprawl on the west bank.

"There aren't many views of the city this spectacular," I said, as Ames came up and stood next to me. I looked for the Tower. It was harder to find from here than from Sandra's condo because we were farther away and higher up. By sighting down Ames's arm, I finally saw the tower's roof poking up out of the trees.

"It's generous of you to support the Tower," I said.

"My support consisted of donating the mansion, but that's the extent of it. Before he died, my father set up a foundation. I'm not a member of the board, however, and I have no say in what causes the foundation supports, so the Tower has to compete for grants on its own merits."

"Just how badly off is the Tower?" I asked him.

"No worse off than many other artistic institutions of

its kind, I imagine. I only know what Tamara tells me. She runs that show, and believe me, she runs it well. She works late many weeknights, and on weekends too. She wants the Tower to be the best of its kind in the country, but it's not easy. With grant money and private funding drying up, Tamara's had to be more creative in her fund-raising. Why do you assume the Tower's so badly off? You don't believe everything Niobe Tigue tells you, do you?" he asked with a knowing smile.

"Because Tamara felt she had to hustle Harris, to use him to bring in the crowds. She let him stay at her home for two weeks. That sounds like desperation to me."

He winced at "hustle." "You're wrong, Miss O'Neill. Don't you believe in letting bygones be bygones? Tamara and Mr. Harris had been lovers in the past. Everybody knows that. But that was a long time ago. Tamara is ambitious. She wants to put the Tower on the map, and she saw Mr. Harris as a way to start. She hoped that, with his reputation and contacts, he'd bring the Tower greater prominence—perhaps by bringing writers of national and international repute here."

"Harris was planning to put the Tower on the map, all right, but not exactly in the way Tamara intended."

He shook his head, as if he didn't understand what the world was coming to. "You're referring to the novel he was writing when he died—his 'gift' to the Tower. I seriously doubt that something so childishly destructive would have hurt the Tower. Indeed, it might even have helped publicize it. You know what they say: Any publicity is better than none."

"Do you think that extended to Tamara's private life?" I asked. "After all, Harris was planning to make her a laughingstock too—in the chapter of the novel he was going to read the night he was murdered."

"Tamara was devastated when she learned about that.

I was there when the policeman told her its contents, and I could see how shocked she was. And John as well." Ames's face twisted in pain at the recollection, his round, brown eyes searching mine for evidence that I believed him.

"After that night, if he'd lived, Harris couldn't have expected to be a part of the Tower again, could he?"

"I'm afraid you're wrong. From what little I know of him, I think he would have been surprised if the Towerites, including Tamara, hadn't forgiven him. Language seemed to mean nothing to him, so he underestimated its power to hurt. Or so Tamara says. Perhaps it was that blindness that got him killed. And Tamara would have swallowed her pride and let bygones be bygones—or at least pretended to. For the sake of the Tower. She is a strong and determined woman. The one thing she would not have done, I can assure you, is murder him. Believe me, Miss O'Neill, I know."

"How about her husband? Would he have taken Harris's novel so calmly?"

"John?" He laughed uneasily. "John concerns himself even less with what goes on among the writers than I do. I'm not even sure he's read Tamara's novel—or any other work of fiction, for that matter. Tamara once confided in me that John has never mentioned the book to her."

"And yet he paid for its publication, didn't he?"

"Who told you that?"

I said I couldn't remember. "The subject just came up when I was discussing the book's merits with somebody."

He gave me a smile that told me he knew better. "Again, Miss O'Neill, I caution you to take Niobe Tigue with the proverbial grain of salt. She's a fine writer, but intolerant of others."

"Are you saying you think *Romance and Reality* is a good novel?"

He looked uncomfortable. He lowered his eyes, as if in sorrow, and said, "No. In my opinion, Tamara is better suited to arts administration than to being a writer herself. I think perhaps we have that in common, Tamara and I, although she is not quite ready to admit it yet."

I asked him about 'the other woman' in Tamara's novel, but he agreed with Niobe Tigue on that. "She has certainly never indicated that there was such a woman. She just outgrew Mr. Harris."

"When John Meade came courting."

"You can't blame her for that," Ames said fiercely. "However much I love the plays of Henrik Ibsen, we can't always live in his bleak and idealistic world, can we? Tamara came from a poor family and wanted to rise above that. So John's money and position certainly played a role in the choice she made. However, had he not come along when he did, Tamara would have eventually perceived Mr. Harris's hollowness, and seen her attraction to him for exactly what it was, a schoolgirlish crush. If she'd married him, she would have suffered enormous heartache sooner or later. But she was incapable of showing John's essential goodness of character clearly in the novel, so she had to bring in 'the other woman' as evidence of the artist's fickleness of character. That was a mistake, in my opinion."

"Maybe you're right. However, it is a sad fact of life that 'essential goodness of character' doesn't always go together with an exciting personality. I wonder if Tamara ever regretted her bargain, after Harris became a successful writer."

"Tamara would have been less than human, I imagine, if she sometimes didn't fantasize about what life might have been like with Mr. Harris," Ames agreed.

"But she's a bighearted woman. She chose John Meade and, I'm sure, has every intention of remaining true to that choice."

Ames was the first person I'd encountered who'd claimed that Tamara Wallace Meade was bighearted.

"It's really quite absurd, isn't it?" Ames said suddenly, nodding out his window. "The tower, I mean. My father added it on. Utterly useless, but he wanted it and so he had it built. Good gracious, how the neighbors did holler! He had a lot of political influence, however, so the building inspectors came out and took a look around and determined that it fit within the limits of the building code."

"Do you ever miss the place?"

"Not at all; I was glad to get rid of it. It's haunted, you know."

I turned and gave him a questioning look that made him laugh.

"Oh, not in the literal sense, of course. But it's got too many memories for me. I lived there alone, with Father. Which means I lived there alone with the servants, and with the few friends I could sometimes convince to come over and play."

"John Meade?"

"Sometimes."

"Somebody told me you've known Frank Ott since you were both children. Was he one of the servants you played with when you were little?"

"He wasn't a servant. His mother worked for my father as a bookkeeper." Ames smiled and shook his head, remembering. "We played together a lot, as children. I was his only friend. As soon as he finished school, he became my father's handyman-gardener, and then mine. When I gave the Tower to the Towerites, I made it a condition that Frank be allowed to stay on.

Tamara would prefer somebody a little less eccentric, I suspect, but she manages to put up with him."

"So John Meade knew Frank when you were children too."

"John didn't enjoy Frank's company then any more than Tamara does now. When Frank would come over, John usually left." Ames got a distant look on his face. "It's funny. Frank was a nuisance, and I was sometimes cruel to him too, I'm ashamed to admit. I still go to the Tower once a week, on Saturday mornings, and we have breakfast together, Frank and I. Frank buys freshly baked rolls from that wonderful bakery down the street from the Tower, and makes coffee and sets the table— white linen, real silverware from my father's time—and we sit and reminisce about the old days. I'm not always sure what Frank is telling me, but that doesn't bother us. Frank enjoys it."

"But you don't."

He stopped, then nodded, reluctantly. "Yes, I also enjoy it. But sometimes I feel a little . . . ashamed of how much I do. It seems childish, doesn't it?"

"No," I replied, "I don't think so."

Ames seemed almost grateful. "He's my only connection with the past. John has no time for nostalgia. I would miss Frank, if he weren't there." He added, "You could join us some Saturday, Miss O'Neill, if you wanted to."

"Thanks, I just might. But isn't Frank angry with you, for handing your father's house over to a bunch of godless and immoral fiction makers?"

Ames looked at me, and for the first time, I heard something hard in his voice. "He's unhappy that I gave up the mansion and that I gave it to them. But he had nothing whatsoever to do with Mr. Harris's murder. Frank is quite content to wait for God's judgment upon sinners. He thinks he is trying to save people with his tracts and his warnings. He wouldn't hurt anybody, Miss O'Neill."

"Okay."

We stood there in the window a minute longer. It reminded me of how I'd stood at Sandra's picture window with Arthur Tigue, looking down at the Tower. It was easier to find Sandra's condo than it had been to find the Tower. From this height and distance, the two buildings seemed closer together than they really were.

We sat back down on the couch and drank our coffee, cold now, under the mild gaze of Chris Ames Sr. Then it was time for Ames to go to the boardroom and announce his resignation. He walked me to the elevator. I wished him luck.

Eighteen

When I got home from work the next morning, there was a message on my answering machine. He didn't give his name, but I recognized Rich Oliver's voice by the pseudo-Harris drawl and the verbosity. "Are you still interested in the whereabouts of Cam Harris on the afternoon of his endlessly deferred reading? Well, I just might have a few tidbits for you. Give me a call, if you're interested." He added his phone number and hung up.

I made coffee, toasted an English muffin, and returned his call. It was a few minutes after eight, time for all good people, except night-blooming cops, to be up and about.

A sleepy voice groaned something that might have been "Hello."

"Hi!" I said, with horrid cheerfulness. "It's Peggy O'Neill. You left a message for me to call you."

"Oh. What time is it? Jesus, you can't sleep nights, or what?" Suffering was making Rich Oliver talk like a real person. Maybe that's why it's so good for writers.

"I work the night shift. I just got home."

"Oh. Okay." A pause while he mumbled something to somebody in the room with him. "Listen," he got back to me, "I know a person who saw Cam the day he

147

died. It's probably nothing huge, but if you want to talk to her about it, we'll be at the Whale tonight. Anytime after seven-thirty."

Why not? My appointment with Arthur Tigue wasn't until ten-fifteen, and I had nothing much to do before that. I could eat dinner at the Via Appia, and meet Oliver and his friend after that.

"You said a couple of tidbits," I reminded him.

"That's right." And he hung up.

When I left my apartment at a little after six that evening, it had begun to snow. Not heavily, but the weather report promised a real storm later.

The Via Appia is your basic family-owned Italian restaurant: homey, inexpensive, with a piece of the True Cross above the jukebox. They also know how a noodle's supposed to be cooked—all the way through. I ordered melon and prosciutto for an appetizer, fettuccine for the main course, and a sparkling water with a twist to drink, bottled sometime in December, an excellent month. I lingered over dinner, chatted with the owner, whom I know slightly, and finished up, a few minutes before eight, with an espresso and a greasy, sugar-coated Italian doughnut. Who says Peggy O'Neill doesn't know how to eat?

When I got outside and crossed the street to the Whale, Central was brightly lit and crowded with people, mostly students. The street was hushed, the way the world always is in a snowstorm. The Whale was crowded too, but dark and quiet, as befits an English pub serving booze too expensive for the riffraff. Kyle wasn't behind the bar that night, but I spotted Rich Oliver at once, sprawled in a chair at the same table he'd occupied before, watching a young woman tossing darts at the dart board. There was a small, superior smile on his face, probably because she was good. When he saw me coming, he hoisted a mug of beer in a kind of salute. A large pitcher stood in the middle of the table, nearly empty. The two people I'd met before were there too, Liz and Eric. Last time, they'd been smoking and discussing the possibility of a female voice in a phallocentric world. Now they were sucking on unfiltered cigarettes and discussing the latest Norman Mailer novel. They glanced at me, then returned to their discussion.

"That's Victoria," Oliver said, pointing to the darts thrower. "She'd give you more competition than I did. She's the person I was telling you about, who saw Cam. Vicky, you're wanted."

She threw her last dart and came to the table and sat down next to Oliver. She had short, straight hair, glossy and almost black, and an olive complexion. I introduced myself, and she told me the story. "It was that Friday, okay?"

"Sure," I said, and nodded encouragingly and made myself comfortable.

She'd been standing on Central and Elm Street, she continued, waiting for a bus, about ten blocks down the street from the Whale. She was on her way downtown to the Greyhound bus terminal, to go home for semester break. When a bus pulled up across the street, Cameron Harris got off.

"It was a surprise, because I didn't think I'd see him again, okay? At least, not until he moved back here, which he said he was thinking of doing. So I called to him and asked him where he was heading. I figured he was probably coming here, okay? Except why would he get off the bus that far down on Central? We stood there talking for a little while."

"Was anybody with Harris?" I asked.

She shook her head. "No. Another guy got off the bus too, but he went in the other direction."

"About what time was this?"

"It wasn't even one-thirty. One-twenty, I guess. Anyways, we stood there, okay? And I told him I was sorry I wasn't going to be at his reading that night, I had to go home, but I hoped I'd see him again if came back here to live. And I asked him if he was going to the Whale, but he said no, he was going to visit a friend."

A bartender came to the table with another big pitcher of beer, and a frosted mug for me. Victoria filled Oliver's mug and started to fill mine, but I put my hand over it.

"She's on duty," Oliver said. "Not even undercover cops like O'Neill drink on duty. Right?"

"Right. And then what?" I asked Victoria.

"I picked up my suitcase and said I'd walk with him a little ways, even though I'd probably miss my bus, okay? He said he was sorry, but he wanted to be alone. He was trying to focus his thoughts on what he was going to read at the Tower, and walking helped him do that. I was kind of disappointed, but I didn't want to be a pest, in case I needed him someday to help my career—"

Rich Oliver blew into his mug loudly, splattering beer on his granny glasses.

"Well, you never can tell, Rich." She glared at him. "Besides, you spent the whole semester kissing his butt." Satisfied, she turned back to me. "Cam said he'd enjoyed having me in class and that I had real promise as a writer." A triumphant look at Oliver, who was studying his fingertips to see if there was any nail left to nibble on. "And then he headed down Elm, and I got on my bus, which pulled up just then, okay?"

I asked her if he'd said anything about coming to the Whale that night.

She nodded. "He said he'd be here, but he might be late. He said 'around six.' He said he hoped some of us would be here, so he could have a last basket of fish and chips, and an Old Nick, before his reading."

"That's what he usually drank." Oliver smiled, reminding me that I'd sprung for an Old Nick for him the week before.

I asked Victoria if she'd told the police all this. She said she hadn't known it might be important until last night, when she'd told Rich about it.

"Vicky and I broke up for a while. We only just got together again last night." Oliver put his arm around her and gave her a congratulatory squeeze.

I got her last name, wrote down her address and phone number, and told her the homicide cop working on the case would probably be getting in touch with her.

"I've already told you everything I know," she protested.

"Ah, but, Victoria," Oliver explained, "by going over it a second time, you sometimes remember an important detail you forgot the first go-around. And it's just those little, apparently unimportant details that put the bad guys away for life. Right, Officer O'Neill? Which brings us to the other tidbit I mentioned on the phone."

He stopped and looked up at something behind me, his mouth still open. At the same moment a hand fell gently on my shoulder. It was Tony Verdugo, his dark eyes staring down at me from his long, mournful face.

"You get around, don't you?" His mouth was smiling, but his deep, close-set eyes weren't. "I've never seen you in here before. I suppose it's just a coincidence?"

I plucked his hand off my shoulder. "What's a coincidence?"

"That I bump into you so often. Outside my classroom, at Sandra's party, now here. These friends of yours?" He looked around the table. "No, they're

Cameron Harris's old students—or that one is, at least."
He pointed at Rich Oliver. "Holding a vigil for your
fallen idol, are you? I watched you hanging on Harris's
every word most of last semester, and heard you echo
his braying laughter whenever he said something funny.
It got so bad, I finally had to switch bars. And just
when I thought it was safe to come back to the Whale,
here's Peggy O'Neill, sitting right where ol' Cam used
to sit, trying to figure out what it was that put an end
to him. Don't you ever get tired of trying to make sense
of the world?"

"Until the University pays me as much as it pays you
to teach that it can't be done, I'll keep plugging away
at it," I said.

"When do I get my turn to assist you in this futile
enterprise?"

I glanced at my watch. I still had plenty of time until
my appointment with Tigue. "How about in a few minutes? Where're you sitting?"

He pointed to an empty booth next to the front windows. He said he'd order me a beer. I told him to make
it a Coke.

"Great." And he slouched away.

When I turned back to Rich Oliver, he was looking
confused. "You know him? He's the guy I was telling
you about last week, the one Cam said he punched
out."

"I know. At one time or another, everybody beats up
Tony Verdugo." I was remembering the sound of Sandra Carr's open hand meeting Verdugo's face. "It must
be his fatigues and paratrooper boots. You'd think he'd
catch on. Now, what's this tidbit you have for me?"

He gave me a big, moist smile. "It's thirsty work,
helping a bounty hunter earn a reward. Make it an Old
Nick again, will you?"

"Oh, Rich!" Vicky said, apparently appalled by the nasty little cadger's behavior.

"It's in honor of Cam," he protested.

I got him what he wanted and waited for him to go through the ritual of getting the head just right before taking a sip.

"It was about a month before he died. One night we all stayed here a little late, and Cam and I were the last to leave. I drove him home because he didn't drive—he claimed he never learned. As he was getting out of the car, I glanced at the house. I'd swear somebody was in there. I saw her shadow against the curtains."

"Her?"

He shrugged. "I assumed it was a her, but who knows? I sort of hoped he'd invite me in for a drink, but he thanked me for the ride and let himself in the house. So I never got to see if there was anybody real behind the shadow."

I prodded Rich Oliver for more, but that was all I got for my four bucks: the shadow of a woman—or maybe a man.

"You didn't just make that up, did you?" After a week of trying to get the truth out of a bunch of writers, I was feeling a little distrustful.

He shook his head. "I'd do a lot better than that, if I were making it up."

"Not better," Vicky stuck in. "Just less convincing."

Nineteen

A red neon beer logo surrounded Verdugo's head like a halo; he looked like a Spanish mystic in a postmodern painting. I wondered if that's why he'd chosen to sit there. A bottle of beer sat in front of him, and a can of Coke at my place.

As I slid into my seat, he said, "I like being stalked by women with gorgeous red hair. It makes 'em easier to spot. What were you expecting to learn by staring into my classroom last week?"

I played dumb. "I don't even know where it is."

He told me, and I pretended to recall the incident after a moment's thought. "But it really was just a coincidence." I am never more earnest than when I'm lying. "I was in the building, visiting a friend, and after I left her office, I must have glanced into all the classrooms as I passed them, not realizing that one of them was yours. You were up on your desk, weren't you—sitting cross-legged?"

"A friend." He sounded skeptical. "Who?"

"Professor Silberman, my adviser when I was a student. You can ask her."

"Silberman? Oh sure, Edith. I just might do that. I've known Edith quite a long time."

"Go ahead."

"She was your adviser? I understand she was quite a good scholar in her time."

"She's still a good teacher," I said. "She's taught a lot of students the love of reading."

There was a pause as he tried to figure out what that had to do with good teaching. Then he shrugged. "You can't blame me for being suspicious, though, can you? You're a cop—even if you're only a campus cop—and you're obviously helping the police with Cameron Harris's murder. I even thought of calling your supervisor to complain, after seeing you at Sandy's party. And I still might, Peggy," he added playfully. "It's okay if I call you Peggy? You can call me Tony, of course."

"Sure." It was a small price to pay for not being summoned before Lieutenant Bixler, a man who has taken blind stupidity to the point of high art.

"You've probably talked to a lot of people by now," he said. "Even Melody. She's angry with me, but I don't think she hates me. She's just confused." He took a moment to pour beer. "You remind me a little of her, you know." His amused eyes glanced across the table at me.

That came as a surprise, being compared to Melody, with her bouncy blond hair and squirrelly face. I told him I couldn't see any similarities.

"Oh, not physically, of course. But she puts everything that happens to her in her journal, no matter how trivial. And later, when the mood's upon her, she tries to construct a poem on the basis of what she's written down. That's what you're doing too, isn't it? You go around collecting bits and pieces of highly dubious reality, and on that basis, you think you're going to construct a story, and in the penultimate chapter—the next to last chapter, to you—you hope to name Cameron Harris's killer. Am I right?"

"I hope so," I said. "Are you saying that the conversation we're having right now isn't real?"

"Each *moment* of it is real, perhaps, as it happens, although some of my colleagues would question that too. But let's both recount this conversation tomorrow—or ten minutes from now—to some other person, and let that person decide which of our versions of it is the more accurate. Whoever describes the conversation the best—creates the most vivid fiction, that is—wins. Truth, or reality, is always like that, just a fictional text. You and Melody don't understand that. Melody thinks she keeps journals in order to preserve reality, but she's just creating fictions as she writes the fluff of her little life down. And when she turns this fluff into poem, she's just creating one fiction based on another. That's what you're doing too."

"Mass murderers would sleep well, with a philosophy like that."

"They do," Verdugo replied. He took a slug of beer. "You keep a journal too?"

I shook my head and grinned at the thought of what Lieutenant Bixler would say if both Paula and I came in one night carrying journals covered with bright crayon drawings.

"Then how do you keep all the crap you vacuum up from the Towerites straight?" Verdugo asked. "Or don't you try? Do you let it all tumble around in that lovely head of yours until enough of it sticks together to fool you into thinking it means something?"

It wasn't a bad description of what I did. I'd figured things out like that a couple of times before. Mozart once said he worked that way too, letting snatches of music float around in his head until suddenly they came together in a meaningful way. I couldn't hope to do any better than that.

"Yeah," I said.

"Your problem," Verdugo went on, "is that you can't know if the pieces you collect even belong in the same story! It's like trying to make a pot out of shards of ancient pottery that have all been jumbled together. Some pot it's going to be!"

"Everybody needs a hobby. One such shard is that there wasn't much love lost between you and Cameron Harris. I wonder what pot that one belongs to."

"I can't imagine. It wasn't hard to make Harris's hit list, you know."

"But he beat you up, at an English Department party last September."

I glanced across the room where Rich Oliver was in the process of launching a dart at the target on the wall. He was wobblier than usual on his high-heeled boots, and the dart missed the target by a foot. Victoria applauded. Eric and Liz paid no attention, talking intently through clouds of cigarette smoke.

"Harris didn't beat me up; he sucker-punched me." Verdugo pointed to his jaw. "I wasn't expecting it."

I buried a smile in my Coke can and asked him what the fight had been about. "You want my version? That's promising. I suppose you've heard that I reviewed Harris's first novel for the *Times*. That was before I knew Melody or any of the other local writers. I thought I was being kind! Apparently he didn't think so." Verdugo shook his head in mock sorrow at this misunderstanding.

"That was a long time ago. It's no reason to pick a fight with you now."

"Tell him that—if you see him in hell! He hadn't forgotten. The first thing he did when Melody introduced us was to remind me of it."

"And then he slugged you, right?"

"Not immediately. First he had more to drink and then he came back and made fun of what I do for a living, the way second-rate writers will do. They're afraid of those of us who know something about literature. I made the mistake of pointing that out to him."

"What'd you do after he hit you?"

"I picked myself up, complimented him on his communication skills, and went off to the bathroom to repair the damage. And no, I did not nurse a murderous grudge for the next few months, and then beat in his head with a fireplace poker, if that's what you're thinking."

That's exactly what I was thinking. "You said Sandra Carr was there. Why, if it was an English Department party?"

He looked at me in surprise. "You don't know? Nobody told you she and Harris were an item in September? I suppose they were trying to rekindle the fire from their Second Story days. Do you think your homicide friends have thought about checking on Sandra's whereabouts when Harris was murdered? It's quite possible to fly to and from L.A. in a day, you know. I've done it on more than one occasion myself."

"What would her motive be?"

He rubbed the side of his face, as if recalling the slap she'd given him at her party. "I wouldn't know. The fury of a woman scorned?"

"You ought to visit a battered woman's shelter sometime to see what the fury of a man scorned looks like. Or the morgue."

"Ouch," he said, and tried to look repentant.

"I was at the Tower the night Melody read her penis poem. Harris laughed at you when you walked out at Melody's reading."

"You were there too? Why?"

"Friends of mine are taking writing courses at the Tower. They took me."

He shook his head. "Are you often in the right place

at the right time?" His hand came down on mine and held it lightly.

"Often." I slid my hand away and wiped it on my jeans. "Would you mind telling me, Tony, what it was about the poem that upset you? After all, it was only a text, wasn't it—a fiction?"

He made a face. "Very clever, Peggy. But when Melody writes a poem that draws from the intimate details of our married life—"

"You think the poem was about you?"

His reaction to the question was the same as Melody's. "Who did—?" Light dawned, or seemed to. "Oh, you thought it was about—*Harris?*" He tried a laugh. "Well, I suppose I can forgive you for thinking so, but you're way off the mark. I didn't like Melody airing the intimacies of our private life publicly. That's understandable, isn't it? If she'd told me she planned to read that poem beforehand, I'd have put a stop to it—or not shown up. But she didn't. All it achieved was a certain amount of salacious whispering among the audience, and an excuse for Cameron Harris to laugh at me."

"You thought they were having an affair," I said, as if he hadn't spoken all that.

"Damn it, Peggy, haven't you been listening?" He saw the skepticism on my face and leaned across the table at me, giving me a look so sincere, I might have bought a used car from him. "Get this through your pretty head, Peggy. Cameron Harris had a nasty streak in him, and he never forgave real or imagined slights. He never forgave me for my review of his book. If I'd been found murdered, he'd be my prime suspect, but I had no reason to murder him."

"Not even if you were going to play a featured role in his next novel?"

"How would that have hurt me, Peggy? Tell me."

Sandra Carr already had, so I decided not to answer that one. Instead, I said, "How about Melody?"

"Melody wouldn't kill anybody for any reason whatsoever."

"That's good to know, but it's not what I meant. I mean, would you kill Harris to keep Melody from appearing in his novel?"

"Of course not! Why would she appear in his novel?" His eyes stayed on my face, unblinking.

"I don't know. Maybe you can tell me."

"I told you, there wasn't anything between them. There never was. They hardly saw anything of each other while he was here last fall."

"How do you know?"

"I don't believe it," he repeated, his little, close-set eyes boring into mine.

"Okay," I said. "The night Harris was murdered, I saw you talking to Melody up by the stage. You were begging her to go with you for a drink somewhere. She turned you down."

"You're everywhere, aren't you?" He ran a hand through his long hair. "Yes, I begged her to go out with me that night. That shows you how much I love her, to let her humiliate me like that in front of all of you."

"I'm curious about why a man like you would marry a woman like Melody."

"Call it the attraction of opposites. She was nice to come home to. I wanted a woman who'd bandage my wounds after a bloody day in the trenches, and she led me to believe she'd be that woman. She fell madly in love with me, at her graduation. After that, we bumped into each other fairly often. Now I realize she was stalking me. After a while, I let myself be caught." He shrugged, smiled at the memory—or at the fiction he'd created on the basis of a lost reality.

His story of their courtship and Melody's didn't exactly jibe.

"I enjoyed her babble," he was saying. "It's like verbal elevator music. You're not like Melody in that respect, at least, Peggy. I doubt you know what small talk is."

Confirming that, I asked him what he thought Melody had seen in him.

He looked at me as though I had to be pretty dumb to have to ask. "Power and stability. Her parents died when she was a child, and she lived with her sister. Whatever else you can say about Sandy, she wasn't much of a mom." He took a long swallow of his beer. I watched his Adam's apple bob up and down under his scraggly, graying beard. "Married life was wonderful until the Tower began to encourage her to think she was a real poet, and helped her get that slim volume published."

"In other words, Melody began neglecting you."

"Shouldn't I have been unhappy about that? Wasn't I supporting her? You've seen that journal she carries around with her everywhere she goes, haven't you? She didn't want children because she had that. I don't think she has any idea of what her life is like until she reads about it afterwards in her garbled notes!"

"Did you ever read her journal?" I was trying not to laugh and at the same time trying not to show that I was trying not to laugh.

"How could I?" he wailed. "She always carried the current one with her. I would have had to wait until she fell asleep some night and then read it by flashlight, praying she wouldn't wake up and catch me. And she kept her old journals locked up somewhere."

I did laugh then. Verdugo looked offended. "What's so funny?"

"You tried."

"Of course I tried! Wouldn't you, if you were in my shoes? Everything that goes on in her life goes on in her journals. I wanted to know!" His long face, awash in neon, was contorted in agony, like an El Greco martyr.

I got up, dropping a couple of dollars on the table. "And yet, you want her back."

"Yes." His shoulders slumped. "Yes, I do. It's crazy, isn't it?" Bringing his glass with him, he got up too, and followed me outside. I could have arrested him for that.

It was good to be out in the cold air, in the clean falling snow. I said to Verdugo, "She's in therapy now with Arthur Tigue."

His laugh was scornful. "Another one of her phases. It won't last. She's been looking for a guide all her life, and now she's found Arthur—the would-be King Arthur. Let him make the best of it; she'll realize what a phony he is, sooner or later. Everybody sees through Arthur, eventually. All the Towerites have, even Cameron Harris. And so will you. Where're you off to now?" He'd left his coat inside, so he wrapped his arms around himself.

I pointed to my car, covered in fresh snow, on the other side of the street. I told him I had some desk work to do before starting my patrol.

He laughed shortly. "Is that what you call paying a late visit to dear Dr. Tigue? Desk work?"

"How—?" Then I remembered that he must have overheard Tigue and me discussing our meeting at Sandra's party. Caught fair and square in a lie, I grinned, said good night, and started across the street.

"Hey, are we friends?" he called after me.

"Sure." I kept walking.

"You think Gary'd mind if I gave you a call sometime?"

I stopped in the middle of the street and turned around. "I thought you wanted Melody back."

"What's that got to do with it? You think monogamy is natural for a man—or a woman?"

"You think sitting in a bar—or a classroom—is?" Some people think they can pick and choose what's natural, according to their needs at the moment.

"See?" He had to holler now, because by then I was on the other side of the street. "You don't know how to make small talk, do you?"

Not with jerks.

Twenty

I had about half an hour to kill before my appointment with Arthur Tigue, so I drove up to the Tower. I like driving in snow; I'm good at it, and winter's the only season my Rabbit thrives in. I turned in to the Tower's parking lot and got out.

The floodlights weren't lit, so the tower itself was almost a part of the falling snow, but there were a few lights on inside the mansion. Night classes would have ended about half an hour ago. I leaned my back up against the tower's rough plaster surface and tilted my head back to let the clean snow fall on my face, washing off the smoke and stink of the bar. The tower fascinated me. It was an irrelevant appendage on what would otherwise have been a pleasant old mansion.

I thought about what I'd learned from Victoria at the Whale. Her story had only cut an hour or so off Harris's unaccounted time, since John Meade had said that Harris had left the Meades' home around noon. But Harris also told Meade he was going to the University, and that wasn't true, not if Harris had been telling Victoria the truth. And he'd also told her he planned to come to the Whale that night, before his reading.

Rich Oliver thought he'd seen "the shadow of a woman." Had he? And if so, who could it have been?

Tamara Meade? Why not, if she regretted her dumping Harris for John Meade and thought she had a chance to get him back? Would Harris be that cruel? Resume his affair with her and plan to read a story that ridiculed her? He probably would.

Or Melody Carr. Every time her name came up at Sandra's party, Sandra got tense and defensive, and so did Tony Verdugo, tonight. Could she have been the shadow Oliver thought he saw?

The side door of the Tower opened and a tall figure emerged. Niobe Tigue. It must have been her turn to close up the Tower that night. I watched her for a moment, a striking figure in a long, dark overcoat and hat against the whiteness of the snow. I cleared my throat to get her attention without startling her.

"What're you doing up here, sleuth?" She came over to me. "Gary left twenty minutes ago, and your literary campus cop friends did too."

"The place fascinates me, and I have some time to kill before going to work."

"Things this ugly and foolish hold no fascination for me," she said. "But then, neither does murder. Making any progress in finding out who did in Cam?"

"I don't know. Somebody just told me that he once saw Harris with a shadow. He thinks it was the shadow of a woman."

Niobe stared at me for a moment, before laughing. "I guess that's progress. But Cameron wouldn't be satisfied with the shadow. Where and when did this sighting supposedly take place?"

"At the house Harris rented while he was here, a couple of weeks before he was murdered. I don't suppose you'd know of anybody—"

"I'd have told you the first time we talked, wouldn't I, if I did," she snapped, "or I'd have told your friend from homicide when he came calling. And I was never in that house, if you're wondering about that." She looked at me curiously. "Don't you have anything better to do with your life than this?"

I was tired of hearing that. "You seem to know what's best for everybody, Niobe. Doesn't that kind of superiority weigh you down?"

That set her back on her big feet for a moment. She made a noise somewhere between a bark and a laugh. "No. When you think you know what's right, you're morally obligated to tell people about it. They can take it or leave it. Enjoy your lonely vigil up here, Peggy. Don't forget what Tamara always says about towers: They're useless, but from them you can read the stars. Maybe the tower will speak to you through its cold walls. Good night." She stalked across the parking lot and disappeared down the street in the direction of Central, seeming to shove aside the snow, falling thickly now, as she walked.

I stayed up there another five minutes or so, but the tower told me nothing, its chill just seeping through my coat into my body. Then I went back to my car and drove down the hill. I didn't see Niobe. She'd either had her car parked on the street, or had disappeared into one of the businesses on Central that stayed open late.

A few minutes after ten, I pulled into the parking lot behind the Psychology Building. Another car was leaving, a dark convertible, its wipers pushing snow off the windshield.

The lights were on in the secretaries' office, and the computer on the desk with Pam's nameplate on it was on too, but the office was empty. It occurred to me that I'd never asked the receptionist what her name was. It looked as if she'd just stepped out for a moment or two.

I walked down the hall toward the stairs. Tigue's office was on the second floor. The women's rest room door opened suddenly and the receptionist came out, almost bumping into me. She looked harried.

"Still looking for Arthur? You just missed him."

"I had an appointment to see him tonight. After his seminar. Did he say he'd be coming back?"

She shrugged. "He didn't say anything. Looks like you got stood up." She didn't look very sympathetic and started to go around me.

"Maybe he forgot. I know you won't give me his phone number, but would you call him at home and let me talk to him?"

She looked even more aggrieved. "I've got work to do. I have to finish typing a grant proposal for some asshole who waited until the day before the deadline to get it to me. Besides, Tigue won't be home for at least ten more minutes, since he just left."

A young man came down the hall. "Tim." She grabbed his arm. "This woman had an appointment with your master tonight, but he skipped out on her. Tim's one of Tigue's postdocs," she said to me. "He knows the creep inside and out."

Tim winced at her language, glanced nervously around, as if the walls had ears. "You must be the one Dr. Tigue called before his seminar tonight," he said. "He left a message on your answering machine, canceling the appointment. I was in his office doing some work and heard him."

Damn Tigue! First he'd made it hard for me by agreeing only to meet late at night, and then he'd canceled on me.

"Did he say why?"

"Call home and listen to the message, if your machine'll let you do that. All I know is, right before he called you, he was talking to someone else on the phone. I heard him say he'd be there as soon after ten as he could make it."

"Where?"

Tim grinned at my futile tenacity. "On a hill, I'd guess. Apparently whomever he was talking to was concerned about Dr. Tigue's car making it up a hill in this weather. Dr. Tigue said his car thrives on snowy hills."

Twenty-One

I drove back to the Tower carefully, through the heavy snow. As I turned in to the parking lot, I could see light, softened by the snow, glowing behind windows on the first floor. I parked next to Tigue's car. Wet snow had already begun to cover the windshield. Ours were the only cars there.

I opened the storm door on the side of the Tower. The inside door was closed but unlocked, so I pushed it open and went in. The entryway was dark, and so were the stairs that went down to the offices and classrooms in the basement. Light, as yellow as the old varnish on the floors, came from the hallway leading to the front of the house. As I scraped the snow off my boots, I noted a pair of galoshes sitting in a puddle of melting snow. I went down the hall, past the dark kitchen where Gary and I had sat with Buck after finding Cameron Harris's body. I made no attempt to walk softly, but I didn't exactly stomp my feet either. As I came to the front of the house, I thought I heard sounds, too muffled to identify, coming from someplace on the second floor. The auditorium doors were open, the room softly lit but empty.

I stopped at the bottom of the stairs, suddenly indecisive, wondering what I was about to interrupt. I figured Tigue probably wasn't with Melody, since her office was in the basement. Tamara's, however, was on the second floor. I didn't want to annoy Tigue any more than necessary—even though he deserved it for standing me up—since I wanted him in a good enough mood to talk to me about the Towerites. Surprising him in a compromising position with somebody in the Tower would probably qualify as "annoying him more than necessary." I also didn't want to annoy Tamara Wallace Meade. So as I started up the stairs, I called out, "Dr. Tigue? Tamara? It's Peggy O'Neill."

No answer. The upstairs hall was dark, but light streamed from the open door of Tamara's office. I didn't call out again, but walked down the hall as nosily as I could.

In the middle of the room, a man's overcoat lay in a heap on the Oriental rug. I stepped in, looking around, then went over and bent to pick up the overcoat. What was next to it didn't look like melted snow. I touched it. The light went off.

I fell forward onto my hands and knees and crawled blindly to where I remembered Tamara's desk was. When I felt a corner of it, I reached out and groped until my hand found a leg of her chair. I maneuvered around it carefully, wanting to put the desk and chair between me and the door. I hadn't heard a switch click when the room went black, so either the lights had been turned off at the fuse box, or else Tamara's switch didn't make noise. In the latter case, whoever had turned off the lights could be in the room with me now or standing in the door.

It could have been a power failure, too. We get them often enough in weather like this. Every molecule in my body wanted to think that's what it was.

Thanks to the heavy drapes that covered the wall and the window, there was no light in the room at all, and the hall was just as black. I crouched in the corner between the drapes and the desk and listened for the presence of somebody else in the room. I tried to relax, to open my body to whatever danger might be coming for me. The falling snow and the drapes shut out all outside noise. The minutes passed. The silence of the house was absolute, but alive, like an old person dying in her sleep.

My fingers fumbled on the bottom shelves of a bookcase, making whispery noises that seemed loud to me. They were looking for a weapon, but they found only books with soft bindings. I pulled one out. I reached up and felt into the darkness until I found the top of Tamara's desk. I tried to pull open the middle drawer, hoping to find something sharp, a letter opener or just a ballpoint pen, but the drawer was locked.

One hand in front of me, I rose to my feet. Using the desk as a guide, I found the overcoat on the floor. I squatted and searched its pockets for a weapon of some kind. Metal jangled suddenly as my fingers found a key ring, and I glanced up quickly as if staring into the darkness would protect me. Then I rose into a crouch and groped my way toward the door, leaving the useless book behind, gripping the handful of keys in a fist, one key protruding between fingers squeezed tightly together. At any moment, I expected to be blinded by the sudden beam of a flashlight or worse. I found the wall, flattened my back against it, and moved along it until my fingers touched the light switch. It was still on.

Somewhere down the hall, a board creaked. Old houses creak, especially when you're alone in them and it's night. I thought again of the crumpled overcoat behind me on the floor and the puddle of blood next to it. Was it Arthur Tigue's blood, or the blood of his victim? Either way, I didn't want to be in that room any longer. I had no options in there, if somebody was after me.

Outside the office there would at least be the option of the unknown.

I slipped off my boots and stepped around the doorway into the hall, crouched, and waited for something to happen. Nothing. The only thing happening was darkness. I've never been afraid of the dark. It's always been a good place to hide, but you can't expect it to last. I continued moving, down the hall toward the stairs, using the wall against the back of my hand as a guide.

My hand bumped against the doorframe of the office next to Tamara's. The door had been closed when I'd passed it earlier. I groped for the door and felt nothing but darkness. Realizing the door was open, I pulled my hand back. My fingertips felt something rough—cloth that moved with breathing—in the doorway.

I screamed and dove past the open door, hitting the floor hands first. The keys flew out of my hand and clattered away on the floor. I felt more than heard the soft, quick footsteps behind me. I half scrambled to my feet and ran forward, holding my hands out in front of me.

Suddenly I felt cold air against my face, smelled damp earth like a grave, and I realized I'd passed the stairs going down to the first floor and was at the door to the tower itself. It was open. I couldn't go back, so I scrambled over the threshhold. I felt the splintery wooden banister against my hands. Without looking back, I plunged down the two steep flights of stairs, sobbing and muttering incoherently.

The basement of the tower was filled with weak light seeping in from little windows almost covered with snow. Shadowy shapes littered the cement floor. I stepped on one and almost lost my balance as it rolled away from under my stockinged foot with a loud, hollow noise. It was a piece of pipe, a couple of feet in length. I picked it up and turned to face the stairs. As I did, I heard, high above me, a door shut.

There was no place to hide and the widows were too high to reach and probably too small to squeeze through anyway, so I went back to the stairs and stood at the bottom, the piece of pipe in my hand. I looked up to see who was coming down. The stairs were empty.

I sat down on the bottom stair and stayed there for a few minutes, panting, sobbing maybe, and listening to my heart beat, grateful that it still was. Then I looked at my watch. Somehow I'd shattered the crystal, but the second hand was still moving. It was a few minutes before eleven. I'd been in the Tower only about twenty minutes.

In a few minutes, Paula would begin wondering why I hadn't shown up for roll call or called in. She'd call my apartment. How long after that until she'd get really worried? And what could she do about it? Nothing.

There was blood on my hands, more than what I'd picked up from touching the little puddle in Tamara's office with a finger. I thought I must have hurt myself upstairs, but I couldn't find any cuts or scrapes. There was also a damp spot on one of the knees of my jeans. That was blood too, and it wasn't mine.

I went over to the window that faced the parking lot and looked out. Tigue's car was still there, slowly being swathed in snow.

I didn't want to spend the night in the Tower's basement, so I started up the stairs, taking them slowly, one at a time, the heavy piece of pipe ready for use. When I got to the first-floor landing, I listened at the door for a minute. I remembered that Gary had told me it opened into a storage room, across the hall from the kitchen. I pushed it open a crack. I used my foot to open it all the way, and stepped in, the piece of pipe ready.

In the gray light from the stairs behind me, I could see that the room was cluttered with the junk you find in the attics of old houses: boxes and broken lamps, chairs and tables, an ancient typewriter on an old desk. I started across it to the door in the opposite wall.

A man was sitting on the floor in the middle of the room, his back resting against a box. His legs made a crooked V in front of him, his head was cocked to one side, and his eyes were closed. He might have been a child who'd dropped off to sleep while playing, except for the blood on the floor beside him. A small trail of fresh blood dotted a path from the tower door to where he was lying.

It was Arthur Tigue. His hands were in his lap, and one of them was clutching something, something red and white and plastic. I squatted to get a closer look.

It was a child's rattle.

Twenty-Two

We were back in the Tower's kitchen, Buck and I, sitting at the same old table we'd sat at the night I'd found Harris's body. Burke, Buck's assistant, was there too, taking notes. Across the hall, in the storage room, homicide people were going about their business in the bright glare of police floodlights, brought in to supplement the room's dim light. I could see Tigue's body, more or less as I'd found it. Bonnie Winkler, the assistant ME, squatted next to it, speaking into a little tape recorder.

Buck's face was drawn, and there were dark shadows around his eyes. He didn't need another serial killer on the loose; he'd had his share for the month.

I told him everything I'd picked up on Tigue, from the day I'd first seen him at the Tower until I'd found his body. Buck's eyes, with their lizard wrinkles, stayed on me the whole time, almost as unblinking as Tigue's.

"Arthur Tigue used to be one of my favorite suspects in Harris's murder," I concluded.

"If he'd been killed somewhere else, and if the killer hadn't put that toy in his hand, there'd be the possibility that his death was unrelated to Harris's. Then he could have gone on being your favorite suspect. He must have made a few enemies of his own over the years, unrelated to Harris and this damned place. Someone's obviously trying to send someone else a message, in a very sick way. I wonder who has the key to that storage room, and who'd be most likely to open the door and find Tigue. One of our people is at the Meades' home now. That's one of the questions he's asking Mrs. Meade."

Bonnie Winkler came across the hall then and told Buck she was finished here. Behind her, medics were slipping Arthur Tigue into a body bag.

"You're getting faster, Peggy. This one's still warm." Turning to Buck, she said, "Same MO as Harris's—struck on the head from behind, more than once, by something heavy. That piece of lead pipe found behind a box in there suggests itself, but you never know."

By the time Bonnie had arrived on the scene, it was about a quarter to midnight. I told her that Tigue had been alive at ten, when I'd seen him driving away from the Psychology Department. He'd probably been killed just about the time I arrived at the Tower, half an hour later.

"Great. The next murder, you'll probably be in time to watch, won't you?" She graced both of us with a pleasant smile, and left, swinging her bag, as if she didn't have a care in the world other than the corpse she'd soon be carving up like a Thanksgiving turkey. She was a single parent, with two kids just hitting their teens. There are many bizarre ways in this world to pay for orthodontia and college.

The indications were that Tigue had been killed in Tamara's office and his body dragged to the tower door and down to the storage room. That's where I'd picked up the blood on my hands and jeans. The killer must have been in the storage room, arranging his grotesque tableau, when I'd gone up to Tamara's office.

I told Buck that Niobe had locked up the Tower that

night and then walked down the hill to Central. I didn't know where she was heading. I also told him about meeting Tony Verdugo in the Whale, and that Verdugo had several good motives for wanting Cameron Harris dead: the fact that he was probably going to appear in Harris's book, their long-standing "literary" quarrel that had already caused a fight, and the possibility that Harris might have been moving in on Melody.

"And Tony's clearly worried about Tigue—or was, I mean."

I also told him what I'd learned at the Whale from Victoria, Harris's former student, and gave him her address and phone number.

"And there's something else," I said. "Three weeks before his death, Rich Oliver gave Harris a ride home, to that house he rented before he moved in with the Meades. Oliver thought he saw a woman waiting for Harris in the house."

"He thought he saw a woman," Buck echoed dully.

"Well, a shadow that could have been a woman."

"Better and better. I've questioned this Oliver lad too. He had a hangover. I guess I should have waited until he'd drunk more coffee or more beer. Maybe he would have told me about shadows too."

I gritted my teeth. "You told me you talked to a woman Harris dated last fall. She thought the relationship was going somewhere until he dumped her. Do you know when he dumped her?"

"Why?"

"I'm interested in shadows."

"It was about six weeks before he died. She couldn't be more specific than that."

"Then if there was somebody real behind the shadow Rich Oliver saw, it wasn't the woman you talked to, unless she was lying about when they broke up."

"As I told you the other night, Peggy, she's got an ironclad alibi for the night Harris was murdered."

"Okay. Then that means we're looking for somebody else's shadow. Isn't that progress? Damn it, Buck! You said there was wine in Harris's body when he was killed. That means he was probably having a farewell bottle of wine with somebody. Near the Tower and the University too, if he was telling Victoria the truth about where he was going when she saw him that afternoon."

"I realize that," Buck said. "You've brought him closer now. I'm not being sarcastic, though, when I say that I don't know how we're going to find the reality behind the shadow, assuming there is any. Do you?"

No. I didn't.

"There's somebody else I think you ought to talk to," I told him reluctantly. "Frank Ott, the Tower's custodian."

"We checked into him pretty closely in connection with Harris's murder, but couldn't find anything. He didn't have an alibi for much of the time when Harris could have been killed, but neither did anybody else. And the only motive we could come up with was he's some sort of religious nut who thinks writers are immoral and fiction is of the devil, or vice versa. But he's been surrounded by writers at the Tower for years and has never done anything violent to any of them. Just leaves tracts around and makes mostly incomprehensible but vaguely threatening noises."

"He loves Melody Carr. And he hangs around her a lot. I think he thinks it's his job to look out for her. Maybe he thought Harris was moving in on her. And Melody herself told me he thinks Tigue's a bad influence. He thinks she ought to turn to Jesus for salvation, not a shrink."

Buck said he'd talk to Ott, but he doubted he would know enough about Harris's books or have a warped enough sense of humor to put a rattle in Tigue's hand after killing him.

"How do you know? He's got a speech problem, but that doesn't mean he can't read or do something creative." It sounded ridiculous to call what the murderer had done to Tigue creative, but Buck knew what I meant and agreed with me. "See if Ott owns a copy of *Lost Letters Home*," I told him. "But even if he doesn't, the Tower's a gossip mill, and I don't think Frank misses much that's going on. He could have overheard somebody talking about Harris's satire of Tigue's therapy methods—satire that wasn't all that exaggerated, either."

When I told him what I'd seen of the inside of Tigue's office, Buck could only shake his head.

He'd talked to Chris Ames about Ott at the time of Harris's murder when he learned that Ames had known Ott since they were both children. Ames had assured Buck that Frank had never shown any signs of violence.

"Ames is a curious bird himself," I said. "I talked to him too. It was Tamara Meade who got him to donate the Tower to the Second Story writers. He's an old family friend—John Meade's his lawyer—who chaperones her about and apparently listens to her problems. He claims there's nothing more between them than that. Apparently John Meade's not interested in much except his hobbies and his law books."

"Meade had a heart attack a couple of years back, and that's slowed him down some. He used to be a pretty athletic guy. Which naturally makes me wonder if he could have negotiated the tower stairs, dragging a corpse around with him."

"Heart attacks don't slow people down the way they once did," I said.

Buck asked me what I'd expected to learn from Tigue that night. I told him I'd just wanted to get his version of Harris's years with the Second Story, and some idea of what he was like, to go with the bits and pieces I'd picked up. "I was interested in seeing how much what he said about the others would reveal about him. I expected to have to listen to a lot of psychobabble about the Towerites in the process. Tigue's diagnosis of Harris was that he was unaware of the power he had to hurt people, and the killer resented this. My own simple-minded diagnosis is that Tigue was projecting, and that what he said about Harris was true of himself too."

Buck listened, but seemed to have something else on his mind. When I'd finished, he said something that took me completely by surprise. "I want you to stay out of this now, Peggy."

"Why?" Your entire face cracks in half when you say that loud enough.

"Because it might not be only a coincidence that Tigue was murdered just before he was going to talk to you. Why not the day before yesterday? Why not tomorrow, or the next day?"

"But he wasn't going to talk to me. He'd changed his mind."

"Right. But only after talking to the killer, apparently," Buck reminded me. He wasn't being reasonable. He got up and came around the table and looked down at me. "Tigue might have been killed because he knew something, and the killer found out he knew it. But whether that's true or not, we're dealing with a multiple killer who must know who you are and what you're trying to do. Whoever it is could have left the Tower tonight without you ever knowing he was here. But he stayed—and tried to kill you too. Which means he may think you know more than what's good for him—or her. So I'm asking you to give it up now."

"No. Besides, that doesn't necessarily follow. Maybe

he'd left something incriminating in Tamara's office, and he was afraid I'd call the police on account of Tigue's coat—which I would have done. So he scared me into the basement."

Buck wasn't impressed. "Maybe, Peggy. But we can't be sure of that. I know you well enough to know that you probably won't do what I'm asking. So I'm going to talk to your chief and ask him to reassign you to a day shift—preferably inside—until this is all over."

I couldn't believe what I was hearing. I jumped up. "You've got to be kidding! I don't need a big, hairy man like you to take care of me, Hansen! You probably think women shouldn't be in combat either, that we should stay pretty and intact, so that the guys, all bloody and with their guts hanging out, have something to come home to after a hard day on the battlefield. That's just the way that asshole Tony Verdugo likes his women." I poked him in the chest while I caught my breath. "Well, maybe if you didn't *have* women at home, all dolled up and sitting naked in bathtubs full of lime Jell-O, waiting for you to come back from the wars, you wouldn't go off to them in the first place!"

I'd backed him up against a cupboard. "I'd do the same thing if you were a man," he bleated.

"Maybe so. And if I were a man, I'd probably be grateful. Unfortunately, because women never had a choice before, I don't think I've got a choice now. And, Buck, you don't have any choice either, and you know it." It's always important to give them a hand up, after you've knocked them down.

His face was scarlet. "Well, I suppose you're just as vulnerable at home as you are walking around campus late at night with a pistol." We were standing very close, almost lip to lip.

"Exactly. And you'll recall that once I almost got

murdered in my own apartment. Mrs. Hammer won't stop talking about it."

"She raise the rent?" He tried out a smile.

"No. She thinks I'm great."

"I'd never come home, Peggy, if I thought you were waiting for me, naked, in a bathtub full of lime Jell-O."

"Not to worry. And another thing, Buck." My breathing was almost under control. "You didn't wait for me to come in and get the manuscript you found on Harris's body. You had one of your cops make a special trip to my place to give it to me. And you gave me more than I'd asked for. You also gave me the notes for his new novel."

He blushed again and looked over my shoulder at a cop who'd come in and was waiting for permission to come closer.

"That was different," he said. "That was— Oh, hell. I'm sorry. Do what you have to do. Just be careful."

I slid my arm around his waist. The first time we'd met, several years ago, he'd tried to do that to me, but I'd pulled away. We'd come a long way since then. I'd never hollered at him before or called him "Hansen" either.

I glanced at my watch. It was almost six o'clock. "You ought to go home," I said, knowing he wouldn't. "You ought to get some sleep."

"I will. When you leave town."

Twenty-Three

I finally got home from the Tower at 7:00 A.M. The snow had stopped, and the morning air, noisy with the racket of snowblowers, sparkled with ice crystals. After I'd showered and put on my pajamas, I microwaved a bowl of shredded wheat into hot mush and, while eating it, listened again to the message Arthur Tigue had left the previous evening on my answering machine. Buck had listened to it at the Tower, but I'd decided I could wait until I got home to hear it.

"After mature deliberation, Ms. O'Neill," the corpse said in his best couch-side manner, "I have concluded that we should leave murder to the people trained to deal with it. Accordingly, no purpose would be served by our meeting tonight. I am sorry for any inconvenience this may cause you. Good night."

"Good night," I said, through mush. It's very weird listening to a man, found dead with a child's rattle in his hand, talk about "mature consideration." It makes you think you shouldn't take life too seriously.

My answering machine has a time and day feature that told me Tigue had called at 6:35, after I'd driven off to dinner at the Via Appia.

I made a mug of hot cocoa and took it to bed. Pulling the quilt up to my chin, I gradually calmed the images

183

of the night enough so I could fall asleep. I slept until almost two-thirty in the afternoon and would have slept longer if the phone hadn't rung.

It was Gary. He'd heard the news via the Tower grapevine and wanted to come over. That's what I wanted too. By the time he arrived, I had a fire going in my fireplace. We sat in front of it and drank coffee and held each other. He didn't ask me to tell him about the night before. I called police headquarters and asked to speak to Sergeant Hiller, the duty officer that day, one of the good guys. If it had been Lieutenant Bixler, I wouldn't have done it; I'd have gone to work. When I told Hiller I needed the night off, he said I'd probably earned it. I realized I was going against the tough-woman position I'd taken with Buck, but even heroes take the occasional time out. And I had some sick days coming anyway, so I wasn't asking for anything that wasn't mine.

Later that evening, I told Gary I wanted to go skiing. We drove the snowy, slippery roads into Nichols Park and skied deep into the woods, as I continued to work the previous night out of my body and mind. It was bitterly cold, but so quiet and beautiful that we didn't complain. Besides, you can dress for cold; you can't dress for terror.

We ended up at Gary's place, watching the Marx Brothers on his VCR and eating pizza from a hole-in-the-wall pizza joint that delivers the real thing, not the stuff formulated by chemists to sit in a car for a long time.

"Can you have nights like this in that place you think you want to live?" I asked Gary.

"It's a different way of life."

"But you'll be the same guy there as you are here. A nice talented guy who likes the *idea* of being natural.

Once you get the idea of natural, you lose the thing itself."

"Don't you ever want to be someone else?" he asked. "Even after what happened to you last night?"

"No."

I'd been home only a few minutes the next day when the phone rang. It was Sandra Carr.

"I tried to get you a couple of times last night. I figured you must've left town. If I'd gone through what you did the other night, that's what I would've done. Some life you lead! I'd like to talk to you about it." She was trying to sound flippant, but couldn't quite bring it off.

"You'd like to talk about my life or Arthur Tigue's murder? And why? Material for another novel?"

She didn't find that funny. "Your friends, the cops, have been all over, upsetting everybody. I guess I'd just like to talk to a friend about it. How about it?"

I hadn't realized she thought of me as a friend.

"Of course they've been upsetting everybody. Don't they do that in your books when somebody gets murdered? And who've they upset? You?"

"They haven't found me yet. I wouldn't be able to tell them anything helpful anyway."

"I suppose you have an alibi for Wednesday night."

"I stayed home, alone—the way a lot of innocent people do."

Recalling the layout of her building, I thought she could have ridden in and out of her condo on an elephant without being seen or heard. "Well, if the cops haven't been upsetting you, who have they been?"

"The Towerites."

"Your sister."

There was a brief pause. "Yes, Melody too. He was her therapist, you know, and he was advising her on a book she was writing. She liked him. They met for an hour or so Wednesday afternoon."

"They did?"

"Your friend, the homicide dick, questioned her about it—what they'd talked about, what his mood had been like, where she'd been the rest of the night. I assumed he would've told you by now. Doesn't he tell you everything?"

I smiled to myself. "You want to get together now? We could have coffee, or dinner later."

She hesitated. "I can't now. I'm going over to see Melody for a little while, to hold her hand. How about I come over to your place afterwards? Say around five?"

I told her that would be fine.

I live a couple of blocks up the hill from Lake Eleanor, and I can see a piece of the lake from my living room window. I had a couple of hours to kill before Sandra Carr was due, so I skied down to the lake and over to the Meades' home on the west side. A stiff wind blew fresh snow in my face, and I was sweating by the time I got to the Meades'.

I removed my skis and walked up the flagstone steps to the house, remembering the candles in the ceramic paper bags illuminating my path the last time I'd been there. I stuck my skis and poles into a bank of snow, rang the doorbell, and heard it chime deep within the house. Half a minute later John Meade opened the door. I told him my name and reminded him that I'd been at their dinner party for Cameron Harris.

A pained look crossed his face. "I know who you are. You found his body the next night, and you found Arthur Tigue's too. I suppose I should view your breathless, red-faced appearance on my doorstep with trepidation. What do you want? Tamara isn't here."

I could talk like that too. "I found the two bodies; consequently I feel I have a proprietary interest in finding out who murdered them. Unless you are that person, you have no reason to view me with trepidation. I'd like to ask you a few questions. It won't take long."

Something that might have been a smile momentarily flickered on his lined face. "I'll give you fifteen minutes."

He stepped back to let me enter, waited while I took off my ski boots and brushed snow off my pants, and then ushered me into the living room. I stood in the entryway for a moment, recalling what I'd seen the last time I was there. I knew a great deal more about the people I'd met here that night—and one of them was dead. Logs smoldered in the fireplace, softly crackling.

"The police have been here," Meade said after we sat down. "Questioning Tamara—and me too. Understandable, but upsetting to Tamara. She's worried about the impact these crimes will have on the Tower." He smiled grimly. "I tried to make her see that they will more than likely draw huge crowds to Tower events for a time, given the human animal's seemingly insatiable need for sensation. I suggested to her that she strike while the iron's hot. Perhaps have a reading by that woman who writes the novels about homicidal maniacs. Tamara thought I was joking. I wasn't."

"How well did you know Dr. Tigue?"

"I didn't know him at all. I married Tamara after he divorced his wife. Tamara knew him because he continued to hang around the Tower."

"Around Tamara too. I understand he tried to get her into therapy."

"When he couldn't get her into bed, yes. And failed at that too."

I asked him where he'd told the police he was Wednesday night.

"I appreciate the way you put that," he said. "Not 'Where was I,' but 'where did I tell the police I was.' A nice distinction. Tamara and I went to the theater. I've already shown the detectives our ticket stubs, for what it's worth. We arrived back here sometime before eleven-thirty and went to bed."

He smiled at something that seemed to occur to him. "I did not spend the other evening killing Dr. Tigue and then playing hide-and-seek with you in the old mansion's dark halls and on the stairs. Although, as it happens, I have played hide-and-seek there—many, many years ago."

He pulled himself back to the present. "Tamara and I have separate bedrooms, so I can't swear that Tamara didn't leave the house again, perhaps climbing out a window and sliding down the rain drain. I'm sure she's physically capable of it, given all the exercise she does, but I don't think she owns an outfit appropriate for the task. Maybe one of our neighbors was up and watching our place from their windows, to see if either of us drove off in the dead of night. The fact that I am still standing here talking to you, rather than trying to raise bail for myself or Tamara, suggests that no neighbor has yet come forth."

Just listening to him talk made my mouth dry. "Wasn't it a little awkward, having Cameron Harris living in your home for two weeks?"

He gave me a pitying smile, one of snooping's occupational hazards. "You surprise me, Miss O'Neill. A woman of your age, of your generation, attaching such importance to Tamara's affair with Mr. Harris so many years ago."

"I was wondering how much importance a man of your age, of your generation, attached to it."

He didn't like being reminded of his age. "You must understand that I went into my marriage to Tamara with open eyes. I wanted her, and I didn't care that she'd been with another man—or other men—before me. That was none of my business. I was married once, you know, before I met Tamara, and I continue to mourn my first wife's death. Tamara doesn't bear me a grudge or hate my late wife."

"But you didn't write a novel about your first marriage," I pointed out, "in which your second wife is unfavorably compared to your first. And there's also no danger that your first wife will come back, either."

Harsh lines I'd seen before gathered around his mouth. "I'm not concerned about losing my wife to another man. People may think what they will of the truth behind Tamara's novel. I held no grudge against Cameron Harris. I could even see why Tamara found him attractive when she was younger. I certainly would not kill him, not for something that happened years ago, and I would certainly not kill him on account of my wife's silly and rather indiscreet novel."

"I didn't realize you'd read it."

He gave me an exasperated look. He went to the fireplace, picked up the poker, and stirred fire into the logs.

"You knew he was writing a new novel," I went on, speaking to his back, "about his Second Story days. And I'm sure you know that the story he was going to read the night he was killed told his version of Tamara's story in *Romance and Reality.*"

He turned to glare at me. "Yes, I know that now. The policeman in charge of the investigation felt under some obligation to inform Tamara and me of the contents of the story. I assured him that, if I had known of it, I'd have thrown Mr. Harris out of my house on his ear, regardless of what Tamara thought of the idea. Also, from what I gather, the story was probably libelous. If he'd lived to read it publicly, I would have sued him for a great deal of money. You see, Miss O'Neill, I'm a lawyer. I don't need to kill people."

A door slammed, somewhere in the back of the house. "Here comes Tamara now." He grimaced, and his eyes darted around the room, as if he were looking for someplace to hide, or to hide me. "I'm afraid that she's not going to like finding you here."

Fe-fi-fo-fum, I thought.

Tamara stopped dead when she saw me. She was wearing something that had cost a lot, the biggest price paid by the animals who'd been born with it. Her face was haggard, as if she needed sleep, and something dark and angry moved in her eyes.

"You showed her in, John," she said levelly. "You can show her out."

"Tamara," Meade said, gently but firmly.

Chris Ames came into the living room behind her and put a hand on her arm. She shook it off.

"Now," she said to me, her voice beginning to rise. "Or I'll call the police—the real police. I'll have you arrested for trespassing."

"I'm sorry," I said. I nodded a quick good-bye to Meade, who was standing at the fireplace, the poker still in his hand. He was staring coldly at his wife.

I headed for the front door. Chris Ames hesitated a moment, darted to the door, and held it open. His face looked pained, the way a child's does when one of its parents has done something humiliating, but his eyes appealed to me for understanding.

"Go talk to Niobe Tigue!" Tamara hollered after me, near hysteria. "She hated both of them. She hates the Tower too. She wants to destroy everything, everything I stand for!"

Twenty-Four

I arrived back at my place in time to take a shower and make coffee before Sandra Carr arrived.

As I took her coat, she glanced around my living room. "You live here, or are you just passing through?"

I pretended not to know what she meant. She wouldn't be the first visitor I'd had who'd noticed the absence of things in my apartment.

She went over to the large framed photograph hanging above the fireplace of a closed door in a wall in Morocco. It's in shades of blue that match the wall-to-wall carpeting that was here when I rented the apartment and which I like a lot. I was curious to hear Sandra's reaction. She didn't say anything; she just looked at it for a few seconds, then reached up and adjusted it slightly. It didn't need adjusting. She drifted over to the bookcase that holds a few books I return to often and the ones I'm reading now.

She finally flopped down on my beige sofa, and I brought the coffeepot in with two cups.

"You must have a rich inner life," she remarked dryly. She was wearing a skirt and matching jacket in a bold, mostly shocking green pattern that set off her fire red hair and angular features.

"My mother collects things. Precious Moments figu-

191

rines and wall plaques that assert that a house is not a home, but without spelling out the difference. She's got cabinets full of souvenirs from places she's never been. When I was a kid, we often moved, and I had to help her pack all that stuff up and load it into the truck. I promised myself I'd never live like that."

"Well, you've certainly stuck to your promise so far," Sandra said. "Our mother collected Hummel figurines. The effect on an impressionable child can be life-threatening. And, of course, she was into crafts: When she died, she was working on a giant macramé wall hanging embedded with driftwood, rocks, and seashells. I had it buried with her. But you've seen my place, Peggy, how cluttered it is. I'm not letting anybody, not even my mother, cheat me out of the pleasure of surrounding myself with the things I love." She flashed her big smile. "You have anything you love that you're not showing?"

I said, as nicely as I could, "If you're the Welcome Wagon, you're too late. And frankly, I find this conversation a little surreal. Maybe it has to do with how I spent Wednesday night."

"You brought it on yourself. Nobody told you you had to look for murderers in dark places."

"Is that why you're here? To tell me to stop?"

She shook her head. "I wouldn't do that. Do you think poor Arthur's murderer was hoping to kill you too because you're on to something?" She tried to make it sound like a casual question, but that wasn't easy to do.

"If I'm on to something, I don't know what it is. And I'm not sure the murderer wanted to kill me, either. I don't know what she wanted to do."

"She?"

We live in an age when the choice of pronoun can be shocking. It's kind of nice.

"She or he," I said. "If you're not here to warn me off, what do you want?"

She set her coffee cup down firmly. "You mind telling me if you or your cop friend have any theories about the murders? Forgive my curiosity, but somebody I know killed Cam Harris and Art Tigue, and that's not a comfortable thought."

"I feel the same way. I think that somebody I've talked to, gotten to know a little, is a double murderer. It's a creepy feeling."

"Who's your most promising suspect?"

I smiled. "I haven't eliminated anybody yet, including you. I don't think Homicide has either."

"How about Tony Verdugo?"

I guess that shouldn't have surprised me. I'd seen the tension between them at her party, and I'd watched it explode too.

"I thought you were friends—in a twisted sort of way."

She shrugged. "He used to amuse me, but not anymore. Maybe his leaving my sister had something to do with it, as well as his promise not to give her a cent. You know, don't you, that Cam was going to slam Tony in his next book?"

"You sound like you have inside knowledge."

"I do. Cam told me. I went out with him a couple of times last fall, after he arrived in town, for old times' sake." She laughed. "In the old days, Cam and I used to talk about Pulitzers and National Book Awards and how we were going to write the Great American Novel. Last fall, our postcoital chitchat was mostly about agents, editors, and advances."

"And he told you about his new novel."

"It was going to be a dark comedy. That's what he called it. The story of an innocent country boy who comes to the Big City and how everybody spots his genius and wants a piece of it. And how he evades and escapes them all."

"And do you think it was true? Did people like Niobe and Tigue and Tamara—and you—want a piece of Harris?"

"Not me!" She held up her hands. "And not Tamara either. Tamara dumped him, remember, before he could dump her. But Niobe certainly, and Tigue. Each of them saw the genius in Cam, and wanted to use it, or direct it. And he made them both look like fools."

Niobe had told me the same thing. "If there are so many other promising suspects, why is Tony your favorite—aside from the fact that he's done your sister wrong?"

"Because he's the only person who was going to appear in Cam's novel who really had anything to fear from it." Sandra's voice throbbed with conviction. "Tony's a big name in literary criticism in this country, you know. That doesn't mean anything to you. It doesn't mean anything to me, either, or any normal person. But it means everything to men like Tony. To be savagely caricatured in a best-selling novel would be the worst thing that could happen to him. He wants to be the next president of the Modern Language Association, and I guess he's got a good shot at it. Playing a comic role in a best-seller wouldn't help. His fellow academics don't like to sit too close to one of their number when he's being laughed at. That kind of thing could be contagious."

"But what exactly was Harris going to say about Tony? I mean, that lit. crit. stuff can only be funny to the few people who know what it's all about. Cameron Harris's readers wouldn't know anything about it. Harris probably didn't know anything about it either."

"Cam was going to describe Tony as what he is," Sandra said. "A letch, a satyr. His reputation for scoring, or trying to score, with young female academics at literary conferences is legendary. You can talk about sexual harassment codes all you want to, but an ambitious woman had better be damned careful how she says no to a man as high up the ladder as Tony, who has so many powerful men in his field indebted to him."

"Cameron Harris told you all this?"

She nodded. "And Melody's told me a few stories too."

"Do you think Melody might have fed Harris some of those stories?"

Sandra shook her head quickly. "No, Melody wouldn't do that. She keeps it in the family. And she didn't see all that much of Cam while he was here, either."

"Okay," I said, reserving judgment about that. "According to Verdugo, he published an unflattering review of Harris's first novel. Was that Harris's motive for wanting to put Verdugo in his book?"

She nodded. "It was the first national review Cam got—and it was devastating. In some ways, I think the novel succeeded precisely on account of Tony's review; people wanted to read the inspiration for such a venomous piece of writing."

"And Verdugo has another motive for killing Harris." I watched her closely. "He thought Harris was keeping Melody from coming back to him."

"Yes," she agreed eagerly. "That's another reason why Tony hated him. But he was wrong about her. She didn't leave Tony on account of Cam."

"She left him on account of Arthur Tigue?"

"No! No, but Tony—after he'd killed Cam—I think Tony might have realized that he'd been wrong about Cam, and decided it was Art who was keeping Melody from returning to him."

For some reason, a line she'd used against the mystery writer at her party popped into my head.

"Nothing in real life's quite as simple as your plots," I said.

"Tony's motives are complex enough for me," she retorted. "Cam was a major author, with three best-sellers in less than five years, and he was going to hang Tony out to dry in his next one. And Tony thought—mistakenly—that there was something between Cam and Melody. That's two good reasons for Tony being Cam's murderer."

"And he killed Tigue because he discovered, after he'd killed Harris, that Tigue was moving in on Melody?"

"I think there was more than that. I think Art knew something that threatened Tony, and he tried to use it against him."

"Blackmail?"

"Not for money, no. But Art wants—wanted—power over people. He was a parasite. He wanted to 'empower' us, he said, but it didn't take most of us long to figure out that what he really wanted was for us to empower him. He tried to fill his emptiness by sticking his claws into other people's lives. He tried to get his claws into Cam too, but Cam was too clever for him. Until he got himself murdered, I thought Art had probably killed Cam. I think he just wanted power over Tony."

"The big problem I have with that theory," I said, "is that it can apply to anybody—even you. Having power over a miserable Comp. Lit. professor wouldn't be worth the risk. Having power over somebody like you might be. A skeptical person, like myself, might also think you had a reason for wanting Harris dead. Arthur Tigue might have come upon some evidence that you killed Harris."

She smiled. "But I didn't want him dead, Peggy. I

liked Cam. If you're thinking I was upset over the breakup of our affair, you're wrong. That was ten years ago. Cam was five years younger than me. The first time we hopped into bed together, he was just a kid, but even then I saw that he'd be a damned unlikely subject for a serious relationship. There was one thing, one thing only, I wanted from him, and that's exactly what he wanted from me too. It worked out fine, for both of us, as long as it lasted. And there wasn't anything he could do to me in his fiction that would hurt me. You'll notice, I've never appeared in any of it."

"But we'll never know about the one he didn't finish writing, will we? You weren't, by any chance, in that house he rented while he was here a few weeks before he was murdered, were you?"

She shook her head. She'd never been there, she said. Their little fling in the fall had been at her place.

I asked her if her affair with Harris had been before or after his affair with Tamara.

"Why?"

"Ever since I read Tamara's novel, I've wondered if, maybe, you enjoy making love in the lilacs, in springtime. That's all."

She got up suddenly. "No. Much too damp, I imagine." Sandra had no face for lying, and she knew it. But what was she lying about? She went over to the photograph of the blue door and made another minor adjustment to it.

It seemed that bringing up Tamara's novel made the sisters, Sandra and Melody Carr, nervous.

Before I'd finished that thought, I knew why. Sandra turned. She saw the look on my face, and knew what it meant. She looked at her watch. "Where's my coat? I've taken up enough of your time."

"I keep forgetting to ask Tamara if she has a younger sister," I said. "Does she?"

"I have no idea."

"When I asked Melody about Tamara's novel, she tried to explain the difference between art and life and that the younger sister existed only in the fiction. Niobe told me the same thing. She thought Tamara just made up the younger sister to justify dumping the fictional Cameron Harris for the fictional John Meade. And Chris Ames thinks the same thing, or pretends to. There really was a younger sister, wasn't there?"

Sandra didn't say anything, but she started to smile, and there was fire in her blue eyes. "Your younger sister," I went on. "I'd begun to suspect that Harris and Melody were having an affair this past fall, but maybe not. But before Harris went to New York he and Melody were lovers, weren't they?"

"Lovers? No. One-night stands don't lovers make. You're really good, Peggy. Cameron seduced Melody the day before she started college. I suppose you'd like to hear about it."

"Why, yes, Sandra, I would."

She laughed at my sarcasm. "I don't have to tell you anything, but I will. I think you deserve a story, as a reward." She sat down again, making herself comfortable for the first time since coming into my apartment.

"I pretty much raised Melody," she said, "and, frankly, it was a drag. She kept a journal back then too. She always called the poets she liked by their first names—Emily, for example. Edna. Tess. So when she got ready to go off to college—a private school, at my expense—I threw a party to celebrate her moving out. I called it a 'Going Away to College Party,' with Melody the guest of honor.

"It was a comedy, really, or would have been if Melody weren't such a damned romantic. Tamara came, and Cameron too. They had been together for about a year. Cam and I had broken up peaceably before that. So there were no hard feelings among any of us.

"Around one A.M., Tamara wanted to go home. She looked around for Cam. No Cam. She left after a while, a lot more pissed off than worried. After all, she had John Meade in the wings. She had her car, of course, since Cam didn't drive then either. I'd noticed that he'd been flirting with Melody all evening, and Tamara had noticed it too, but I didn't think anything of it. I thought Cam was just trying to make Tamara jealous, because of John.

"But Melody was also missing, and Tamara noticed that before I did. To make a long story short, she drove straight to Cam's apartment, used her key to get in, and caught them in bed together."

"Not lilac bushes." For some reason, I was disappointed. Before, I'd wanted the fiction to conform to the reality. Now I wanted it the other way around.

"Cam's apartment," Sandra said with a rueful smile, "was in one of those hundred-year-old piles of brick over near the Old Campus that always have romantic names carved over their entrances. It was called 'The Lilacs.' "

I burst out laughing, in spite of myself. Tamara Wallace Meade was more inventive than I'd thought—and a lot nastier, too.

"You told me," I said, "that Harris seduced Melody. That's hard to believe. They met at your party, somehow sneaked out and over to his apartment, and from there into the sack. What'd he do, hypnotize her?"

"Pretty nearly. She told me she was sitting on the stoop out front of my apartment building, trying to sober up—too much champagne. Harris came out and found her there. He'd probably followed her out. They decided to walk for a while, and ended up at his place. Big surprise. It's not a very new story."

No, it wasn't. I'd taken a man away from a woman at a party once myself. I guess I'm lucky that women named Dierdre can't write.

So now I had still another version of *Romance and Reality*. This one sounded the most convincing of all, which probably said more about me than the story.

"I can see why you laughed at your party last Friday," I said, "when I asked if Harris had turned bitter because Tamara dumped him."

"But Tamara *was* going to dump him, for John Meade. And Cam knew it. That's why he went after Melody. We'll never know what his writing would have been like if he and Tamara had stayed together." She grinned. "Knowing Cam, I suspect it would have been exactly what it was. He was no saint, either!"

"What you're saying, then, is that Tamara wrote a fiction blaming him, he wrote a fiction blaming her—and they were both wrong."

"Or both right." She shrugged. "Not knowing themselves worked out just fine for both of them."

"Until Harris got murdered."

"Yeah, until then. But what pisses me off the most is that Tamara convinced Melody that she's responsible for breaking up the 'romance of the century.' She's got Melody eating out of her hand. I've tried to explain to Melody that she actually did both of them a favor, but she thinks I'm just being cynical. She didn't want to go to the dinner party at the Meades', to sit there at the table with Harris and pretend nothing had ever gone on between them. But Tamara begged her to—she wanted to show Harris, she said, that there were no hard feelings on anybody's part. So Melody decided that she deserved to suffer."

"There's no love lost between you and Tamara."

"No. When I was just starting out as a writer, and needed all the exposure I could get, I asked to have a reading at the Tower. Tamara tried to get the board of directors to turn me down, on the grounds that what I wrote 'couldn't really be called literature.' The board supported me. After all, I was a founding member of the Tower. I still pay dues, too."

"Why? You don't need the Tower anymore. You can have book signings and readings just about anyplace you want."

"It's just to annoy Tamara." She laughed and stretched. "But you know what? Tamara called last night and asked if I'd do a benefit reading at the Tower. 'You mean, you want me to read my trash in your sacred temple of Art?' I asked. I can't help it; she brings out the worst in me. I agreed only because Melody begged me. Besides, I owe the collective a lot, in spite of Tamara. It's there I learned not to mind rejection slips. When you write alone, it's just you, your ego, and your naked little manuscript, and you think a rejection slip means the end of the world. But if you work within a writing community, you see writing that you think is really good get rejected too—sometimes many times before it's accepted, if it ever is—and you realize that all a rejection slip means is that on a particular day, a particular editor didn't like your work."

I remembered what Melody had said at the Meades' dinner party, when Cameron Harris sneered at Chris Ames's aborted writing career. "It's funny, isn't it? If Chris Ames had had that kind of support, he might have devoted his life to writing, and he wouldn't have had his father's home to donate to you."

Sandra shrugged. "Without Ames, there wouldn't be the Tower, but there'd still be the Second Story. Art's like dandelions. The only way you can keep them out of your nice, boring lawn is to use poison that kills everything *but* your nice boring lawn. So I'll do a reading at the Tower since Cameron has another engagement."

"Even though you raised Melody, you're not the best of friends."

"Oh, we do okay, I guess. But Melody's so damned earnest. And, of course, she claims to be allergic to my cats. I make her sneeze just being close to her, which doesn't make it any easier for us. I had to get rid of the two cats I had when she came to live with me after our parents died, and the first thing I did when she moved out was go to the Humane Society and get Jim Bob and Pierre."

"Yet you asked her to take care of them the month you were gone."

"So? I couldn't think of anybody else I'd trust in my place for a month. Melody agreed, and the cats and my houseplants survived, and so did she. The cats stayed away from her, which made it easier."

I couldn't help smiling. "Is that what she told you?"

She looked at me curiously. "Of course. They ran and hid whenever they saw her. I guess they know when they're not wanted."

If that's what Melody told her, and if Sandra wanted to believe it, that was their business. The family, as a unit, wouldn't exist if there hadn't been deception first.

Sandra stayed another half hour or so, talking about her various writing projects and another one of her books that was going to be filmed for TV. Finally she got up to leave.

"You need wallpaper in here. That's the problem—or one of them. There's nothing to hold the eye. We'll go down to a paint store I know, and I'll help you pick it out. And you're going to have to get rid of this stuff too," she said, scuffing at my royal blue carpeting. "Hardwood floors and big, bright throw rugs. I'll give it some thought."

I laughed. I didn't plan on getting rid of the carpeting. But wallpaper was a possibility.

"And where were you the night Harris was murdered?" I asked her.

She smiled back. "Los Angeles."

"Can you prove it?"

"I don't know. I may have stayed home that night. I may have had an idea for a new book, and it's possible I didn't leave my place for several days and nights around that time. I suppose your cop friends could check it out, if they haven't already."

"Cameron Harris seduced your little sister, fresh out of high school. Right under your nose, her guardian's nose. And what was he up to with her during the past four months? And what did he have in mind for your little sister, if he'd moved back here? And what was your interest, really, in Cameron Harris, besides a roll in the hay for old times' sake? Maybe I'll wait to let you redecorate my apartment until we catch the killer."

"You're so damned conventional, Peggy." She tried to sound flip. "Once all this is over, we're going to have to do something about that too."

Twenty-Five

After Sandra left, I tried to read, but it was hard to concentrate. I thought of calling Gary; that didn't appeal much either. I stood at my window for a while, staring out at the night and the corner of Lake Eleanor through the lightly falling snow. Finally, at a little after nine, I microwaved something for dinner, took a shower, and got ready for work, even though it was much too early. There'd be someone in the squad room I could talk to.

I don't have to drive to the University along Central Avenue, but I did. I had no reason to drive up the hill to the Tower, either, but I did that too, even though the place had almost killed me. It couldn't keep me away on that account. Besides, it was still early and there'd be people around.

The parking lot was full of cars. Light fell in great yellow patches from the windows onto the snow. Now full of writers and would-be writers, the mansion seemed warm, almost cozy. The teaching of writing, in its many guises, was going full blast inside; murder hadn't been able to stop it.

I leaned up against the tower, my gloved hands deep in my down jacket pockets, only my eyes and pointy nose visible through the fur-lined hood. Through the snow, the city's skyline looked like silver etched on gauze. I looked for the cluster of the tallest buildings, one of which housed the offices for Ames hardware. I found it, taller than most of the buildings around it. I'd looked down here from up there, and managed, with Chris Ames's help, to locate the tower I was leaning against now. "It's haunted," he'd told me. It wasn't hard to imagine him and Frank Ott playing in and around the place. It was a little harder to imagine John Meade playing in the tower's dark halls and on the stairs, as he'd put it. They'd all three probably played in the tower itself.

Chris Ames worked in a tower, Cameron Harris died in one, and Sandra Carr lived in one. Thinking of Sandra, my eyes moved to the left, to the condominiums about half a mile away. Hers was the middle one of three identical buildings, and there were lights on in it. I could see the window where I'd stood with Arthur Tigue the night of Sandra's party. I imagined I could see her clutter, her houseplants, and her two cats, although, of course, I couldn't.

She'd come to see me because she was worried about her sister, and wanted to know what Buck knew. But maybe that was only what she wanted me to think. Maybe she was really worried about herself. I wondered if, even as I stood down here, speculating on murder, she was up there, bent over her word processor or typewriter, hard at work on another thriller. I'd have to read one someday, I thought, although I didn't care much for books that scary.

Melody lied about the cats to Sandra, and Sandra had believed her—or wanted to. Melody probably talked somebody else into going in and feeding them. If she had, and if Sandra ever found out, she'd kill her. I wondered who Melody had recruited for the job.

As I pushed myself away from the tower wall and started back toward my car, I smiled at the thought of

Melody's small deception. And then I stopped, waiting for the bits and pieces of accidental reality, as Tony Verdugo had called them, to come together in my mind and form something recognizable.

Melody lied about the cats, the voice said. *Start with that.*

She'd told her sister that they'd stayed away from her, when she'd come in to feed them. I'd seen those cats, and they were not shy. The only reason they would avoid somebody who came in to feed them would be if that person was mean to them. I doubted that Melody was mean to her sister's cats.

But even if they'd hidden from her, she would have reacted to them. I have a friend so allergic to cats that he once got a severe reaction just touching a coat a cat had slept on several weeks before.

Melody had lied about that to her sister. So what? It might only mean that Melody didn't want to make her sister feel bad about putting her through such an ordeal—as if Sandra would care—but it might also mean she had somebody else go in and take care of them. *Don't argue,* the voice said, *just listen.*

Nobody knew where Cameron Harris had been the afternoon he was murdered, and Sandra's condo was a brisk ten-minute walk from the Tower.

Melody might have asked one of the Towerites to take care of Sandra's cats for her: Tamara, Niobe, even Arthur Tigue—or any one of a dozen other Towerites— might have done it. No big deal, especially with so many people who thought Melody needed taking care of. They would have promised Melody not to tell Sandra.

It could be quite innocent. A joke played on Sandra, for Melody's sake.

For that matter, Cameron Harris could have taken care of Sandra's cats for Melody—for old times' sake.

I wondered if Buck had found an unidentified key on Harris's body.

I thought back to Sandra's party. Tigue had been eager to talk to me about the Towerites and get *his* licks in too. He also seemed anxious to find out what the others, especially Niobe, had said about him.

It suddenly dawned on me. That night Tigue must have arrived at the point I was at now. Until I told him, he hadn't realized that Harris's whereabouts the afternoon he was killed were unknown. He found that interesting.

We were interrupted by Sandra and Tony and some of the other guests, and then the fat woman who wrote romantic suspense novels—Ursula?—joined the group. She said something about Sandra's houseplants, and Sandra said that Melody had come in and watered them. Verdugo brought up the cats and Melody's allergy to them, laughing at Sandra for asking her sister to come to her condo every day during the time she was gone. Arthur Tigue seemed interested in that conversation too. And, when I reminded him of our appointment, he'd lost all interest in both me and it.

Sandra had just told me that Melody met with Tigue the afternoon of our appointment.

I looked at my watch. It was a few minutes to ten now, and the Tower classes were almost over. I walked around to the front entrance and went inside. A few students were coming down the stairs from the second floor, laughing about something. I stood at the foot of the basement stairs and waited for Melody's class to end.

After a while, students began coming out of her classroom. Paula was among the last. I watched her stand in the doorway and say something to another student. She frowned when she saw me.

"How are you?"

"I'm fine," I said. "A couple of scrapes here and there."

"What are you doing here?"

"Nothing. I just want to talk to Melody for a few minutes."

She nodded, as if hearing something entirely different. "Uh-huh. Something's up. You've got a theory about the murders, don't you?"

"The start of one. It's about time, isn't it?"

"I guess so." She smiled. Suddenly she grabbed me and gave me a long, hard hug. "I was worried about you, Peggy. Where are you going after you leave here?"

"Roll call."

She looked at me a long time, then nodded. "See you there."

Melody came out of her classroom then and walked down to her office. I waited until she'd gone inside, and then I followed her. She was standing at her desk, loading student papers into her big bag. She looked up when she heard me tap on the doorframe and, as Paula had done before her, frowned when she saw who it was.

"What do you want?"

None of the Towerites seemed to enjoy the sight of me anymore. Only the big happy face on Melody's wall seemed glad I was there.

"I talked to Sandra. She told me you were one of the last people to talk to Arthur Tigue—besides his students, of course. And his killer."

She closed her eyes, as if fighting pain. "Don't. No more, please. I've told the police everything I know. There wasn't anything to tell. Dr. Tigue was no different than on any other occasion when I saw him."

"What time was your appointment?"

"At four. We only discussed my book, that's all. Now please—"

"Did he ask you who took care of your sister's cats while she was in California?"

The words straightened her up as if I'd slapped her, and the blood drained out of her already pale face. "What?"

"You heard me. You told your sister the cats hid from you when you came in to feed them. But that's not true, is it? Not unless you did something to frighten them, and you're incapable of that. I know something about cat allergies, and I spent an evening at Sandra's trying to avoid her cats. You're a lot more allergic than I am. You're so allergic, you don't even visit your sister. So you didn't take care of them; somebody else did. Who?"

I thought she'd be scared, but she was angry instead. "Just who do you think you are?"

"Come off it, Melody. You either tell me, or you'll tell Homicide. You decide."

"Homicide?" Her brow furrowed, her large eyes widened. "I've already talked to them. I told them everything I know. What do the cops have to do with this?"

She wasn't kidding. She really didn't know. "Nobody knows where Cameron Harris was the afternoon he was killed. I think he was in your sister's condo."

"No!" Then she laughed, a mixture of hysteria and relief. "You think Cam was feeding Sandra's cats?"

"You know the answer to that better than I do. Was he?"

"I told you, I fed those cats! Nobody else. Just me!"

Her eyes refused to meet mine. They returned to her cluttered desk, landed on her journal, its cover decorated with a big, childish sun and happy flowers. She picked it up and stuffed it into her purse. "I'm leaving now. I'm very tired. Teaching's exhausting work, and I have to be here early tomorrow morning for the business meeting. And some people I care about have been murdered." She started toward the door, as if to leave me behind in her office.

"Dr. Tigue did ask you who fed the cats, didn't he?"

She tried to ignore the question, but then she stopped at the door and turned and looked at me. She asked, in a small voice, "What's so important about who fed Sandra's cats?"

"At Sandra's party, I told Tigue that Harris's whereabouts were unknown on the afternoon of his death. He found that interesting. A little later, he discovered that you were supposed to feed your sister's cats, even though you're allergic to them. After that, he seemed to lose interest in discussing Harris's murder with me. I think he put two and two together and guessed that Harris was in the condo that afternoon. And yesterday, right after your session with him, he canceled his appointment with me. Several hours after that, he was dead."

She was listening to me as if I were explaining the secret of the universe, and it had some immediate and profound relevance to her life.

"You should be a writer, you know," she said, finally. "You really should. You've got the imagination for it. But even imagination requires some anchoring in reality." She tossed her curly blond head. "What if it were true? I mean, what if I did ask somebody else to take care of Sandra's cats? And what if Arthur did know who that mythical somebody was? Does that mean that somebody murdered him?" Her voice was mocking, but her eyes were afraid of my answer.

"I don't know. I'd probably know more if I knew who that mythical somebody was."

She smiled. "If your theory's correct, then why haven't I been killed? Or do you think I'm an accomplice?"

"If you're not an accomplice, and if I'm right that

you didn't take care of those cats, you might be killed next, Melody."

"If you're right," she echoed. She held the door for me.

I didn't know what else to do. My theory was as thin as spring ice. I held on to it because it was the only one I could come up with. I was caught in "the tyranny of the original idea," as my old teacher Edith would say.

As Melody locked her door, I said, stubbornly, "I am right. You didn't take care of your sister's cats. You're lying to me. I don't know why. Not yet."

"I can see that you're concerned for me," she said as we walked down the hall to the stairs. "But you don't need to be." Her eyes were clear and wide-set, like Barbie's, and large, like Bambi's.

At the top of the stairs, Tamara Meade was talking to Niobe Tigue. It didn't look like a friendly chat. They stopped when they saw me. I nodded to both of them. Only Niobe nodded back. I felt their eyes boring into me as I walked out into the cold.

As I drove down the hill, a car pulled out of the Tower's parking lot behind me. Paula was at the wheel, with Lawrence beside her.

Twenty-Six

As soon as I got to headquarters, I went into Ginny Raines's office, empty that time of night, and used her phone to call Buck at home. He listened without saying anything as I told him what I'd figured out.

When I'd finished, he asked why I thought Harris would want to be in Sandra Carr's condo.

"I don't know. Maybe he was having an affair. At first they met at the house he was renting. It was secluded, ideal for meeting somebody who didn't want to be seen with him. But when he had to give that place up and move in with the Meades, they had to find someplace else to meet. Harris might have talked Melody into letting him have the key to Sandra's place."

"Why?"

"Because he was too well known for them to meet in a public place. And maybe he didn't want to flaunt his lover in front of the Meades, or maybe the woman didn't want the Meades to know about her. So they met at Sandra's condo. It's perfect, Buck. I've been there. The chances of them being seen are small, and they wouldn't need to come in together, either. Whoever had the key could go first, then let the other one in. Even if someone recognized Harris, they wouldn't know who he was visiting."

"You've asked Melody about it, and she denies it. After two murders, why would she do that? You think she's involved?"

"No. I mean, I don't know. You'll have to ask Sandra if she gave her key to anyone else, but I'll bet she didn't. Melody got someone to take care of her sister's cats for her, and that person used the condo to meet Harris those last two weeks. Unless Melody gave the key to Harris."

Buck didn't say anything. Except for the absence of a dial tone, he might have hung up. "Buck, are you there?"

"So what," he said, "if I find out that Melody did commit this monstrous crime? She farmed out the care and feeding of two cats, and the watering of a lot of houseplants, to somebody else for a month. So we go look up this cat-sitter, and she—if it is a she—says, 'Sure, I took care of the cats, but Cameron Harris was never up there with me.' What do we do then, Peggy? Torture a confession out of her?"

"Damn it, Buck, I know it's a long shot! But at least I've come up with a theory. That's more than you've done!" There was a pause after that. "Sorry. I guess I'm getting carried away."

"Part of your theory may be correct. We talked to Ni-obe Tigue, and she told us she ran into Dr. Tigue the day he was murdered, at the Tower. She says he told her he had some ideas about Harris's murder that the police might find interesting."

"What!"

"You heard me. She said he had the gleam in his eye he always got when he knew something damaging about someone else."

"Did she know why he was at the Tower?"

"To pick up Melody Carr. They were working on her book that afternoon."

"And that's when he got the information out of her that confirmed his suspicions," I said. "Will you at least call her in and lean on her a little? She's lying about taking care of those cats. I know she is."

Buck took pity on me. "If you're right, there could still be any number of innocent reasons for it, but I'll pay her a visit and ask her, politely. And I'll send a detective over to Sandra Carr's condo, with a picture of Cameron Harris, to see if anyone in the building remembers seeing him there."

It was the least he could do.

As I patrolled my beat that night, I couldn't get my theory out of my mind. I was as sure Cameron Harris had been in Sandra's condo the afternoon he'd been murdered as if I'd seen him there. And if we knew who he'd been with, or why he'd been there, we'd be able to figure out who murdered him.

At a little after two, Paula and Lawrence rescued me from my thoughts and we drove off to the Donut Whole for our coffee break. I told them my theory.

"Buck's right," Lawrence said. "You can't put the thumbscrews on somebody on the strength of something that flimsy."

"Thanks, Larry," I muttered into my coffee.

"Speaking of Gary," he said, "are you two still a couple? He told us in class tonight that he's returning to South America. You going to quit your job and go with him?"

"No."

"Good." He shoved a piece of coffee-soaked doughnut into his mouth.

"It might've been Cameron Harris himself who took care of those cats for Melody," Paula said.

"Then there'd be no reason for Melody to keep it a secret," I said.

"Maybe she's just afraid her sister'll be mad, because she let somebody else go into her place alone," Lawrence put in, "especially if it was somebody Sandra had once dated."

Then Paula dropped her bombshell. "If Melody did anything she felt was underhanded, no matter how small and unimportant, she'd agonize over it. She's that kind, Peggy. I know it's hard for you to understand. And anything she agonized over would be in her journal. She puts everything in it. Everything. I know because she reads from it in class. She reads us stuff that never amounts to anything, as well as the stuff she's turned into poems."

"You think she'd write who she gave Sandra's key to in a journal?"

"She would, yes. Especially if she didn't think what she was doing was right."

"She took her journal home with her tonight," I said. "I saw her put it in her purse."

Lawrence wiped greasy sugar off his lips with a napkin. "It won't do you any good to break into her apartment and sneak a peek at it, Peggy, if that's what you're thinking. How'd you explain in a court of law how you got whatever you got, if you got anything at all?"

"Don't even think about it," Paula said as we walked back to the car.

They couldn't stop me from doing that.

Twenty-Seven

It was still snowing when I finished my watch and returned to police headquarters. I changed out of my uniform, then went down to the squad room to fill out my report and have a cup of coffee to help me stay awake until I got home.

Paula and Lawrence were there, working on their reports.

"Any brainstorms?" Lawrence asked me.

I shook my head.

"You didn't sneak away and break into Melody's apartment, did you," Paula asked, "while she was sleeping?"

I don't think she was kidding.

"It wouldn't have worked anyway," she continued. "If you're right about her getting somebody else to take care of those cats, it would've been in one of her older journals, not the one she's carrying around with her now. And you wouldn't know where to look for those."

Right.

At my car, I started it up and scraped the new snow off the windows. I was thinking about what Paula had just said.

She was wrong. I did know where to look for Melody's old journals. They were in her office at the Tower,

216

in one of the boxes she'd stashed there when she left
Tony Verdugo.

I glanced at the cheap plastic watch I'd bought the
day before, to replace the one the Tower broke. It was
almost seven-thirty, if the thing could be trusted. Would
Frank be there yet? Saturday was a big day at the
Tower—a business meeting followed by workshops,
and a reading by some local authors in the evening. The
walk would need to be shoveled and the heat turned on.
I remembered too that Chris Ames and Frank met for
breakfast in the Tower on Saturdays. I wondered how
early they started.

I parked across the street, in front of one of the old
mansions there, and considered what I was about to do
and why.

Melody had asked me why she hadn't been murdered, if she had the same information that killed Arthur Tigue. I didn't know. Maybe because the killer
didn't know Tigue got the answer from her. Or maybe
the killer planned to kill her but hadn't got around to it
yet. Or maybe I was wrong, and my mind was laboring
under the tyranny of the original idea.

I was prepared to break into the Tower, but I didn't
have to. Frank Ott was in the parking lot, shoveling the
snow as it fell. He looked like a figure in a glass snow-
ball. I sat in my car and waited until he disappeared behind the house. I crossed the street quickly and ran up
to the front door. It was locked.

Staying close to the wall, I ran to the side door.
Frank had left it ajar. I slipped in, and closing it carefully behind me, I tiptoed down the hallway to the
stairs that led to the basement.

I'd watched Melody lock her door the night before.
The lock was as old as the building itself and yielded
easily to a credit card. Inconsequentially, it occurred to
me that Niobe Tigue would never be able to break into

an office like this, since she didn't believe in plastic money. I went in, closed the door behind me, and switched on the light. The room looked exactly as it had the night before.

With a black marker, Melody had carefully labeled the cardboard cartons and grocery bags containing the remnants of her marriage. The carton on the floor next to her desk was labeled "Journals."

I set it on top of her desk and opened it, watched by the happy face on the wall. It contained about two dozen notebooks, their covers decorated with childish drawings: flowers, sailboats, mountains, and rainbows and suns everywhere. I pulled them out one by one. Each journal held one month's worth of Melody's effusions, regardless of whether the journal was filled or not. An exercise in futility, her husband had called it, fiction masquerading as reality.

The journal for January, the last month of Harris's life, was missing.

My first reaction was anger. Melody must have come back after talking to me and taken that journal home with her. My theory was correct; she was protecting somebody.

I started to leave, to sneak out the way I'd come in, when another thought occurred to me. What if she hadn't done this? What if the murderer had? If that was true, then it wouldn't do any good to destroy the journals without also destroying Melody, since, once she discovered the theft, she'd realize I was right.

I searched her desk until I found a list of the phone numbers of the Towerites. I dialed her number, and held my breath as I listened to it ring. I was just about to break the connection and call Buck when a sleepy voice came on the line.

I let out my breath. I'd been convinced she wouldn't

answer, that she was dead. I didn't know what to say to her.

"Hello," she said again.

"Hello," I replied weakly. And then I pulled myself together and decided to risk it. "This is Peggy O'Neill, Melody. I'm in your office at the Tower."

If I was wrong, I was finished as a cop, and I could easily end up in jail for breaking and entering.

"What do you mean?" The sleep was gone from her voice. "You broke in? You have no right to do that!"

"I know that, and if I'm wrong, I won't blame you if you swear out a complaint against me. I'd do the same thing. But please, Melody, just answer one question. Just one."

"What is it?" Her voice was like ice.

"Paula told me you always carry your journal for the current month with you. You're keeping the old ones here in your office, temporarily. Is that right?"

"Have you been reading my journals?"

"No, but that's why I broke in here, to read your January journal. Did you take it home with you last night?"

Dead silence for a minute. "This is a trick, Peggy, isn't it?" A pleading note entered the coldness in her voice.

"No, it's not. Listen to me, Melody, please! The journal for January is missing. Whoever took it has probably destroyed it by now, but that won't do him, or her, any good, as long as you're alive. You have to believe me, Melody, or you're going to die too. Whoever you're protecting has got to kill you now. The only way you can save yourself is to tell the police who it is. Once you've done that, you're safe. There's no reason for anybody to kill you anymore."

She'd tried to interrupt me several times, but I overrode her. There was a brief silence. "You're just trying to get me to admit that it wasn't me who—"

"No!" I hollered down the line. "We don't have time for that now. After I talked to you last night, you talked to whomever it is you're protecting. Didn't you?"

"How—?"

"Quit acting stupid, damn it, and tell me who it was! Now, or you're going to die, just the way Arthur Tigue and Cameron Harris died!"

"How do I know you're even in my office? For all I know, my journals are all there, intact, and you're no-where near the Tower."

"I'll hang up, and you can call me back."

And I hung up.

I waited for what seemed like forever, and then the phone rang.

In a very small voice, Melody said, "Tamara."

Relief that she'd spoken the name was greater than the surprise.

"She knew I'd promised Sandra I'd take care of her cats, because I complained about it so much. One day she offered to do it for me. I shouldn't have agreed, be-cause I know Sandra doesn't like her, and wouldn't want her in her place alone. But it was really awful be-ing around those cats, and I trusted Tamara, I really did. Sandra should never have asked me to take care of the cats in the first place, and I shouldn't have agreed to do it, but . . . I made Tamara promise not to tell anybody. Sandra would've killed me if she found out. Tamara said she hoped I wouldn't tell anybody either. She didn't want Sandra madder at her than she already was."

"When was this?" I asked, although I could easily guess.

"About two weeks before Cameron was murdered."

"Just after he moved in with the Meades."

"I guess so. She admitted it to me last night. She said she and Cam started having their affair a couple of weeks before that. She was working late one night at the Tower and he came in and they talked about old times. He invited her over to his place for a drink—and that's where it began. Something just came over them. It was bigger than both of them, she said."

I tried to imagine how big that could be.

"But when Cam had to give up his house," Melody went on, "they had no place to meet. Tamara wouldn't carry on an affair in her own home."

"And that's where you came in."

"Yes. But Tamara told me—and I believe her, Peggy—that Cameron was alive when she left the condo."

People keep insisting that Tamara tells the truth, I thought. First Chris Ames, now Melody. It's the consequence, I suppose, of having three names. Maybe I could try it, except that Peggy O'Neill is all I've got.

Melody continued. "She told me she left the condo first, and went to the Tower. She and Cameron always left separately because she couldn't risk being seen with him. She begged me not to tell you or the police. It would ruin her marriage if John found out, and anyway, it would be for nothing, because she didn't kill Cameron. I said I'd think about it. I believed her. I trusted her."

Because you owed her so much, I thought, since you thought you'd broken up her relationship with Harris.

"How long did you say you'd think it over?" I asked.

"I said I'd call her today, tell her my decision."

"Call the police instead, Melody. Call them now." I gave her Homicide's number. "Ask for Buck Hansen. If he's not there, tell whoever is. And keep your door locked. If Tamara comes calling on you this morning, don't let her in. No matter what she tells you or how she looks or sounds, don't let her in. Tell her through the door that you've already informed the police and there's nothing she can do now to keep it from coming out. Then she won't have any reason to kill you. But don't let her in anyway."

"She wouldn't kill me, Peggy. She's not like that."

"Melody!" My voice rose out of control.

There was a long silence that seemed to stretch for minutes. "All right, Peggy, I'll do what you say." She sounded as if she was worried about my mental health again.

Twenty-Eight

I hung up and sank into Melody's chair, exhausted. A few minutes later, I heard footsteps outside, coming down the hall. Frank. I wasn't anxious to meet him and explain what I was doing in Melody's office, so I waited until the hall was silent. I opened the door a crack and peered out. The hall was empty. I slid out, closed the door silently behind me, and went down the hall and up the stairs.

I walked out the side door and followed the path Frank had shoveled to the sidewalk. As I started to get in my car, I took a last look, my eyes following the shaft of the tower up to the room at the top.

Coming out of the little chimney pipe on the roof was a wisp of smoke, a streak of dark gray against the lighter gray of the clouds.

I ran back across the street and into the Tower again. I went up to the first floor and hurried down the hall. As I passed the kitchen, I glanced in and saw a coffee maker cheerfully perking on a counter. It smelled great, but I didn't stop to consider what it meant. I ran up to the second floor. The door leading into the tower was open. I took the stairs two at a time and was out of breath by the time I burst into the little room at the top.

In the middle of the floor stood a small table covered

with white linen, and two kitchen chairs facing each other across it. There were two place settings, with white napkins and ornate old silverware, plates, cups, and saucers.

I went across to the stove. Small birch logs were stacked neatly next to it. The poker, of course, was gone, locked in the evidence room at police headquarters downtown, so I used my foot to open the fire door. A fire was burning inside.

I started to close it when something caught my eye; it was a piece of cardboard decorated with a brightly colored flower drawn the way children draw them, big loops around a circle. The flower was red, the circle bright yellow. I reached in and snatched it out, the heat scorching the tips of my fingers, just as one torn edge was starting to catch fire. I dropped it on the floor and stepped on it carefully, then stooped to pick it up.

As I did, I noticed the legs of the stove. They looked like the paws of an animal. I'd seen them before, on Chris Ames's desk, in the photo of Ames as a child, playing on the floor where I was standing now.

"What a pleasant surprise."

I spun around. It was Ames—the adult Ames—standing in the doorway, a smile creasing his round face.

"Were you planning to join Frank and me for breakfast—or are you sleuthing, so early in the morning?"

My mouth was dry and I was still breathing hard from the climb. I swallowed twice before answering. "Breakfast would be nice, if you've got enough for one more."

"Frank only just went down to the bakery. We like our rolls fresh. But he always buys more than enough, so there'll be plenty."

"I didn't realize you and Frank met up here. I assumed you would eat in the kitchen."

"Didn't I mention it the other day? Frank and I haven't let what happened to poor Mr. Harris keep us out. Absolutely not! What did you find of interest in the stove? May I ask?"

"A piece of cardboard with a flower drawn on it. It looks like the cover of one of Melody Carr's journals."

"Really?" Ames frowned. "I wonder what it's doing up here. You think it might be related to the murders?"

I stuck it into my jacket pocket and shrugged. "Who knows? Perhaps I could go downstairs and bring up another chair."

"Let's leave that to Frank." He smiled. "He enjoys being of use. In the meantime, why don't we sit down? You look like you need to rest. I assume you were patrolling the campus all night. How cold you must have been!"

Not as cold as I was now. I didn't want to sit down. Cameron Harris had been sitting in a chair when I'd found him, in that closet to my left.

Either Chris Ames was a killer, or he wasn't. I could find out quickly enough by telling him I couldn't stay for breakfast after all, and walking toward him. He'd either let me pass or show me what he was holding in his jacket pocket. I wanted very much to believe he'd let me pass, but you can get badly hurt playing a card, when you don't know what's trump. Instead, I decided to try to keep him entertained until Frank came up with breakfast. Not because I thought Frank wasn't Ames's accomplice, but because—trapped the way I was—the more confusion, the merrier.

"You read Tamara's novel, *Romance and Reality,* in manuscript, didn't you?"

He looked startled at the change of subject. "Did Tamara tell you that?"

"No. Niobe Tigue mentioned that you'd introduced Tamara to Ibsen. Tamara's novel is so—Ibsenian. I know how much you love Ibsen."

"Yes, I do love Ibsen," he said, still puzzled. "But Tamara's novel is not very good Ibsen, I'm afraid." He cocked his head expectantly, waiting for what I was getting at.

"Well, that wasn't your fault. Did she follow any of your suggestions?"

"No, alas, she didn't."

"You didn't advise her to burn it—the manuscript, I mean?"

"Burn—?" He laughed, but the merriment was gone from his little eyes. "Good heavens, no! Why would I?"

"Well, doesn't Hedda do that with her manuscript?"

He shook his head. "No. Not her manuscript. It was—"

"I know. She burned some guy's manuscript. To tell you the truth, I didn't like *Hedda Gabler* very much. I mean, why couldn't Ibsen just write a play about his own fear of sex and scandal and all the other things that make life interesting, instead of dumping it on a woman? But you know what I mean. I thought, since you burned your manuscript . . ."

He stared at me. "How did you know that?"

"Magic." I waved the question away. "So you read Tamara's manuscript, and you didn't think much of it. Yet you paid to have it published."

"How—?" He grinned suddenly. The merriment was back in his eyes. From the first time we'd met, he'd enjoyed my company, the way my mind works. He seemed to be enjoying both now, too.

"Why, Mr. Ames?"

"Well, it's not what you think," he replied. "I'm not in love with Tamara. And I wasn't then, either." He stopped. "Actually, I suppose I am in love with her, but it's not the kind of love that wants anything, or expects anything. That's probably a good thing. I certainly wouldn't care to be married to her!" He shuddered. "Do you believe me?"

"Yes. I don't imagine you'd want her to have the kind of power over you that marriage brings with it. I'm sure you're most comfortable being her loyal friend, her confidant. So why did you pay for its publication?"

"I'm not really sure." He frowned. "Not because of its literary merit, certainly."

"Let me tell you why. May I?" I waited until he nodded, obviously puzzled but curious too. "You paid for its publication because the novel was about selling out. I'll bet that's why you loved her, too. She gave up a man she loved for a man who could give her the financial security and respectability she needed."

" 'Craved' is more like it," he corrected me, a slightly aggrieved tone creeping into his voice. "And what's wrong with that, Miss O'Neill? After all, as I told you in my office, we don't live in Ibsen's plays, do we? Life and literature aren't the same at all. Tamara needed what John had to offer her more than she needed the life she imagined she would have with Cameron Harris. You have no idea the kind of life she had, before she married John."

"Don't be so sure of that. But I'm not judging her. It's actually you we're talking about now. Isn't it about time? You've spent so much of your life in the shadows, your gifts hidden. You loved Tamara Meade for the choice she made, and that's why you paid to get her novel published."

He shrugged. "I suppose that might have been part of it. Maybe you should become a psychologist, like Dr. Tigue."

I ignored him. "You sold out too. You gave up your

dream of becoming an author because your 'kind and gentle father' wanted you to."

"Don't speak of him in that tone of voice, Miss O'Neill," Ames said, sharply. "Please. You've heard me say it before, and I'll say it again. I didn't have talent enough. There is nothing worse than to be able to see characters and scenes in your mind's eye and yet know you can't bring them to life! The world doesn't need another second-rate author, and I didn't want to be one, either."

"How would you know you were, unless you'd given it a try?"

He was still standing in the doorway, barely filling it, although it wasn't a very big door. He seemed to be slumped into himself, but he kept his eyes on me, across the room, the table and chairs between us.

He said, as if I hadn't spoken, "My father was the kindest man I ever knew. He never raised his voice, or a hand—not to me, not to anyone else. And he never tried to discourage me from becoming a writer, either." His voice rose suddenly. "But I could see the hurt in his eyes, whenever I tried to talk to him about it. As I've told you, he turned his father's hardware store into a regional chain. He was enormously proud of that, prouder of that than of becoming wealthy. And I was his only son. If I didn't carry on the business after him, it would have been lost, all of it. It would have fallen into the hands of strangers. There would have been nothing left to remind the world of who he'd been and what he'd done. The thought of that was incredibly painful to him."

"The business is in the hands of strangers now."

"Yes."

"And you burned the manuscript of your novel."

"But only after it had been rejected."

"Once."

"Yes."

"And later, you donated your father's mansion to the Tower, as a kind of atonement, I suppose, for your betrayal of your dream and your integrity."

"Not my integrity, Miss O'Neill." He pulled himself up and glared at me.

"Okay. But you burned your manuscript here, in this stove."

He gave me a startled look. "Who told you that?"

"This was your room as a child, wasn't it?"

"How—? Oh, the photograph on my desk." He laughed, perhaps relieved that I wasn't magic after all. "You're very observant."

This was the room in which Chris Ames had never really grown up. It would have hurt his father too much if he had.

"At dinner," I went on, "at the Meades', Cameron Harris told us how you'd destroyed your novel after one rejection. He was appalled, or pretended to be. Then he started to ask you how you'd destroyed it, but someone interrupted him—Melody, I think—and you didn't get a chance to tell him. But you told him the next day, didn't you?"

His head moved slightly, and his lips twitched, as if fighting a smile.

"You met Cameron Harris that evening and offered to do more than just tell him how you destroyed your manuscript. You offered to show him where. Tell me, Mr. Ames, did you bring the subject up, or did he?"

He thought a moment, then gave me the puckish smile I'd first seen at the Meades' dinner. "He did. He asked me again how I'd destroyed my novel. I teased him; I wouldn't tell him, but I'd be happy to show him if he was so interested. He wanted me to tell him, right then and there, but I wouldn't. I let myself be guided by circumstances, Miss O'Neill, let it be a little . . . impulsive."

He smiled at the memory. "Mr. Harris boasted of his gift for improvisation at the Meades'. You remember that, I'm sure, since he used his gift at your expense that night. I discovered that I have a little of that gift myself. You see, I knew that Mr. Harris was meeting Tamara at Sandra Carr's condominium. They had been for two weeks, ever since he moved in with Tamara and John. Tamara tells me everything. She enjoys sharing her life with me because she knows I'm discreet. I'm very fond of her, and I enjoy the time we spend together. And of course, I don't want her life to be upset any more than she does. It's too comfortable for us the way it is. So I was there, waiting, when he came out of Miss Carr's condominium and started walking towards Central Avenue. I assumed he was going to get dinner at one of the restaurants there before the reading. Tamara had left the condominium earlier and had come directly here. She was very concerned that his reading proceed smoothly.

"When Mr. Harris saw me, I pretended to be surprised and claimed I was on my way to the Tower. We walked together. It was he who brought up my manuscript; I didn't have to, although I would have if he hadn't. His tone of voice the night before rankled.

"As we walked over here, I said to myself that I wouldn't do it, kill him, if we encountered anybody who might recognize us. We waited behind Mr. Mallory's car in the parking lot until Frank moved out of our sight, and then I used my old key to let us in through the side door. We crept down the hall and into the kitchen, where I took the key to the tower. I made a real production out of it, and Mr. Harris—Mr. Harris played along! We were two boys sneaking around, not wanting anybody to know we were there. I'd done that often enough as a child, pretending someone was there who actually cared what I got up to.

"We peeked into the auditorium, at Mr. Mallory fiddling with the loudspeakers up by the podium. We watched him until we heard a car pull into the parking lot. It was Niobe Tigue, arriving with the chairs from the funeral parlor. 'Come on!' I whispered, and gave Mr. Harris a nudge. We tiptoed quickly up the stairs to the second floor. Every creak our steps made seemed magnified a thousandfold."

Ames paused and he gave me a look of childlike awe. "It was the oddest thing. I hadn't done anything bad yet, and I wasn't even sure I was going to do anything bad. Nothing would have happened if we'd been caught sneaking up into the tower, and yet my heart was in my throat, I could hardly breathe, and I'd never been so scared before in my life. Mr. Harris saw my terror, and laughed at me silently. He was having the time of his life! Later, when it was all over, I had to laugh when I thought of how he'd laughed at my terror.

"Upstairs, we could hear Tamara talking on the phone in her office down the hall. She was talking to John, explaining why she hadn't come home for dinner, lying to him, as she so often did. We looked at each other, and laughed silently at the shabbiness of life. And then we climbed up here. I closed the door behind us. Mr. Harris saw me do it, and laughed out loud. But that was all right, for sound doesn't carry well from up here.

"Mr. Harris looked around this room and said, 'So this is where you did it.' He'd never been up here before.

"*Yes,* I replied, *in the stove,* over there where you're standing, Peggy. *That's the same poker I used to stir the ashes thirty years ago,* I told him, and he picked it up and opened the fire door. He laughed again. I'm sure you remember Cameron Harris's laugh. It was quite distinctive, offensive. Then he went over to the windows, to admire the view, he said, to get 'atmosphere' for the novel he was working on."

Chris Ames stopped and smiled expectantly. I waited for him to go on, but he didn't say anything more. The story seemed to lack something.

" 'Atmosphere' for the novel he was writing about the Tower," I prompted.

"Yes."

"Go on. I want to hear how it ends."

"You do?"

I nodded.

"Isn't it obvious?"

"I'm afraid so. But I'd like to hear it, anyway."

"He stands at the windows a long time. He's bent over, of course, to see out, for he's very tall. I take the poker from his hand, so gently he scarcely notices, and wait until he steps back and straightens up. I raise the poker and hit him with it. And hit him again as he falls, and then again and again."

Ames paused, and his eyes, which had been seeing the murder of Cameron Harris, came back to me. "It was so easy, and it gave me such great pleasure." The glow of that pleasure died slowly in his eyes. "The rest you know. You found the body, you saw him."

"How'd you get back out of the building?"

"The same way I came in, of course."

He looked annoyed, as if he would have preferred to leave the details to my imagination.

"But then you were a real murderer. You'd just done something bad. And if anybody had seen you leaving the Tower, and recognized you, you'd have been in trouble, too. That must have made it scarier than when you came in."

"No." His eyes were dull. "It was much scarier the first time, when it was just pretend."

Twenty-Nine

Without much enthusiasm, he told me how he killed Tigue.

"Dr. Tigue pried the truth out of Melody about who took care of Sandra Carr's cats." He stopped and gave me a sharp look, as if something occurred to him. "I wonder if he had you to thank for that—or am I giving you too much credit this time?" He saw by the look on my face that he'd guessed correctly. "Well, so you too have Dr. Tigue's death on your conscience. I'm sorry. In any case, Dr. Tigue wormed what he wanted out of Melody so cleverly that she didn't even realize what he was doing. She's such a trusting soul. Protected from life's cruelties by her sister—who writes thrillers!"

Ames shook his head. "Dr. Tigue went to Tamara with his knowledge. He was 'curious' to know if she'd done more in Miss Carr's condo than just see to the needs of two cats and some plants. Tamara tried to convince him that she hadn't met Mr. Harris there, that it was all perfectly innocent. Tigue indicated that he accepted this, but she didn't believe him. She knew him too well."

"What did he want from her?"

Ames shrugged. "We'll never know, for sure. But it must have been what he always wanted: power and control over people. He was an empty man. Some empty men try to fill their emptiness with money, and some with power. I think that if there had been a choice between the two, Dr. Tigue would have chosen the latter. He'd once been in love with Tamara, and she'd rejected him. I didn't ask him what he wanted. As you can imagine, Tamara was panic-stricken. She feared that, if he did go to the police with his suspicions, they might think to check the key to see if it fit Sandra's condo. I tried to—"

I interrupted him. "What key?"

"The key to Sandra's condo, of course. As I told you, Tamara left the condo before Mr. Harris, and she left the key with him, expecting him to return it to her when they met here later. But, of course, they never did."

"I haven't heard anything about a key." Had Buck held something that important back?

"No, well . . ." Ames cocked his head and smiled again, a child's smile, full of mischief and shame. "I took the key from Mr. Harris's body after I killed him. But Tamara couldn't know that, and I could hardly tell her without also telling her I'd killed him, could I?"

He shook his head in something that looked like sorrow. "She did so worry about that key. I tried to reassure her, as best I could. I told her the police had probably forgotten all about it; we all carry keys that belong to locks we have left behind, and poor Mr. Harris would be no exception. But she was obsessed with the possibility that the police would figure it out, and that would lead them to Melody and then to her. You saw how she behaved when she found you in her home yesterday."

He shook his head, remembering how badly she'd behaved to me. "I tried to assure her that even if the key did lead the police to her, it would not be sufficient evidence to convict her of murder. She would simply insist that Cameron Harris was alive and well when she left the condo. But Tamara was concerned with her reputation, and she also knew her marriage would not survive John's learning that she had resumed her affair with Mr. Harris.

"So I had to act, to keep Dr. Tigue from going to the police with the story—or otherwise using his knowledge. You see, he didn't really believe Tamara had murdered Mr. Harris. For all his psychology, Dr. Tigue thought that murderers were not people he would know, much less have been in love with. So I simply called him and told him that Tamara would like to meet him at the Tower that evening, in her cozy office, to discuss the matter of the condominium and Mr. Harris's murder at greater length. Dr. Tigue agreed, in a voice in which triumph competed with lust in a manner I found most unpleasant. I think, had you heard it, you would agree, Miss O'Neill. I had no compunctions about killing him. I used a piece of pipe from the basement, left there from when the house was being remodeled for the writers."

"What was the point of the child's rattle?" I asked. "More of your creativity oozing out?"

My sarcasm pained him. "I'd read Mr. Harris's book, *Lost Letters Home*. I make it a practice to read everything that has to do with the Tower, so I knew about his satire of Dr. Tigue's rather unorthodox therapy. I couldn't resist. I simply couldn't resist, just as you couldn't resist calling pasta 'noodles' that night at the Meades'."

The similarity didn't exactly leap out to the normal eye. "Your hanging around to make art out of Tigue's murder almost cost me my life," I said. "You could have killed me that night too. Why didn't you?"

"Yes, I could have, couldn't I?" The quirkly little

smile came and went. "I knew where you were at every moment you were crawling down the hallway. I know that hallway, and its darkness, well. But why should I have killed you? I didn't know you were the one who'd told Melody about Tamara and the cats. Dr. Tigue did not share that knowledge with Tamara." Chris Ames hung his head, but kept his eyes on me from under his thick gray brows. "I simply wanted to play with you for a moment or two. Indulge myself, perhaps for the last time, in a game of hide-and-seek in my old home. I didn't believe I would be doing you any lasting harm."

The number of people I'd encountered recently who deserved their own playpens seemed to be multiplying.

"Why haven't you killed Melody yet? That would cut the connection between Tamara and Cameron Harris completely."

His round eyes met mine. "For the longest time, I was hoping that wouldn't be necessary. Melody has always been such a good friend to Frank. She's the only Towerite who really cares about him. But now I'm going to have to do it. You made it necessary," he said, reproachfully, "when you explained it to her last night, so I'm afraid you're going to have that on your conscience too. Right after you talked to her, Melody went to Tamara's office, to demand an explanation. Tamara did exactly what she'd done with Dr. Tigue. She begged Melody not to go to the police. She swore that she hadn't killed Harris and that Sandra's condo had nothing to do with Harris's murder. She told Melody that if her husband heard about her affair, it would kill him. He does, after all, have a heart condition. What she meant, of course, was that he would divorce her. She played on Melody's compassion—and the fact that Melody seems to think she broke up the love affair between Tamara and Mr. Harris—and it worked. Melody said she'd think it over. If she decided to go to the police, she promised to let Tamara know first."

"And then Tamara told you," I said, "so that you could handle it the same way you handled Tigue."

"Oh, no, no! Please, you mustn't believe Tamara knows anything about this. She told me, yes, but not because she knows that I killed Dr. Tigue. She was in a panic, and she didn't know who else to turn to. She needed to talk to somebody about it. To open her heart."

"But when you kill Melody—then she'll know you killed Tigue, and Harris too."

He thought about that. "I wonder." He smiled sadly. "Somehow, I doubt it. When it isn't convenient, Tamara has the remarkable ability to not know what she knows. I'm sorry about Melody, of course. She isn't a gifted poet by any means, but I wouldn't hurt her on that account. However, I cannot let Tamara suffer the consequences of what I've done, either, can I? How could I live with that? Tell me!"

He paused, to give me time to come up with a solution that would be mutually satisfying to both of us. I couldn't. I could only keep him talking.

"After you killed Harris, you put the story he was going to read that night on his lap. It was a story about Tamara."

He smiled proudly. "Of course. But I knew it would do her no harm. Nobody would think Tamara had arranged it like that, and it would confuse the police. Plus, it was a nice touch."

"Symbolic."

"I think so, yes."

"Well, killing Melody isn't going to help Tamara, I'm afraid. Tamara's at police headquarters right now, being grilled, just like any common, garden-variety multiple killer."

"What!" Ames took a step into the room, as if he'd been pushed from behind.

"Before you came in, Mr. Ames, I was in Melody's office. I found the box with her old journals and saw that January's was missing. I understood what that meant, and realized Melody was in danger, so I called her. I managed to convince her to call the police, and she did." At least, I hoped she did. "It's all going to come out now, and whether or not Tamara's convicted of murder, she's in for a rough time. If you're really concerned about her, there's only one way to save her: You'll have to confess to the murders yourself."

He stood there, a few steps in the little room, his round boy's face screwed up in thought. Then it lit up, as if a light bulb had literally gone on overhead. He pulled the little, expensive-looking pistol he'd been holding out of his jacket pocket and pointed it at me.

"That's quite a comedown for you, Mr. Ames, from Daddy's tower to that toy."

"It's not a toy, Miss O'Neill." He was all business now, his father's son. "Do you think they have arrested her now? The police? Tamara?"

"Yes. Why?"

He nodded, pleased. "Then if you're found dead, in that little closet over there, just like Mr. Harris, they'll know it wasn't Tamara who did it. They'll have to let her go."

"Somebody'll hear the shots."

Ames shook his head. "No. It's remarkable how little sound escapes from up here. This is where I spent my childhood, so I should know."

I started to say something but stopped. I didn't have anything left to say. Ames watched my face and saw the dismay growing there. "I'm sorry," he said, as his pistol steadied on my chest.

I gave the card table between us a kick that sent it

over, and lunged at Ames through the falling debris, tripping over one of the table's legs and crashing at his feet. He pointed the pistol down into my face. Staring up into the muzzle, I tried to scramble to my feet, the final futile act of my life.

Loud footsteps on the stairs came up fast. Ames spun around, stepped away from me, and shoved the pistol back into his jacket pocket just as Frank Ott burst into the room. He was holding a large tray with a silver coffee service on it. He'd shaved, his hair was combed, and he was dressed in a threadbare navy blazer and dark tie.

Frank looked at the mess I'd made and said something I couldn't understand to Ames in an anguished voice.

"Go back downstairs, Frank. It's all right. Miss O'Neill's had an accident. We'll have our breakfast in the kitchen today. We'll be down in a moment."

Frank looked from Ames to me and back to Ames and then started to leave the room.

"Do you know what this is, Frank?" I said. He stopped and turned back. I held up the scrap of Melody's notebook I'd rescued from the fire. "It's your friend Melody's. Chris burned her notebook in the stove over there and he was going to kill Melody too, to keep her from telling the police who killed Cameron Harris and Dr. Tigue. And he has a gun in his pocket that he's going to use to kill me too, when you go downstairs."

Frank turned to Ames and gave him a look that begged him to tell him it wasn't true.

"Go downstairs, Frank," Ames said, his voice harsh. "Now."

"No, Chrissy." Frank backed up against the wall next to the door and stood there stiffly, still holding the coffee service in front of him, his mouth set in a determined line. They stood like that for a moment that stretched into forever. Then Ames gave Frank a loving smile, shook his head, and said, "You always did show up at awkward times, Frank, didn't you? Like a curse."

He turned to me and said, "I'm really not myself this morning, Miss O'Neill. I've had so much on my mind lately. My retirement ... and all the rest. I'm sorry. You're not hurt, are you? I'm glad. I'll see you to the door."

He was suddenly the perfect host in his father's house. He swung his left hand in a gesture that invited Frank and me to go first.

"Let me have the pistol, Mr. Ames." I held out my hand.

He smiled regretfully and shook his head.

I lunged for him, caught his wrist, and started to twist his arm behind his back. Suddenly I felt myself grabbed from behind, my arms squeezed painfully to my sides, the noise of Frank's coffee service loud in the little room as it joined the mess on the floor.

"Thank you, Frank," Ames said, stepping back. "Please take her outside." He gave me a look that told me he'd expected more of me, somehow. That was the last I saw of him. Frank carried me to the tower door and partway down the stairs, before setting me down and letting me walk the rest of the way on my own.

Thirty

As we stepped out onto the porch, the door slammed behind us. Frank turned and stared at it, as if expecting it to open again for him. We heard the deadbolt click into place.

"Come on," I said, taking him by the arm. We crossed the street, and I pounded on the front door of an old mansion until an elderly man in a robe opened up. I showed him my badge and asked for a phone.

I called Homicide. The desk sergeant told me Buck was busy and couldn't be disturbed. He was probably in an interrogation room with Tamara Wallace Meade. I told the sergeant it was urgent, a matter of life and death, and he put me through. Buck didn't sound as if he enjoyed being disturbed. I told him the situation. He asked some brisk questions and hung up. I figured a morgue car would be more useful than a SWAT team, but there wasn't any point in telling Buck that. He had to play it by the book, as I'd done when I tried to get the pistol away from Ames.

A gray-haired woman in a nightgown was standing in the kitchen door, listening as the man who'd let us in explained that it had something to do with the bohemians and hippies that damned fool Ames had sold his house to across the street. Frank and I went back out-

242

side. He hadn't said anything since we'd left the house. He knew that the situation was out of his hands now.

An old van labored up the hill and slowed at the Tower's driveway, its turn signal winking. I ran over to it, waved it to a stop. It was Niobe Tigue. I explained enough of the situation so that she backed down the street the way she'd come. After parking, she walked up and stood next to me. I told her a little more of the story. She listened, nodding solemnly. She stared at the Tower for a moment and then said, "You told me you've read some Ibsen, didn't you? How about *The Pretenders?*"

Ibsen again. I shook my head. I'd never heard of it. I was watching the windows in the tower room, looking for Ames or his shadow. From where I stood, I could also see if he tried to leave the Tower by the side door, but I knew he wouldn't.

"Hardly anybody has," Niobe said. "Too bad. It rivals some of Shakespeare."

"What does?"

"*The Pretenders.* One of Ibsen's early plays. There's a scene in it where the king begs his fool to give up *his* dream, and live for the king's instead."

I could hear sirens down on Central, growing louder.

"You know what the fool says?"

"What fool?"

"The king's fool, in Ibsen's play! Aren't you listening?"

Suddenly Frank shouted and ran across the street. I grabbed for him, missed and started after him, until I realized he wasn't running toward the Tower. He was running to intercept Melody Carr, walking up the hill. He took her arm and spoke softly to her. He began to cry, and she began to cry, too.

Wisps of black smoke were seeping out around the

basement windows of the mansion, and light flickered behind them. I hadn't thought of that.

Niobe continued. "The fool replied, 'I could die for your dream, sire, but if I am going to live, I must live for my own.' "

The cop cars would get there with their uselessly armed men before I could get to a phone to call for firemen, so I didn't move. It was a very old house, and Ames had had time enough to set a good fire.

"And that's what Chris Ames did," Niobe shouted, over the scream of sirens, her eyes shining. "He tried to live for his father's dream, instead of for his own."

What's a story without a moral to Niobe Tigue?

The cops arrived, saw what was happening, and radioed for fire trucks. A cop came over and asked me where I thought Ames was.

"He's dead."

Writers and students began arriving then, hurrying up the hill on foot through the snow and the police barricade, for classes that wouldn't be held that morning.

Black tendrils of smoke coiled out of cracks in the tower walls. Suddenly the room at the top exploded into flame.

"Look," Melody exclaimed, her eyes sparkling. "It's like a giant flower opening." She was holding Frank by the hand.

Standing next to me, Niobe muttered, "It's just a rotten tower going up in smoke."

Maybe they were both right.

Thirty-One

And that's all she wrote, as my father used to say, whenever something in his life ended abruptly, which it often did. I never thought to ask him who "she" was. Fate, maybe.

By retelling Chris Ames's story to Buck, I got Tamara Wallace Meade off the hook for Harris's murder almost as fast as I'd got her on it, but she had a lot of explaining to do anyway. She admitted to Buck that she'd fed Sandra's cats for Melody, although at first she denied Harris had ever been in Sandra's condo with her. When Buck pointed out that it wouldn't be necessary to make the facts public if she cooperated, she admitted everything.

She and Harris met, off and on, at the house he was renting, the last several weeks he was there. They met in the afternoons, when Tamara was supposedly at work. She'd fallen in love with him again, and she thought he'd fallen in love with her again too.

"She didn't know how it would end," Buck told me. "She didn't know how she wanted it to end, either. For her, this love was like 'a madness in the blood.' " There was no inflection in Buck's voice when he said that. You had to look hard to find the irony in his eyes—or else add it yourself. I recognized the line from Tamara's novel.

When Harris moved in with the Meades, they had to find another place to meet, since they couldn't continue the affair in her home. That would have been sleazy, Tamara told Buck, and besides, her husband rarely left the house anymore since his heart attack. Meeting in a motel would be sleazy too, and of course, there was the risk of Harris being recognized.

Then she remembered Melody complaining about having to take care of her sister's cats.

Tamara admitted that she'd told Chris Ames about her affair with Harris, but she never for a moment suspected that he'd murdered Harris.

Buck said, "Ames must have feared that if Tamara left her husband for Harris, he'd be shut out of her life, just like he was being shut out of his father's business."

"Maybe," I said, "but I think it's more likely he really loved Tamara so selflessly that he killed Harris because he thought Harris was playing with her, and that she might actually leave John Meade for Harris, and then Harris would dump her. That would explain why he left the manuscript on Harris's lap. By making it a part of the murder scene, he ensured that Tamara would find out what a bastard Harris was."

"You're a romantic, Peggy, in a bent sort of way."

"I'm glad somebody understands me."

Tamara insisted that she really believed Arthur Tigue when he promised he wouldn't go to the police with his suspicions, so she had no reason to want him dead. Yes, she had told Chris Ames of Tigue's visit to her, but it wasn't true that she was panicked about it or that she feared he would blackmail her in some way. And she never dreamed that Ames would murder Tigue to get him off her back. The poor deluded man, she added.

She hadn't told the police she'd been with Harris that

last afternoon of his life because it was simply too embarrassing, and because she was afraid the discovery of her affair would kill her husband. She'd behaved irresponsibly—she knew that!—but Cameron Harris had been such a vital man, such a creative man. She knew Buck would understand.

The story Buck made public was based on what Chris Ames had told me, sanitized slightly to protect the guilty. Ames had killed Harris because he was jealous of his success as a writer and because Harris had planned to write a novel satirizing the Tower, Ames's childhood home, his gift to the artistic community of the city. He'd killed Tigue because Tigue had information that threatened him. That was, in its way, the truth.

The membership in the Tower had grown immensely since its Second Story days, so it couldn't go back to its old quarters above the bookstore. Temporarily the Towerites are holding their classes in odd spaces all over town—scattered like the dandelions to which Sandra Carr likened the creative impulse—until they find another building they can agree on. The insurance money for the Tower, and Ames's estate, which he left for the upkeep of the Tower, ought to be enough to buy something pretty grand. Melody Carr is agitating for an abandoned church that's on the market, Niobe Tigue for an abandoned school.

Sandra Carr's become something of a pest. She thinks I saved her sister's life—I haven't told her I was the reason she nearly lost it—and she wants to reward me, since I'm not going to get the reward promised by Ames for solving Harris's murder. She's offered to redo my apartment at her expense, if I give her a free hand with it. No way. But I did agree to let her help me pick out new wallpaper, and pay for it.

Epilogue

One night a few weeks after the Tower burned down, I was patrolling the Old Campus. It was a little after midnight when I walked into the Humanities Building and down the dimly lit hall on the first floor. I'd passed Edith Silberman's office when suddenly the door in front of me opened, light spilled out, and after it stumbled Tony Verdugo.

"Hi, Peggy." He held on to the doorframe for support. He had a bottle in one hand, something stronger than beer. He wasn't surprised to see me.

"Hi."

"Congratulations."

"Thanks."

"But you know," he said, giving me a crooked, drunken grin, "I couldn't help notice something—something interesting about it."

"What's that, Professor Verdugo?"

He gestured with his bottle, one finger pointing. "You were the one who got to tell the story in the end—Ames's story. Ames told you what he wanted you to know, and you told your cop friend what you wanted him to know. And that's all we know. Am I right?"

"Absolutely."

"So tell me this," he said, squinting at me. "Where's the truth?"

The bottle slipped out of his hand and smashed on the floor at his feet. He looked down at it as if he didn't understand how he could be holding a bottle in one moment, and find it in pieces at his feet the next.

"Where's the truth?" he repeated, looking back up at me.

"I don't know. I'm just a simple campus cop. Now, why don't we go outside and I'll call the squad car to take you home."

"S'not necessary. My car's out there someplace."

"I'm sure it is. Let's go find it."

As I led him outside, I used my walkie-talkie to call in Paula, who had the squad car that night. When she arrived, I helped her handcuff Verdugo and get him in the cage.

"Two gorgeous muses," he exclaimed happily, "fluttering about my head. Where are the other seven?"

Paula drove him off to detox.

Oh, and Gary's returning to South America, in search of the simple life. He promises to write.

Meet Peggy O'Neill
A Campus Cop With a Ph.D. in Murder

"A 'Must Read' for fans of Sue Grafton"
Alfred Hitchcock Mystery Magazine

Exciting Mysteries by M.D. Lake

ONCE UPON A CRIME 77520-4/$5.50 US/$7.50 Can

AMENDS FOR MURDER 75865-2/$4.99 US/$6.99 Can

COLD COMFORT 76032-0/$4.99 US/ $6.99 Can

POISONED IVY 76573-X/$5.50 US/$7.50 Can

A GIFT FOR MURDER 76855-0/$4.50 US/$5.50 Can

MURDER BY MAIL 76856-9/$4.99 US/$5.99 Can

GRAVE CHOICES 77521-2/$4.99 US/$6.99 Can